MALICE BY DESIGN

An Authentic Medical Thriller

GARY BIRKEN, M.D.

Erupen Titles

Contents

Prologue

ITHACA, NEW YORK
JANUARY 2009

WITH EACH LABORED breath she drew, the muscles of Dr. Anna Hartmann's barrel chest heaved and jerked as they struggled to force desperately needed oxygen into her failing lungs. With her condition rapidly deteriorating, she lay propped up against the hand-carved headboard of the four-poster bed that had been in her family for three generations.

"My appearance disturbs you," she said to the gaunt man standing at the foot of her bed. "I'm an old woman, and my body has betrayed me, but I assure you, I'm still in full possession of my faculties."

"I know you are, Doctor. Would it be okay if I asked you a question or two?" he inquired taking note of her patchy gray complexion and hollow eyes that had slipped back into their deep-set sockets. Though he struggled to ignore it, the stale scent of lingering illness that thickened the air churned his stomach.

"If you must," she answered.

"It's been many decades since you concluded your work. To your knowledge, has any other individual or group attempted to continue your medical research?"

"If you understood the mitigating circumstances—as I thought you did—you wouldn't be asking that question. But since you did, the answer to your question is no."

"You mentioned the first time we spoke that you were sure there are no other written accounts of your research except your own. I just wanted to make sure I understood you correctly."

With a feeble hand, she gestured at the time-weary Victorian writing desk with tarnished brass handles that sat under the only window in the room. Uttering even a single sentence further weakened her ability to breathe.

"My journals are on the desk. I suggest you take a good look at them. They are without doubt the only recorded evidence of my discoveries."

"I hope you understand that I intend no disrespect, but I have to remain extremely cautious regarding my possible involvement."

"Young man, I'm not trying to sell you anything. If you don't understand that I'm offering you the opportunity to lead one of the most important research initiatives in the last hundred years, then you're a fool."

"Dr. Hartmann, please understand that I didn't mean to imply…"

"I pray I haven't misjudged you. I thought you were a man of vision and inspiration."

Deciding to say nothing, his pinched expression was his only response to her offensive comment. After a strained silence, he started across the room toward the desk where his eyes fell on three jade-colored leather journals that were scuffed and faded by time.

With a hand that quivered with anticipation, he ran his index finger along the gold-embossed border and coarse spine of the middle journal. Fearful of its fragility, he cautiously unknotted the black leather ties and gingerly opened it. He began by examining several pages from each of three divided sections. They were all marked by meticulous handwritten notes and flawless diagrams.

When he was finished, he closed the journal and repeated the same process with the other two. After he'd scanned the final page, he felt reasonably assured he hadn't traveled nearly five hundred miles on a fool's errand.

"This appears to be magnificent work, Dr. Hartmann. You're to be congratulated. If it's still your wish, I'd be honored to continue the research where you were forced to stop."

"Since I'd expect any scientist worth their salt to make the same offer, you'll excuse me if I'm neither flattered nor overwhelmed by your words."

"I'm sorry if I've said anything that has given you cause to regret inviting me here today."

"To be frank, you haven't convinced me you fully grasp the immense responsibility that comes with building upon my work." Between disjointed breaths, she went on. "My journals will take you to a hilltop from which you can make one of the greatest medical breakthroughs in modern history."

Before he could respond, a hefty woman with mousy gray hair walked into the room. After casting a displeased glance the man's way, she went to her mother's bedside.

"Don't try to speak any more, Mom. You're obviously exhausted." Elise Hartmann was her mother's only child and sole caretaker. For the past few years, she had devoted herself mind and body to the task. For most, it would have been a trying existence, but Elise was a kindhearted woman who accepted her dreary life without bitterness, almost as if it were her calling.

"Stop fussing over me. I'm…I'm fine."

"I know you are," she said, tucking the lavish down comforter snugly under her mother's feet. Without turning toward the man, she stated, "My mother's in no condition to continue her conversation with you. I'm afraid you'll have to leave now. I'll meet you downstairs in a few minutes. If it's still her wish, I'll bring the journals to you."

"Of course," he responded, relieved he wouldn't be placed in the awkward position of having to conclude the meeting himself. Just as he was about to step out into the hall, he turned back to the woman in the bed. "It was a distinct pleasure meeting you, Dr. Hartmann. If you allow me to advance your work, you have my word of honor the results will reflect proudly on you."

"Unfortunately, that's something I'll never know."

As soon as he was out of the room, Elise said, "Mother, you have to calm down. You promised me."

"I've accomplished a great deal in my life, but there were grave mistakes along the way." Her words faded into silence for a few seconds. "Perhaps this man will be the one to make the world understand that. In spite of regrettable appearances, my hands and mind were always guided by the highest purpose."

"Nobody will ever question your intentions or the importance of your work."

With Elise's assistance, Anna used what little energy she could muster to lean forward. The skin of her arms was parched and stretched over her fluid-filled elbows. Elise placed a crystal tumbler to her mouth. With barely parted, cyanotic lips, Anna found the tip of the straw and drew two sips of ice water into her mouth.

Tears brimming in her eyes, Anna said, "I pray I haven't made a catastrophic mistake. May God forgive me if I have."

"Get some rest. I love you."

Elise leaned down and kissed her mother's forehead. She then moved to the desk, collected the journals, and slipped out of the room. She advanced along the dimly lit hallway to the ornate spiral staircase. When she reached the first floor, she went directly to the entranceway.

"Miss Hartmann, I have some concerns I'd like to—"

"Your concerns don't interest me in the slightest, sir."

"But you must understand, I have to—"

"Actually, the only thing that matters is what you understand," she told him, gesturing toward his leather computer case. "Either take the journals or leave without them. It's a matter of complete indifference to me. I assure you, my mother's second choice to carry on her work is a phone call away."

It was the look of sheer resolve in her eyes that guided his choice. He was a man who didn't normally tolerate insubordination, nor did he allow anybody to instruct him, but he was also savvy enough to appreciate who had the leverage in a negotiation.

He raised an apologetic hand. "I'm sorry. I certainly didn't mean to imply that I wouldn't be honored to further advance your mother's work." He extended his hand and accepted the journals from Elise.

As he slipped them into his computer bag, she said, "What you carry in your case is the legacy of a great woman. I warn you sir. We've taken you at your word. Don't ever forget the pledge you made never to disclose my mother's identity to anybody. I promise you, if you break your word it will be a tragic mistake."

"My oath to her is forever and unconditional. Nobody will ever learn of her involvement in any of this." He buttoned his coat and stepped out onto the porch. "I only regret your mother won't be here to see her dream come to fruition."

"As per our agreement, don't ever contact my mother or me again."

The sound of the door pounding closed prevented any hope he had of responding.

By the time he reached the end of the driveway, he was chilled to the depth of his core by a gusty wind laced with frozen rain. Hunching his shoulders, he made his way down the slippery side-walk to his rental car. He struggled to remain cautiously optimistic but his elation was mounting. Every particle of his being was telling him the contents of Anna Hartmann's journals would be a shining beacon guiding him to a medical triumph that would be forever attributed to him, and him alone.

Part I

Chapter 1

OSTER CHILDREN'S HOSPITAL
DEFIANCE, OHIO
THIRTEEN YEARS LATER

CONSUMED by a brand of misery that penetrated to the cavernous recesses of his marrow, Dr. Hayden Kubicek walked out of his younger brother's hospital room. He made his way down the broad corridor that ended in an expansive glass atrium, still struggling to believe that five minutes earlier he'd been holding Max's hand when he drew his final breath.

Unable to hold a clear thought in his mind, Hayden stared without purpose at a densely wooded area behind the hospital that stretched, untouched by human hands, as far as the eye could see. Even though he wasn't a particularly spiritual person, he couldn't fathom what divine force would see the need to seize the life from a vibrant teenager who had everything to live for.

At twenty-eight years of age and a second-year family practice resident at Fowler Hospital in Toledo, Hayden had an encyclopedic mind for medical detail that had distinguished him as one of the most talented residents the program had ever recruited. He was tall, with wide-set porcine eyes and a jutting chin that overhung an ample neck. He had a slight crook to his nose, a constant reminder of the three fractures he had suffered during a praiseworthy four-year high school wrestling career.

Two years earlier, his world and that of his parents was thrown into turmoil when Max was diagnosed with leukemia. In spite of the poor prognosis, he'd battled his way to remission through several intensive courses of chemotherapy. But all that changed five days earlier when he was suddenly stricken by an overwhelming illness. For no apparent reason, he'd developed extreme leg pain and difficulty walking from severe muscle spasms. The next day, he'd suffered uncontrollable seizures and bizarre changes in his behavior that ended in a profound coma.

In spite of an Olympian effort on the part of his physicians, Max showed no signs of improving. Eventually, the only intervention left to them was to place him on full life support. The next morning, Max's treatment team met with Hayden and his parents to inform them that Max's passing was imminent. In addition to being devoted parents, Nina and Peter Kubicek were intelligent and realistic people who were already painfully aware their son was close to the end. Maintaining dignity in both life and death was a guiding spiritual principle they shared, prompting them to sign the necessary documents that forbade the doctors from employing any heroic means to preserve Max's life. As soon as the meeting was over, Nina and Peter went to his bedside, tearfully said their goodbyes, and returned to Toledo to wait for the inevitable phone call.

Hayden continued to gaze out on the woodland. With the stark realization that Max was gone, a chilling mixture of sorrow and denial numbed him with disbelief. Even though he had said his final goodbye to his brother, he suddenly felt compelled to see him one last time. Doing whatever he could to gather himself, he exited the atrium and followed the corridor back to Max's room.

When he came through the door, he was surprised to see a man standing next to Max's bed making entries in a small spiral notebook. Hayden didn't recognize him but was quick to notice his sky-blue, knee-length lab coat, which differed from the gray coats that were customarily worn by the attending physicians.

Hayden took a few paces forward. The man crooked his head and locked his eyes on him. Just as quickly, he averted his gaze and slipped the note pad into his top pocket. Hayden moved toward the opposite side of the bed to speak with him, but to his surprise, he hurried toward the door without uttering a word. Hayden craned his neck but was unable to read his identification badge. More than a little stunned, he considered following him into the hall, but after a few moments of reflection, he assumed there must be a logical explanation and dismissed the notion.

Hayden shifted his attention to Max and allowed a lungful of air to escape through narrowly parted lips. His face had taken on the appearance of an ethereal death mask. His lifeless cheeks and lips were as vaporous as an early morning ground fog. Standing there motionless like a child playing freeze tag, Hayden fought back a new stream of tears.

When a few minutes had passed, he reached for the black and yellow American Legion baseball cap that Max always kept on his nightstand. He claimed it was good luck. With the softness of a watchmaker's touch, Hayden brushed the cap's visor with his finger-tips. His lips parted into a hint of a smile as he remembered how he and Max had always shared a fist pump and a high-five when their visit came to an end.

Easing forward a step, he leaned over and lightly stroked Max's cool hand. With his throat drawn taut from unmitigated heartache, he set the hat on the pillow and kissed his beloved brother's forehead for the last time.

Chapter 2

Making his way toward the elevator, Hayden couldn't get his mind off the man in Max's room. Why would an Oster staff member be hovering over him making notes? Even more perplexing was the inexplicable way he fled the room the moment he laid eyes on him. He reflected on the enigma for a few more minutes but finally decided he was overthinking the incident. Surely there had to be a logical explanation for the man's presence.

As Hayden approached the nursing station, he spotted Robyn O'Brien speaking to one of the other nurses. Since Max's first admission to Oster, Robyn had taken care of him through many trying and uncertain days. She and Hayden were of similar ages, and both shared an unbridled passion for medicine. After a few months, it wasn't surprising they had developed a strong friendship.

When he was a few steps away, he noticed Robyn was gesturing freely as she spoke to Lynn Mateo, the assistant head nurse. He stopped to let them complete their conversation, but found himself already within earshot.

"You're overreacting," Lynn said. "We work in a hospital that cares for the sickest kids in the Midwest. Things like this happen."

"Max is the third patient this month we've lost from this horrible illness, and none of the doctors have the first clue what's causing it or how to treat it." With a wag of her finger, Robyn added, "I'm not trying to be argumentative, but I've been taking care of leukemia patients for eight years, and I've never seen an illness that remotely resembles this one."

Hayden's immediate thought was to discreetly retreat, but just as he turned, Robyn shook her head in frustration and caught sight of him. From the uneasy look that jumped to her face, he assumed she knew he'd overheard her conversation. After swapping a regretful look, the two nurses walked over and joined him.

Lynn spoke first. "I'm so very sorry, Hayden. Max was a great kid and so special to all of us. We're going to miss him terribly. I'll pray that you and your family find a way to get through this."

"Thank you. I appreciate your kind thoughts."

"If there's anything I can do, please call me." He responded to her offer with a nod and a well-mannered smile. She continued, "I've got a medication to give, and I'm already late. I'm sorry, but I better get going." Moving forward, she gave him a hug and then headed down the hallway.

"Are you leaving right away?" Robyn asked.

"I really should. I promised my parents I'd come straight home. I don't think they're doing very well."

"I'll walk you down to the lobby."

They walked off the unit and turned down the hallway that led to the elevators. Hayden sensed Robyn wanted to say something about her conversation with Lynn but was struggling to find the right words.

"I know how much it's bothering you that the doctors don't have an explanation for Max's passing," she finally said.

"Things like this sometimes happen in medicine. As physicians, we don't always have an explanation, especially when a patient takes an unexpected turn for the worse. Hopefully, in time, they'll be able to figure out the cause of death."

"You know how I feel about our doctors; if they can't figure it out, nobody can."

Hayden probably wouldn't have said anything to Robyn about

what he'd observed in Max's room, but her conversation with Lynn was still playing in his mind. As the elevator doors rumbled open, he decided to broach the topic.

"Something very strange happened when I went back into Max's room. There was a doctor I'd never seen before standing at the bedside writing in a small notebook. He didn't see me at first, but when he did, he practically bolted for the door. He didn't say a word or even look my way. I should have said something to him, but I didn't. Do you happen to know who he is?"

"His name's Dr. Abel Haas."

"What's his specialty?"

"He's a full-time bigwig in pediatric cancer research. He's an MD, but it's rare he does anything related to actual patient care," Robyn answered. "He's published hundreds of articles and textbook chapters on leukemia. The powers that be at Oster have recognized him several times over the years for his outstanding research contributions, especially in the care of leukemia."

"That surprises me. Why would a researcher even an outstanding one, be in a recently expired patient's room taking notes? And why would he race out of the room without explaining himself when a family member happened to come in?"

"We always have a large number of clinical research studies going on. Maybe Max was enrolled in one Dr. Haas was in charge of."

"I know every investigational study my brother participated in," he said with conviction as they stepped out of the elevator and started across the lobby. "Before my parents gave consent, I went over every one of them in detail with them. I don't recall seeing Abel Haas's name on any of them."

"If he wasn't in Max's room because of a clinical research study, then I have no idea why he was there."

"I overheard you and Lynn discussing the other two children who died of the same illness Max did."

"I kind of assumed you had."

"I had no idea there were other deaths," he said.

"The illness hasn't been a big topic of conversation in the hospital. Whatever this disease is, it has all the physicians scratching their heads."

He stopped her with a hand on her arm. "Do you know if Dr. Haas was in either of the other two patients' rooms around the time of their deaths?"

Robyn averted her gaze, but not before he noticed a hint of uncertainty in her eyes. Wanting an answer to his question and rapidly losing his concerns about being diplomatic or politically correct, he was prepared to press her on the point if necessary.

"I was working the day the first child died. She was a ten-year-old girl. I saw Dr. Haas go into her room a few minutes after the parents left."

"Do you recall how long he was in there?"

"I'd say about ten minutes."

"And the other patient?"

"I have no idea," she answered, as she took his arm and resumed walking. "Look, Hayden, whatever this illness turns out to be, it's become a touchy subject around here, especially in the last several days."

"In what way?"

"Nursing leadership informed us the first two cases were sent to the quality assurance committee for an in-depth review and root cause analysis. I'm sure Max's name will be added to that list. We've been…encouraged…not to discuss the cases with anybody."

"I'm surprised to hear that. I wouldn't exactly call that a culture of transparency."

Even though his mind continued to flood with questions, Hayden sensed Robyn's mounting discomfort and decided to tap on the brakes. He took a few minutes to thank her again for her devoted care of Max and to make sure she understood how much she had come to mean to him and his family. It was a tearful exchange that ended with his promise to call her as soon as the funeral arrangements were complete.

He walked out of the hospital into a gray overcast day. For the first part of his dreary drive home, his mind stayed busy recalling his fondest memories of Max. But as he turned onto Route 24 and headed toward Toledo, his thoughts shifted back to the strange circumstances surrounding Max's passing. He was as much perplexed as concerned that Oster would take steps to silence the nurses regarding an unexplained illness.

As a physician, his mind took him in the inevitable direction of wondering whether Max's passing was the result of more than just an enigmatic illness. Plagued by one unanswered question after another, he cautioned himself not to stray too far from rational thought. Even so, he realized he didn't have to be a card-carrying conspiracist to consider the possibility that there could be those at Oster who had reason to conceal information regarding the sudden inexplicable deaths of three of their leukemia patients.

An hour later, he pulled up in front of his parents' house. Instead of getting out, he placed his hands atop the steering wheel and stared at the home he and Max had grown up in. After a time, he stepped out of his car and made his way up the cobblestone driveway.

Before going inside, he walked to the far end of the wraparound porch that he'd helped his father build when he was a senior in high school. They had selected brown decking, and the structure was adorned with a dozen hanging philodendrons that had been placed precisely where his mother directed. Every two years, Hayden and his dad sacrificed a lazy summer weekend sanding and painting the porch. When he was old enough, Max became an enthusiastic member of the crew.

Curling his hands around the porch's red cedar railing, he set his eyes on the crescent moon that was partially obscured by a low deck of clouds. It had been easy enough to find out the identity of the man who had been in Max's room, but something told Hayden that discovering Dr. Abel Haas's motive for being there wouldn't be nearly as simple. Taking a couple steps back, he turned and started toward the front door, still pondering the chilling question of whether it was possible the death of his beloved brother could have been prevented.

Chapter 3

NELSONVILLE, OHIO

FOUR MONTHS LATER

PETITE IN FIGURE, with a soft face and an unforgettable smile, Leah Dunne had far greater reason to worry about her only child's aches and pains than most parents. It was twenty-three months ago that Charlee's pediatrician informed her that the easy bruising and constant fatigue she was suffering were being caused by acute leukemia. That evening, which was one month to the day after her seventh birthday, Charlee was admitted to Oster Children's Hospital. Before the week was out, she was started on an intensive regimen of chemotherapy.

Since her first admission, Charlee had been in and out of Oster more times than Leah chose to remember. Two months ago, her guarded optimism took an encouraging turn for the better when Charlee's hematologist recommended she be discharged with the plan of readmitting her at a later time to undergo her next phase of therapy. Leah was a stark realist and understood her daughter's ordeal was far from over, but the elation she felt at the prospect of having Charlee home for a few weeks sent her spirits soaring.

The few slivers of light that filtered into Charlee's bedroom from the hallway left it dim and shadowy. As Leah crossed the carpet, she could see her lying on her back with her left leg draped over the side of the bed. The strange configuration surprised her, as Charlee usually slept on her side facing the wall. The stuffed giraffe her grandmother had sewn for her fourth birthday, which she always kept tucked under her arm, had fallen to the floor.

"What's wrong, Munchie?" she asked, sitting down on the edge of the bed and placing her cheek on Charlee's forehead. When she felt it was clammy from tepid perspiration, an all-too-familiar anxiety stirred her gut.

"My mouth and tummy hurt, Mommy."

Leah reached over and turned on the bedside lamp. The instant her eyes fell on Charlee's sallow skin tone, she was filled with breathless fear. Her eyes swung to the right, becoming transfixed on the sticky pools of saliva bubbling at the corners of Charlee's mouth and a dry, scaly rash that covered her neck. Drawing back, Leah pushed a trembling hand against her mouth to cover a gasp.

Grabbing for a tissue, she moved closer and dabbed Charlee's lips. It was at that moment Leah noticed she was grinding her teeth, and the muscles surrounding her mouth were contorted in spasm. Having been at her daughter's side through every moment she'd been in the hospital, Leah believed she'd seen every possible complication that could befall a child being treated for leukemia. For the first time, that conviction was seriously shaken.

With her heart fluttering from the rush of adrenaline surging through her veins, Leah reached down, cradled Charlee, and slowly elevated her torso. But when her head drooped backward like a giant Raggedy Ann doll, she quickly eased her back down on the bed. Taking hold of the blue chenille blanket, she slid it down to her waist. Charlee's usual scaphoid abdomen was tightly distended, looking as if air had been forcibly pumped into her stomach.

Inhaling sharply, she said, "I'll be right back, Munchie."

"Don't go, Mommy. I had a bad dream. I'm scared."

"I'm just going to run to my room and get my phone. I'll be right back. I promise."

"No, Mom. Please, stay with me."

"You're okay, Munchie. I'll be back in two secs. I promise."

Above Charlee's continuing pleas, Leah raced back to her room. Through eyes made blurry by a rush of tears, she scrambled to find her cell phone. Consumed with frustration, her eyes continued to dart around the room. Finally, she spotted it on the dresser, wedged between a messy stack of equestrian magazines. Her hands were shaking even harder, but she managed to grab the phone and call 9-1-1. Fighting to hold herself together, she struggled to provide the operator with the information he requested.

Gulping one frantic breath after another, Leah sprinted back to Charlee's room. With everything around her in an uncontrolled freefall, she knew the only thing that mattered was getting her daughter to the closest hospital, where arrangements could be made to have her urgently transferred to Oster Children's Hospital.

Chapter 4

With its strobe lights flashing red and white and its back-up horn piercing the tranquil fall night, the ambulance carrying Charlee Dunne backed into the receiving dock of Hocking Medical Center's pediatric emergency room. The two paramedics attending to Charlee wasted no time unloading the stretcher and wheeling it into the special treatment room reserved for those children who were the most acutely ill.

"Do you know when the doctor will be in?" Leah asked the nurse who had just finished attaching the cardiac monitor leads. "I'm anxious to make the arrangements to get my daughter transported to Oster Children's as soon as possible."

"Dr. Pope is finishing up with another patient. He knows your daughter's here. I'm sure he'll be in shortly," she said, preparing to draw several tubes of blood.

"I'm worried about the way she keeps grinding her teeth and how fast she's breathing. Are her vital signs okay?"

"Her pulse is a little rapid, but her blood pressure is normal. I don't think she's in any immediate danger. She probably just picked up a virus somewhere and needs some IV fluids. I'm sure she'll be fine."

Leah in no way agreed with the nurse's assessment of Charlee's condition, and was shocked by her relaxed sense of urgency.

"Dr. Pope has ordered some blood tests, which I'm going to draw now. I saw from your intake information that Charlee is presently being treated for leukemia."

"That's correct. She gets her care at Oster Children's."

"Does she have a port?"

Leah nodded. "She went to surgery the day after her first admission and had it placed by the pediatric surgeons. She gets all her IV treatments and blood draws through it. It's next to her left shoulder and easy to feel under her skin."

"I'm quite comfortable with ports. I'd like to spare Charlee any discomfort, so I'd recommend we draw her blood tests through it instead of looking for an arm vein. Are you okay with that?"

"That's fine."

After she'd gathered the blood samples, she turned to leave. "My name's Danielle. If you need anything just push the call button."

"Thank you."

Leah turned her full attention back to Charlee. She was in a restless sleep, fitfully rolling her head from side to side every few seconds. In the bright light of the room, she could see her complexion was even more pallid than it had been at home.

Fifteen minutes passed, and Dr. Pope still hadn't made his appearance. Leah's patience had thinned to the width of a tissue turned sideways. Pacing in a tight circle, she was moments away from storming into the hall and demanding to see the nurse in charge when a butterball of a man with a flat nose dressed in rumpled scrubs waltzed into the room. Without so much as a glance in her direction, he walked over to the bed.

"Ms. Dunne, I'm Dr. Pope. I'll be looking after your daughter."

"Thank you, Doctor. I wanted to make sure I told you that Charlee's presently being treated for—"

"Leukemia," he said. "Yes, I know. I read the intake information on all my patients before coming into the room. How long has she been sick for?"

"She's been a little under the weather for about a week, but I didn't think it was anything serious. She really didn't become seriously ill until tonight."

"What do you mean by a little under the weather?"

"She was slightly more lethargic than usual, and her appetite was off, but as I said, she really didn't get sick until tonight. The moment I saw the change, I called the paramedics."

"I understand she's been home from Oster for a little over five weeks. Is that so?"

"Yes. We're due to go back for her next course of chemotherapy in a couple of weeks. All of her hematologists feel she's doing very well."

"From where I'm standing, I'd say that's hardly the case." In spite of Pope's less than polished bedside manner, Leah cautioned herself not to allow his uncaring manner to prompt her to forget her manners.

For the next few minutes, he continued his examination without asking any questions or offering any comments. When he was finished, he took a couple steps back and folded his arms in front of his chest. His gaze remained directed at Charlee.

The door swung open, and Danielle poked her head in. "The results of the blood tests are back, Dr. Pope."

With a hasty nod, he strolled across the room to a laptop workstation and pulled up the report.

"You mentioned she hasn't been eating well of late."

"She's a leukemia patient. Her appetite's never great, but it kind of depends on her chemotherapy schedule. Tonight, she ate about half of her dinner.

"Has she been vomiting at all?"

"No."

"Abdominal pain?"

"Not until tonight."

"How about fever?"

"Again, not until a couple of hours ago," she answered.

"I see from your information that you own a horse farm."

"I raise quarter horses for barrel racing."

"Has your daughter been injured recently?"

"For obvious reasons, I haven't allowed her near any of our horses since she was diagnosed with leukemia."

He finally looked up at her. "Has she lost any weight?"

"Charlee's always been a thin child. Being on chemo for most of the past two years hasn't helped matters. So, yes, she's lost some weight." Pope shoved his hands into the pockets of his white coat and said nothing for a moment. She could easily read the smug disapproval in his eyes and she thought she heard him humming under his breath. "Do you have an idea of what's wrong with my daughter, Dr. Pope?"

"I was just about to ask you the same question."

"Pardon me?" she said, feeling her face flush with anger. "With all due respect, I'd appreciate a straight answer to my question."

"Have you taken a good look at your daughter, Ms. Dunne?"

"Of course I have. That's why I'm here. What is it that you're not saying?"

"If you were in my shoes, would you believe that a patient who looks as ill as this child had only been ill for an hour or so?"

"I've dedicated my life to taking care of my daughter, Dr. Pope. I'm desperate for her to recover. Why in heaven's name would I lie?"

"I'm an emergency room physician, not a psychiatrist. Anyway, I think you'd be in a better position to answer that question than me." A sour look wrinkled his face. "What about her father… relatives…friends?"

"What about them?"

"Maybe they've noticed something you haven't."

Doing everything in her power not to allow the conversation to deteriorate into a regrettable altercation, she ignored his comment. Divorced for three years, Leah hadn't heard a word from her ex-husband in over eight months; a personal matter, the details of which she hardly felt compelled to share with him.

"Charlee and I live alone. It's just the two of us. Dr. Pope, I hope you're not trying to tell me that…that her blood counts are dangerously low."

"No, that's not the problem," he was quick to answer, tucking his pen back into his pocket. "Your daughter's problem has nothing to do with leukemia. She's suffering from severe malnutrition," he stated bluntly.

"Excuse me, but that's completely absurd."

"I'm confident in my diagnosis, and if we allow it to continue, it could take her life in a matter of a week or so. Perhaps, you didn't notice it."

She felt his eyes moving over her face.

"Surely, there must be some other more…more logical explanation that would account for Charlee's illness."

"I'm afraid not. The swelling of her abdomen, the rash, her blood tests… I could go on and on, but all the classic signs and symptoms of starvation are there. A third-year medical student could have made the diagnosis."

"Children don't act a little under the weather for a week and then suddenly appear as if they're starving to death."

"Which is precisely why it's impossible for me to believe that your daughter's only been sick for a week. She's obviously been deprived of nutrition for much longer than that. You said yourself that she's been home for over a month. Unfortunately, I have no way of knowing whether you simply missed it or purposely caused it."

"Are you accusing me of intentionally starving my child?" Leah's voice cracked with frustration. "Have you lost your mind? This child's the love of my life. How dare you suggest that I'd be capable of such a horrible thing?" Leah suddenly stopped and raised her hand to her mouth. "Dr. Pope, you've made a terrible mistake. Charlee's not starving to death. I'd like her to be seen by another doctor."

"I'm the only doctor here, and as I keep telling you my diagnosis is correct."

Leah fell silent, staring straight ahead as if she were searching for answers on the walls. When she was able to collect herself, she said, "I'm sure this is a good hospital, but it's not a children's cancer hospital, and with all due respect you're not a pediatric oncologist."

"I'm a board-certified emergency room physician. I feel perfectly comfortable caring for children of all ages, irrespective of what their illness happens to be. Be advised, Ms. Dunne, that I'll be contacting Athens County Children Services to report my findings. I'm sure the investigator will be happy to hear your side of the story."

It finally dawned on Leah that it was pointless to pursue a conversation with somebody who obviously had no interest in being bothered by the facts.

"I'd appreciate it if you'd call Oster Children's and arrange for my daughter's immediate transfer."

"I've already placed the call."

"Good. That's the first intelligent thing you've said," she said more to herself than Pope, although a part of her hoped he heard her.

"Ms. Dunne, sling as many arrows my way as you please. I'm required by law to identify the possibility of abuse or neglect and report it to the appropriate authorities. Your daughter's a minor, and it's my obligation to protect her."

"From me? Her own mother?"

"So it would seem. I'm going to order some medications, which I'm certain will improve her condition. Now, if there's nothing else, I have other patients to attend to." Without waiting for a response, he started toward the door. "Danielle will let you know when the transport team from Oster has arrived."

"Supposing you're wrong about Charlee, Dr. Pope?"

"Supposing I'm not," he said with a shrug, as he marched out of the room.

Feeling the same mixture of anguish and despair she'd felt the day she learned Charlee had leukemia, every particle of her being ached with uncertainty. Seeing her suffer a major setback and being accused of child abuse all in the same evening transcended inconceivable. In a fog-like state, she made her way back to the bedside. A new flood of tears spilled from the corners of her eyes.

Struggling to gather herself, she sat down and gently stroked Charlee's ash-brown hair. Her mind took her to the only place she could find solace. Somehow, amid the confusion and panic that inhabited her thoughts, she knew her guardian angels at Oster would do whatever was necessary to prevent her precious Charlee from being taken from her.

Chapter 5

After another grueling twenty-four-hour shift, Dr. Hayden Kubicek opened the door to his townhouse, tossed his time-beaten rucksack in the corner of the entranceway, and made his way to the living room. It was seven a.m., and the only thing on his mind was watching a little mind-numbing television until he fell asleep. Kicking off his favorite work sneakers, he fell onto a lumpy green corduroy couch he'd liberated from his cousin when he started medical school. A nostalgic smile came to his face when he caught sight of a framed photograph of Max and him attending an Ohio State–University of Michigan football game three years ago. It was those types of wistful memories that helped Hayden deal with the lingering grief of losing his only sibling.

It had been four long months since Max had died, and he was no closer to knowing the cause of his death now than he was that fateful morning. His abject failure was not for lack of trying. He had called and sent a litany of emails to a number of the physicians who had cared for Max. They had either failed to respond or did so with a polite dodge of his questions. He had also gone the route of contacting several of the administrators. The response was similar— well-scripted, polite, but vague emails filled with empty promises of a continued investigation into Max's death and their promise to advise the family the moment they discovered anything.

Hayden was disheartened by the brick wall he'd hit but light-years away from abandoning his efforts to uncover the details of how Max had died. He was determined to make sure beyond any doubt that his death wasn't the result of a medical error. If there had been a lethal mistake in his care and a wall of lies had been created by Oster to conceal it, it was his intention to tear that wall down.

After a couple of minutes of channel surfing, he settled on an *Animal Planet* rerun depicting a mother cheetah's struggle for survival on the Serengeti plains. As usual, it didn't take long for exhaustion to crawl out of its box. Before the first commercial, he was sound asleep.

At a few minutes past eight, he was abruptly wakened by several bangs of his brass door knocker. While he shook the sleep from his head, he stared at his noisy ceiling fan. Finally, he pushed himself off the couch and headed for the front door, wondering who could be pounding on his door at this time of the morning. When he opened it, a chubby man of average height stood before him. He had a lopsided jawbone and stubby hands that he held pushed against his sides. He held a white shoebox in his hands.

Hayden recognized him instantly. The mere sight of him caused his blood to simmer.

"Dr. Kubicek, I'm Dr. Abel Haas."

Neither of them extended a hand.

"I know who you are," Hayden was quick to respond, his face a stone mask. "I remember you busily taking notes in my brother's room the morning he died."

"I'm well aware of that. I understand from several people at Oster you've been asking a lot of questions about me and the circumstances surrounding your brother's death."

"You'll have to excuse me, but since you and everybody at Oster have ignored every request for information I've made, I saw no reason to make a secret of it."

"I'm sure we could talk all day about the politics behind why your inquiries have gone unanswered, but I suspect we have more important matters to discuss."

"Maybe it's too late, Dr. Haas. Maybe I've decided to approach the problem through different channels."

The edges of Haas's mouth creased into a dubious smile.

"I didn't come here to play mind poker with you, Doctor. We're both too smart for that. I assure you that your different channels will lead you to more dead ends. Focusing on the past isn't going to help you."

"I've had a long night. Why don't you just tell me why you're here?"

"I'm here to share critical information with you regarding Max's death," he said with conviction. "If you'd rather not listen to what I have to say, well, that's your choice, but I think it's a decision you'll long regret."

With his eyes set on Haas, Hayden steepled his fingers . He quickly surmised that Haas was correct—this wasn't the time for bluffing or idle threats.

Not wanting to wake up tomorrow knowing as little about Max's death as he did now, he pushed the door the rest of the way open, took a step to the side, and motioned Abel Haas to come inside.

Chapter 6

ONE WEEK LATER

CAREFULLY EXAMINING the latest styles in shirts his tennis club's pro shop had to offer, Dr. Jack Wyatt worked his way around the rotating display rack. Having faced a grueling schedule for the last several months without a weekend off had tested his resilience to the constant day-to-day stress of caring for the sickest patients in the hospital. Today, all that changed as his unforgiving schedule came to an end and he began a ten-day vacation.

"Hey, Doc," came a voice from the other side of the shop. Lifting his eyes from the rack, Jack saw Kurt Aubrey, the assistant teaching pro, holding up the phone. "It's your office." Having a pretty good idea why his staff hadn't called him directly, Jack's hand immediately went for his cell phone. It took him only a few seconds to confirm his suspicion that it was dead. He groaned inwardly. Perhaps with the one exception of remembering to charge his cell phone, Jack had an encyclopedic fund of knowledge and the memory of a mentalist.

He strolled over to the counter, thanked Kurt, and took the phone.

"Hello."

"There's a doctor looking for you."

"There's always a doctor looking for me, Meredith," he responded, glaring at the wall in front of him. "I'm on vacation. I thought we talked about this."

"This doctor drove all the way here from Defiance just on the off chance you'd be able to see her."

"She didn't call first?"

"No. She told me she didn't want to risk us telling her not to come. She was a tad anxious to say the least. I've been trying to get a hold of you for an hour."

"Fine. Give me her number, and I'll call her."

"That won't be necessary."

"I don't understand. Didn't you just say—?"

"She's kind of on her way over there to see you. I told her you wouldn't mind."

"Where? Here, at my club? I hope you're kidding."

"Don't blame this on me," Meredith said. "Your phone's been going straight to voicemail all morning. Did you forget to charge it again last night?"

Jack dropped his angular chin, seeing no reason to answer her rhetorical question.

"And you might tell whoever's running your snooty tennis shop that it might be nice if they'd answer their phone every now and then. I've been trying to reach them for an hour."

"Did she mention why she came all the way to Columbus to see me?"

"I didn't ask. All she told me was that she's the chief of staff at Oster Children's and it was urgent that she speak with you. I may be just your bumbling assistant, but that sounded pretty important to me."

Having no filters and an ill-placed informality were the cornerstones of Meredith's personality. It never rubbed Jack the wrong way, and since she was hands down the best practice manager he'd ever worked with, he was more than willing to overlook her quirky temperament.

"I'll give you a call later, before I leave town. And Meredith, don't worry about this. You did the right thing."

"Thanks, boss. Say hi to Madison for me."

Handing the phone back to Kurt, Jack absently thumbed at his ear lobe, a habit he'd acquired too long ago to remember. "Do me a favor, Kurt. There's some big shot from Oster Children's Hospital coming over here to speak with me. When she arrives, could you send her out to the court?"

"Sure, Doc."

Noticing a line forming behind him, Jack turned away from the counter and made his way over to the far wall to have a look at the latest-model tennis rackets.

He had been admiring the rackets for a few minutes when a casually dressed woman walked up, pointed at the one Jack was examining, and said, "Great choice. I've been hitting that model for the past six months, and love it. It has to be the most arm-friendly racket on the market. How bad is your tennis elbow?"

"Always there, but some days worse than others."

"Mine was awful, but that racket cured it."

Jack didn't recognize her, but it didn't surprise him. The club had a large membership, most of whom he'd never met.

"Althea Kavanaugh."

"Jack Wyatt. Excuse my poor memory, but have we played together?" he asked, guessing they were about the same age.

"No. Actually, Dr. Wyatt, I'm the big shot from Oster Children's."

Consumed with embarrassment, Jack squeezed his eyes shut.

"I'm terribly sorry, Dr. Kavanaugh. I didn't realize you'd be here so..."

"Please, call me Althea," she said with a warm smile. She extended her hand. "And I should be the one apologizing for disturbing you like this. I don't normally ambush my colleagues at their tennis clubs, especially when they're on vacation, but what I'd like to speak with you about is of critical importance."

Slight in size and slim-waisted, Althea had a face curved in the shape of a heart and ivory-colored skin. She was a well-intentioned woman who had found her stride later in her career when she was named the chief of staff at Oster. A pediatric dermatologist by training, she'd given up her practice when she'd accepted the offer from the board of trustees to work for Oster Children's full time.

"Let's have a seat," he suggested, pointing to a couple of canvas-backed wooden chairs on the other side of the shop.

Jack was quite familiar with Oster Children's, both for its excellent reputation in pediatric cancer care and the cutting-edge medical research they did. Notwithstanding his admiration for Oster, he was still puzzled why the chief of staff would go to all the trouble of driving down to Columbus to speak with him. His hope was he'd be able to help her with whatever the issue was quickly and get back on track enjoying the first day of his vacation.

He pulled his legs in and rested his hands on his knees.

"We're presently treating a number of our leukemia patients for a strange illness that...well...has all of us pretty well stumped. We admitted our first case about ten days ago. According to the parents, he'd only been sick for five days, but when we saw him, he had obvious signs and symptoms of advanced starvation. In addition, he was demonstrating severe spasms of his facial muscles, marked agitation, and excessive salivation. To put it bluntly, we've never seen an illness like this before."

"I'm not sure I understand. You said he'd been sick for less than a week. How could he be in such a severe state of starvation?"

"That's the same question we've all been asking ourselves every day," she answered. "I know this sounds impossible, but when we first saw him, he looked like he'd been adrift on the ocean in a rubber dinghy without food for a month. The next day, when we were still in a quandary trying to figure out what was wrong with him, we admitted two more leukemia patients with the identical symptoms, and since then, the number has kept growing. At about five this morning, I was notified that another four patients were on their way in." She paused as a pained stare came to her face. "That's when I decided to drive down here and talk to the most renowned expert on elusive diagnoses in the United States."

Jack was a gracious man but not one to accept compliments without being a little ill at ease.

Leaning forward in his chair, he said, "I'm flattered you'd ask for my input, but as much as I'd like to help, my training's in adult internal medicine and neurology. I really have no experience treating children, especially those with a serious illness like leukemia."

"I appreciate your modesty, Jack, but you're not an obstetrician either, and that didn't stop you from figuring out how to cure *Gestational Neuropathic Syndrome* a few years ago. If you hadn't done that, there's no telling how far the epidemic would've spread. It's been estimated you and Dr. Shaw saved the lives of thousands of pregnant women and their unborn babies. Except for AIDS, GNS hit this country harder than any other illness in the last fifty years."

"But that was an epidemic," he was quick to point out. "That doesn't sound like what you're dealing with at Oster."

"Not yet, but I'm well beyond worried that's exactly what we may be faced with before the month's out. Look, Jack, you've proven you have an uncanny ability to unravel diagnostic dilemmas. You come up with answers when all of those around you can do nothing more than scratch their collective heads."

"That's a compliment that I truly appreciate, but I can't think of a hospital that has more renowned experts on its medical staff than Oster Children's."

"That may be true, but none of them have been invited to the White House to receive the Presidential Medal of Freedom," she said with a grin. "I don't need another pediatric specialist. I've got a hospital full of them. I need a Sherlock Holmes—I need Jack Wyatt."

It was clear to him he was sitting across from somebody who combined adept persuasiveness with an unshakable determination to get what she wanted.

In a gesture of contrition, Jack raised both his hands. "Why don't you tell me a little more about the disease?"

The corners of Althea's mouth curled into the beginnings of a smile. She spent the next few minutes giving Jack a detailed description of the symptoms that accompanied the starvation disorder. She emphasized the children were continuing to lose weight, even though they were receiving the standard, time-tested treatment for severe malnutrition.

By the way Althea was looking at him when she had finished, Jack got the feeling she believed he was possessed of divine wisdom and would instantly provide her with the solution to Oster's medical dilemma. Even though some of the symptoms were neurological in nature, Jack didn't have a clue as to what illness could cause such rapid starvation. He had spent most of his career evaluating bizarre illnesses, but they were diseases that medical science had never seen before. That wasn't the case at Oster. Starvation is a worldwide epidemic, but very curable with the appropriate nutrition and medical care, leaving Jack baffled as to why the children being treated at Oster weren't responding to treatment.

"Is there anything in their medical histories that's common to the entire group?" he inquired.

"Aside from their underlying leukemia, the only two things all the kids have in common is they were outpatients when they became ill, and none were sick for more than about a week before they were admitted."

"How many patients have you admitted?"

"As of this morning, we're up to eighteen."

"Are there other children's hospitals in Ohio that are seeing the same illness?"

"We've been making daily calls to all of them. So far, none of them has seen any patients with similar symptoms. The same is true for the dozens of other children's hospitals across the country we've reached out to."

"I'm sorry, Althea but I can't think of anything off the top of my head that might shed any light on the illness. Obviously, not having examined any of the children or reviewing their charts in detail, it's almost impossible for me to offer a truly informed opinion."

"I had a feeling you'd say that, and that's precisely why I'm here. I know what I'm about to ask is a major imposition, but I was hoping you might consider coming to Oster for a few days to consult on the cases." Althea shifted in her chair. With her expression hopeful, she went on, "There are two things for certain, Jack: we're admitting more of these kids every day, and none of them are showing any signs of improvement, even though they're receiving maximal medical therapy. To put it bluntly, they're starving to death in front of our eyes. We're also very concerned that, before we know it, we could have a full-scale epidemic on our hands," she repeated. "We have no idea what kind of time frame we're looking at, but we all share the same fear. If we can't find an effective treatment for this illness pretty damn soon, the result could be catastrophic." Interlacing her fingers, she leaned in and said in a grim voice, "We need your help, Jack, and so do these children and their families."

Chapter 7

Before Jack could respond to Althea's plea, a woman dressed in a yellow tennis outfit and toting a white equipment bag approached. She was thirty-eight years old, had a toned figure, a slender neck, and delicate fingers. Attractive in an exotic way, her sharply curved facial features projected a unique allure.

Jack and Althea came to their feet.

"I wasn't expecting you for another hour," he said.

"My schedule changed, and I was done sooner than I anticipated."

Jack and Madison had first met at the University of Florida when she was a medical student on the neurology service and he was the chief resident. Jack would say they got off on the wrong foot; Madison would more bluntly call it a certifiable disaster. With no love lost, they went their separate ways to advance their medical careers. Their paths didn't cross again until several years later when Jack was summoned to South Florida to consult on the GNS epidemic. Madison, a fully trained perinatologist, was already working on the illness when he arrived.

To serve a higher purpose, they'd agreed to put the past behind them and do everything in their power to work together harmoniously. They were an improbable couple from the start, but as they spent more time together, their relationship took on an amorous pathway of its own. Although Madison was wrestling with some commitment issues, eighteen months earlier, she'd decided to accept a position in Columbus at the Children's Hospital of Ohio. Jack couldn't have been happier about her decision to relocate.

JACK TURNED TO ALTHEA. "I'd like you to meet Dr. Madison Shaw. Madison, this is Dr. Althea Kavanaugh. She's the chief of staff at Oster Children's."

"It's certainly nice to see you again," Althea said, shaking Madison's hand.

"Always a pleasure. You look wonderful, Althea."

He cleared his throat. "I wasn't aware you two already knew each other."

"We serve on several state and national committees together," Althea said.

With a knowing smile, Madison stated, "I didn't get your voicemail until a few minutes ago. Why am I getting the feeling you didn't drive all the way down here from Oster because you're interested in joining our tennis club?"

"I'm afraid your suspicions are correct."

"I attended our executive committee meeting yesterday," Madison said. "We discussed Oster's growing concern about this new condition you're seeing in your leukemia patients."

"I can't think of the last time we faced such a difficult and frustrating problem."

"How far have you and Jack gotten in your conversation about him coming to Oster?" Madison asked. "I assume you left the message for me to join you, hoping I'd help you persuade Jack to consult on the cases."

"Actually, that's only half correct. We'd be delighted to have both of you come."

"I'm flattered. Where do we stand with the arrangements?" she asked.

"As a matter of fact, Jack and I were just discussing that possibility when you arrived." Aletha turned to Jack and added, "As I said, We'd be grateful beyond words if you'd agree to join our team."

Jack regarded them suspiciously. "This feels a little bit like a double-team in basketball."

"Let's call it friendly persuasion," Althea said with a slight head tilt.

After swapping a glance with Jack that silently sealed the agreement, Madison said, "We should be able to be at Oster this evening. How does that sound?"

Althea came to her feet. "That...that would be perfect. I wouldn't know how to begin to thank you both. We have a lovely guesthouse on our campus for visiting faculty. I'll make sure it's ready for your arrival. A few days ago we formed a focus group made up of the key physicians involved in the care of these children. We'll be meeting late this afternoon." The corners of her mouth curled into a smile and she added, "I'll inform the group that Drs. Shaw and Wyatt will be consulting on the cases."

"We look forward to meeting the members," he said.

"It was a great pleasure meeting you, Jack." She handed him her card. "I wrote my cell phone number on the back. Let's plan on meeting at the welcome center in the lobby. Please let me know the moment you've arrived."

"I hate to ask," Jack said with some hesitancy, "but this is kind of short notice, and I don't know if I'll be able to make arrangements for my dog..."

A warm smile appeared on Althea's face. "Please, bring the dog with you. My husband and I raise Gordon setters and are avid dog lovers. We have a robust pet therapy program at the hospital. What kind of dog do you have?"

"He's a bluetick hound."

"Great breed. My brother lives in rural Virginia and always has three or four of them."

"You may regret the invitation," Madison chimed in. "Besides being a major slobberer, I'm afraid Moose is a little short on manners."

She chuckled. "Bring him anyway. I look forward to seeing you both this evening." After taking a few paces toward the exit, she came to a stop and turned around. "And, by the way, we have two clay courts on the campus, so feel free to bring your tennis gear." With a final wave and a thumbs-up, she headed for the exit.

"Grab your stuff," Madison said. "We still have plenty of time for a set or two before meeting your mother for lunch."

He looked down at his tennis bag, but instead of picking it up, he placed his hand lightly on her forearm.

"I saw a strange look on your face. Did you think I would turn down her request for help?"

"Not really, but I was afraid you'd be conflicted because you know we've really been looking forward to this vacation."

"But you—"

"Don't worry, Jack. I know who you are. I was just trying to make things easier for you."

"I understand but sometimes I get an inkling that you don't think I'm as in touch with your feelings as you are with mine."

"You're a great guy and a gifted doctor, but when it comes to relationships, it's sometimes hard to believe you're forty-two years old. It's kind of like your mother says—relationships aren't exactly your strongest suit."

"My mother is a great pediatric cardiologist, but I'm not sure she's an authority on affairs of the heart."

"She's one of the brightest people I've ever met. I'd be pleased to think that someday I'd possess half the insight she does."

"We've been talking about this vacation for a long time. I just want to make sure you're not too upset about us having to cancel it."

"We're not canceling it. We're just postponing it." Kissing him on the cheek, she grabbed her racket and pointed toward the courts. "Don't worry about it. Something tells me there will be plenty of blue-sky holidays in our future."

Chapter 8

Since the day Jack brought Moose home from the rescue center, he'd taken him everywhere that permitted dogs—and some places that didn't. When it was time to purchase a new car, he'd opted for a camper van instead. Although he continued to vehemently deny it, Madison insisted the only reason he'd bought it was to accommodate Moose.

After a two-and-a-half-hour ride, they exited the interstate and were passing through downtown Defiance when Jack stole a peek at Madison.

"You've been a little quiet. Do you want to talk about it before we get there?" Jack asked.

"Same answer, buddy. I have good days and bad days."

"Mentally or physically?"

"Each day's a little different, but it's generally a mixture of the two."

"Since you've had leukemia, how do you feel about taking care of a lot of children with the same illness?"

"I have leukemia, Jack—not had. It's a bit premature to imply it's a thing of the past."

"But your last bone marrow biopsy was normal."

"And it was wonderful news, but it was also only five months ago, and the truth of the matter is, I could relapse at any time."

"I understand, but your genetic profile and other tests put you in the best possible prognosis group. I think we have good reason to be optimistic."

"I'm doing my best dealing with the uncertainty," she said, shifting her gaze out the window. "But it's no fun walking around all day with a very large sword of Damocles hanging over your head."

"I just want you to know that I'm not the only physician in the country who specializes in elusive diagnoses. Any time you feel you want to leave Oster, all you have to do is say the word. We'll be totally honest with Althea, extend our apologies, and be on the next flight to paradise."

"Deal," she said, reaching over to take his hand. "If I'm not feeling a hundred percent, you'll be the first to know."

Somewhat reassured that Madison wouldn't conceal any health issues from him, Jack drove the last ten miles to the hospital without mentioning the topic again. As soon as they turned onto the Oster campus, he called Althea to confirm their plans to meet at the welcome center. They left Moose sleeping on his monogrammed dog bed in the back of the camper van. It was a cool evening, and as he always did, Jack lowered the back window a few inches and left the hound a bowl of water.

Oster Children's Hospital was a wonder of modern construction that achieved a textbook balance between practicality of structure and boundless imagination of design. Before the first drawing was ever rendered, the architects had organized concept meetings with parents, pediatric caregivers, and hospital administrators. The final product was an architectural marvel that included wide-open spaces with celestial ceilings, futuristic fountains, and mystical aquariums, all of which were in the setting of interactive activities. The ultimate cost far exceeded the Oster Family Foundation's projection, but there wasn't a single board member who objected to the overrun.

The moment they entered the lobby, Jack spotted Althea coming toward them.

"How was your drive up from Columbus?"

"Not too bad," Madison said.

"I know you must be anxious to get settled in, but before I take you over to the guesthouse, I thought you might want to take the nickel tour of the ICU and the leukemic malnutrition unit."

"That sounds fine," Madison said.

With an eager smile, Althea pointed toward the elevators and escorted them across the lobby.

"Because our public relations folks are expecting a firestorm of media attention, they suggested we come up with a name for the illness. We tackled their request at yesterday's focus group meeting, and after quite a long discussion, we agreed upon *leukemic malnutrition*. Everybody's already calling it LM." She shook her head. "Why is it that a disease doesn't seem to take on any real importance until medical science starts referring to it by its acronym?"

They departed the elevator on the third floor and walked down a broad corridor that ended at the entrance to the intensive care unit. Althea tapped in the entrance code on the keypad, and the doors swung open with a whoosh. The unit was much larger than most children's hospital ICUs. The seventy-eight beds were arranged in four separate treatment pods. Each had its own nursing station and was equipped with state-of-the-art monitoring equipment.. Althea took a few minutes to show Jack and Madison each of the pods, finishing the tour in front of a large atrium that had been designed as a parent lounge.

"This is certainly a beautiful facility," Madison said.

"We're very proud of it. If you're not too tired, there's one family I'm anxious to introduce you to tonight. Every infant and child we care for is special, but Charlee Dunne and her mom have especially captured our hearts. Charlee just turned nine, and unfortunately she was admitted last week with all the symptoms of leukemic malnutrition."

"We'd be happy to meet them," Jack said.

"This way." She gestured down the central hallway. "To maximize their care, we decided to admit all the leukemic malnutrition patients to the same treatment pod. Because of the number of new cases of LM we're seeing, we're also just about to designate a similar unit on the fourth floor."

Just as Althea raised her hand to knock on the door, it opened, and Leah Dunne appeared. Her shoulders were stooped, and the sclerae of her eyes were tear-stained and a subdued shade of scarlet from hours of crying.

"How are you, Dr. Kavanaugh?"

"I should be the one asking you that question."

"It hasn't been the best of days. The last time Charlee was discharged, I remember praying we'd never see the inside of the ICU again."

Althea took Leah's hands in hers. "We're going to figure this thing out and get her back on her treatment schedule just as quickly as we can."

In a voice consumed with a mixture of doubt and despair, Leah said, "I know the staff is doing everything they can, but to look into their eyes and see the hopelessness is beyond disheartening. I'm sorry to sound so pessimistic, but Charlee lost another pound in the past twenty-four hours, and her tummy's more swollen." Shaking her head slowly, she added, "It's getting harder to hold onto any hope at all."

Jack noticed Leah's chin trembled ever so slightly as she spoke.

Althea said, "I know I'm asking a lot, but please do whatever you can not to lose hope."

Leah smiled sadly. "It's a funny thing when a group of parents all find themselves in the same desperate situation. We talk about everything, and we don't keep secrets from each other. So I think I speak for all of us when I tell you we're all scared, but what terrifies us the most is that none of the doctors have ever seen this illness before, nor do they have the first clue how to treat it."

An uneasy silence followed. Althea lightly tapped her lower lip with her fingertips.

"Let me introduce you to Doctors Wyatt and Shaw," she said. "We've asked them to join our team, and they were kind enough to accept. They'll be consulting on Charlee's case." Leah stepped forward and extended her hand as Althea continued. "Dr. Wyatt's a neurologist who's an expert in a relatively new specialty called elusive diagnoses. Dr. Shaw's a highly experienced perinatologist from the Children's Hospital of Ohio."

"It's nice to meet you both. Although, I don't think there's a mother in this country who doesn't know your names. I thank you both for offering to help Charlee," she said her affect as flat as a skipping stone.

"We'll do everything we can to help," Madison promised.

Leah forced the hint of a smile to her face. "Charlee's an absolute angel. She doesn't have a disagreeable cell in her body. From the beginning, she's done everything the doctors and nurses have asked her to without making a peep. I know how wonderful this hospital is, but I've seen children come into this ICU and never leave. I don't mean to sound ungrateful. Believe me, I appreciate everybody's encouragement, but I feel like I'm holding on to the bottom rung of the ladder. Everybody keeps telling me and the other parents the same thing—we just need more time."

She paused, rolling her hands over to where her palms now faced the ceiling. "The part that's got me terrified is just how much time the doctors are talking about. I'm not a physician, but from where I sit, my daughter's running out of time pretty quickly."

Althea said, "All we can do is keep burning the candle at both ends trying to figure this thing out. I wish there was something else I could tell you, but for now I'm afraid there isn't."

"If you have some time tomorrow," Madison said. "Dr. Wyatt and I would like to spend some more time with you and Charlee."

"Of course. I'll be right here all day," she told them. "If you'll excuse me now, I should be getting back to Charlee. She's been sleeping so restlessly, I'd hardly call it sleep. I'm afraid to leave her alone for too long."

"I'll stop in early tomorrow," Althea said, to which Leah responded with a courteous nod before stepping back inside the room. The look of discouragement that settled on Althea's face spoke volumes.

As they started back down the hall toward the core desk, Madison said, "My pediatric rotation in medical school lasted eight weeks. One thing that has always stuck in my mind about these situations is how quickly the parents of seriously ill children are able to read between the lines of our well-intended platitudes."

"That's one reality I've never been able to navigate around," Althea agreed.

As they approached the exit from the ICU, Jack became lost in thought, struggling to keep himself emotionally detached from the situation. In spite of everything he'd been taught in medical school and during his residency, keeping a safe emotional distance by pushing Leah Dunne's heartache into some remote crevice of his mind was a lot easier said than done. What disturbed him more than anything was that he hadn't even examined his first patient with leukemic malnutrition yet, and he was already shaken to his core.

Chapter 9

Two hours had passed since Leah had been introduced to Jack and Madison. Learning from Althea that they would been consulting on Charlee's case bolstered her optimism, but she was still light-years away from believing Charlee's recovery was a certainty. The room was too warm for her, but since Charlee preferred it that way, Leah left the thermostat where it was. Every few seconds, her attention was drawn to the cardiac monitor over the bed. The way the multi-colored digital displays interacted with each other was almost hypnotic.

It hadn't been her intention, but she had drifted off to sleep for almost an hour. When she awakened, she pushed herself out of the large recliner and walked over to Charlee's bed. The moment she laid eyes on her, she felt her gut tighten. She was awake, but her mouth was clamped shut, her breathing fretful. At the corners, she had formed new collections of foamy saliva.

"You haven't gotten much sleep, Munchie. Why don't you try closing your eyes for a while?"

"I had another bad dream, Mommy. I'm afraid to go back to sleep." she answered, kicking off her covers. "Why's it so dark?" There was a slight slur to her words.

Seeing as the room was well lit, Leah found her comment concerning. With her brow was speckled with beads of perspiration, Charlee rotated her head from side to side across the pillow. Picking up a dry washcloth from the nightstand, Leah softly dabbed her forehead and mouth. She hadn't noticed it until now, but Charlee's gaze seemed vacant, and her sapphire blue eyes, which normally shone, were muted by an opaque glaze. Setting the washcloth down, Leah walked over to her purse and removed her cell phone. Before she returned to the bedside, she turned the dimmer switch on the overhead light up to its highest setting.

"I have a great idea. A little while ago, Barry sent me some terrific pictures of First Lady with her foal. Let's you and I take a look at them."

"Please, Mommy. I really don't feel like it."

"C'mon, it'll be fun. Nobody loves horses more than you do," she urged, holding her cell phone a foot and a half from Charlee's eyes. "This one's really great. First Lady's sure a wonderful mom."

"It's too dark and blurry. I can hardly see her."

"That's okay. How about this one?" Leah asked, swiping to the next photo.

"I can't see it, Mommy."

"That's okay, honey," she told her, staring into her languid eyes. Feeling her chin clench, Leah slowly moved her hand to the left, but Charlee failed to track the movement. Struggling to conceal her mounting panic, she said, "I'll tell you what, Munchie, let's take a look at the rest of these a little later. In the meantime, why don't you try closing your eyes again? I'll be right back."

"Where are you going?"

"I just want to ask Diana something. I'll be back in two minutes. I promise."

Feeling as if she were rooted to the floor, she gulped a frightened breath, set her phone down on the end of the bed, and quietly crossed the room. The moment she opened the door, she spotted Diana a few rooms down checking a medication. With her first step she was out into the hall, with her second she was standing next to her side.

"Something's wrong. Can you please come check Charlee right away? I...I think she's losing her..." Unable to utter another word, Leah covered her mouth with a tremulous hand.

Diana grabbed her stethoscope from around her neck, took Leah's arm, and guided her back toward the room.

"Take a breath and tell me what's wrong."

"There's...there's something wrong with Charlee's eyes," she finally managed in a voice shaking with panic. "My god, Diana—I think she's losing her eyesight."

Chapter 10

In the muted light of his kitchen, Dr. Abel Haas stared down at the bleached white capsule he was gently rolling between his thumb and index finger. Because potassium cyanide was readily available from multiple suppliers on the internet, acquiring it had turned out to be considerably easier than he had anticipated. He'd read extensively on the manner of death caused by cracking a cyanide capsule between one's teeth. Sixty seconds after it enters the bloodstream, the chemical robs every cell in the body of its essential oxygen, which quickly causes an untreatable cardiac arrest. He thought about how he'd seen it dramatized in old movies he'd watched on TV. The way the victims convulsed wildly and frothed at the mouth was exaggerated but not entirely inaccurate.

Haas was an enigmatic man who maintained a solitary lifestyle. Cursed by an incurable uneasiness in the company of others, he had never become comfortable in his own skin and went from day to day insulating himself from the world around him by wrapping himself in his work. His only sibling was a matriarchal older sister who had stopped speaking to him many years earlier for what she claimed was his utter selfishness.

He closed his eyes. Raising his hand to his mouth, he gingerly placed the capsule between his lips. He was convinced he had the courage to take his own life if it became his only option. But for the moment, he still needed time to come up with a solution to the most overwhelming problem he'd ever faced.

Removing the capsule from between his lips, he replaced it in a small plastic bottle. Strolling into the living room, he stopped briefly to gaze into the recessed brick fireplace. He again thought about the errors he'd made over the last thirteen years. He'd never thought of himself as somebody who would allow the past to haunt him. Even so, he constantly thought about what he could have done to make things play out differently. He had the honesty to admit he had made a mess of things. The harrowing thought of having to face the consequences had rendered him of no use to himself or anybody else.

With each passing week, he felt as if he were holding on by the thinnest of margins. The last few days had been particularly painful, as he found himself paralyzed by a maddening mixture of indecision and confusion. Finally, he realized his only option was to put as many miles between himself and Oster Children's Hospital as possible. As he looked across the room at a four-masted schooner in a bottle that he'd spent over two years building, his mind transported him to times that were less troubling.

He made his way into his bedroom, where he finished packing an olive-drab canvas duffle bag. Throwing it over his shoulder, he walked through the living room to the small entranceway. Just as he was about to open the door, he stopped and took a final look around. He filled his lungs to their capacity, held the breath for a few seconds before allowing it to silently slip out.

Having a realistic idea of what the future held in store for him, Abel Haas flipped off the lights and left his home for what he was certain was the last time.

Chapter 11

With the nascent sun burning off a stubborn morning ground fog, Madison and Jack stood at the entrance to the hospital's jogging trail. The two-mile-long path wound its way through eight acres of pristine woodlands, canopied along much of its length by the bowed branches of deep-rooted hickory trees. By eight thirty, they'd finished an ambitious jog and had returned to the guesthouse to get ready to go to the hospital.

As soon as they came through the doors of the ICU, Jack spotted Althea standing next to a portable x-ray machine talking on her cell phone. With a troubled look on her face, she raised a hand and gestured them over.

"I'm afraid there were a couple of rather discouraging developments overnight. To begin with, we admitted three new patients with leukemic malnutrition, and I was just informed two more are being transported to us now. And, for reasons that defy understanding, Charlee Dunne and two other children lost their eyesight." Her posture sagged. "This illness is becoming our worst nightmare come true. Not only are the hospitalized children deteriorating, but we're also seeing a steady stream of new cases."

"Has ophthalmology offered an opinion?" Jack asked.

"Both an ophthalmologist and a neuro-ophthalmologist have already consulted on the cases. Neither of them has any idea what's causing the blindness."

Just as Jack was about to pose another question, his phone rang. "Excuse me for a moment," he said, stepping away.

Just at that moment, a woman wearing a knee-length, immaculately pressed white coat approached with a brisk purpose in her step. "I'm glad I caught you, Althea. I'd like to speak with you about the leukemic malnutrition cases," she said, with no apparent outward concerns that she might be interrupting.

"I'd be pleased to hear whatever's on your mind, but before you begin, allow me to introduce you to Dr. Madison Shaw. Madison's a perinatologist at Ohio Children's." She turned to her left and continued, "Madison, this is Dr. Lennon Armbrister."

"It's nice to meet you," Madison said, to which Lennon responded with a distracted nod and an abrupt hand shake.

Slim-hipped, with probing emerald eyes and a delicately freckled complexion, Lennon was an outstanding hematologist. Recruited by Althea specifically to head up the leukemia program, she'd come to Oster after spending nine years at Los Angeles County Children's Cancer Clinic. Possessing a vast fund of knowledge, she also had an extraordinary instinct for patient care. Unfortunately, at times she conducted herself as if she hailed from a place where good manners were unknown. On too many occasions, her stubborn, unapologetic side created unnecessary tension and conflict. Althea had lost sleep wondering if bringing her to Oster was a mistake, but in the end, she'd always managed to convince herself that Lennon's medical expertise and devotion to her patients trumped her behavioral gaffes.

Jack finished his phone call and rejoined the group.

"And this is Jack Wyatt," Althea said.

"Dr. Wyatt needs no introduction," she said turning toward him. "I've been looking forward to meeting you since the moment Althea informed me you were coming." Moving a couple of steps closer to Jack, she added, "I followed every detail of the GNS epidemic in

Florida. What you accomplished there was one of the great medical achievements of the century."

"That's kind of you to say. It's nice to meet you."

"I know how busy we're going to be working on leukemic malnutrition, but I'd love to sit down with you some time. There are dozens of questions I'd like to ask you about GNS."

While Jack fiddled with the cuff of his shirt, he heard the unique scratchy tone of Madison clearing her throat. She was obviously irritated by the lavish praise Lennon continued to bestow upon him. He'd always been a quick study, and it hadn't taken him long to understand the many ways she cleared her throat was a language unto itself.

"Jack and Madison are going to be working closely with us, so unless you have an objection, I'd like them to hear what you have to say."

"I have no objections."

"In that case, you have the floor," Althea said.

"I know the focus group had a very detailed meeting yesterday, but there have been some recent developments that weren't on the agenda that I feel are extremely important."

"Such as?" Althea asked.

"In the first place, I don't think we should waste a lot of time and resources investigating improbable causes of leukemic malnutrition."

"Don't you think it's a little too soon to be taking that position? We've barely started looking into the disease. The consensus opinion is to take a broad view of things at first and then narrow our focus as we uncover concrete facts that either rule in or rule out a possible cause."

"I believe that would be a mistake," Lennon said. "We simply don't have the time to throw away chasing ridiculous notions down bottomless rabbit holes. You don't have to look any further than yesterday's meeting to see what I'm saying. There were some pretty wild theories regarding possible causes. I assure you, leukemic malnutrition isn't a previously undiscovered side effect of chemotherapy; nor is it some bizarre environmental toxin, or a new variant of leukemia."

"You seem quite convinced of what it's not," Althea stated in an even tone of voice. "Do you have an idea of what it might be?"

"Leukemic malnutrition is being caused by a rapidly mutating virus," she pronounced. "There's no question about it, and unless we get everybody on board with the idea, a lot of innocent children are going to start dying."

Chapter 12

"A rapidly mutating virus? Excuse me, Lennon but why didn't you mention this theory of yours at the focus group meeting?" Althea asked.

"There are still a few loose ends that need tying up, and to be perfectly honest, I'd prefer to discuss it with you before putting it to the entire group."

"With all due respect, Lennon, it's the express purpose of the focus group to discuss these types of issues without a prior review by me or anybody else. At the risk of repeating myself, I believe the smartest thing we can do is take a broad view of things. Later, we can——"

"Later is the enemy; later will mean the wholesale death of countless children; later is simply not an option," she insisted, folding her arms in front of her. "Can't you see that?"

"I think you may be overreacting a little."

"Overreacting? There's no time for a relaxed approach to the worst problem this hospital has ever faced. Can you assure me that a week from now we won't have a hundred of our leukemia patients starving to death and going blind right down the hall from where we're standing at this moment? If you can make that assurance, by all means do so, and I'll go quietly into the night."

Madison laid a subtle hand on Jack's arm, raised her eyebrows, and they both took a couple of steps back.

"I think we both know nobody could make such an assurance," Althea said. "But panicking and shooting from the hip could have devastating consequences. If we have any hope of beating this thing, we need to stay calm and act as a professional team."

Lennon responded glibly with a tilt of her head and an annoyed sigh.

Jack studied her face and manner. She appeared to him as somebody who was convinced she was shouting at the rain.

"Look, Althea, I understand that I remain employed here at Oster at the pleasure of the board of trustees. But I'm not going to remain silent about a life-threatening illness for fear of being labeled politically incorrect or failing to understand the importance of some Reader's Digest definition of teamwork."

Jack glanced over at Madison, whose return look was one of disbelief. If his impression of Althea was correct, she wasn't going to allow her conversation with Lennon to deteriorate into a petulant disagreement in the middle of the ICU, especially in front of two visiting physicians.

Althea's response was measured. "I understand your concern, Lennon, and I appreciate your passion, but it might better for us to discuss this later in my office."

"We can have all the off-line conversations you want, but I'm telling you the cause of leukemic malnutrition is a highly virulent virus that's mutating at an incredibly rapid rate. If we have any hope of curing this illness, that's where we need to focus every drop of talent, resources, and energy we have."

"I'm not saying your theory's incorrect," she said, stealing a glimpse of Jack and Madison. "I'm only saying we shouldn't dismiss every other possibility out of hand."

Lennon took a step closer to Althea and said, "Take a look around. The parents of these children are becoming more desperate and terrified with each passing day, and that's because we've been unable to provide them with any answers that might give them even a speck of hope. And in case you haven't noticed, physician and nursing morale is in a tailspin because everybody's working eighteen-hour days trying to save these children." After halting briefly to take a breath, she continued in a voice barely above a whisper. "And I'm sure you've heard the same rumors I have—that both the nurses and parents are wondering if leukemic malnutrition resulted from some physician error or hospital mishap."

"I think we both know that there's not a shred of evidence to support that. The parents have no reason to believe leukemic malnutrition happened because of some medical mistake."

Shaking her head slowly, Lennon responded, "I think the parents will decide for themselves what they will or will not believe. I've been working on this theory around the clock, and I've made significant progress, but I've reached a point where I need the help of my colleagues...especially an expert virologist."

"Why don't you stop by my office this afternoon? If it's that important to you to discuss your theory with me prior to bringing it to the focus group meeting, I'll make an exception."

"Thank you. I'm confident, once you understand how I arrived at my conclusion, you'll be as convinced as I am." Lennon turned to Jack and Madison. "I look forward to working with you both."

"That's one tough lady," Althea stated, after Lennon had disappeared down the hall. Shifting gears, she said, "The board of trustees authorized a press briefing for early this afternoon. A lot of what's going on has already been in the media, but there's no question it's becoming a much more important story, and something tells me it's going to get worse before it gets better." She looked down at her watch. "If you're ready, why don't I make rounds with you and introduce you to some of the parents?"

"Sounds like a plan," Madison said.

"Give me a couple of minutes," she said as she started away. "I just want to let the nurse manager know we're making rounds, in case she wants to join us."

Once they were alone, Jack asked, "What did you think of that little encounter?"

"From the way Althea just handled Lennon Armbrister, I'd say her leadership skills are pretty sharp, but it's obvious she's worried. I think she knows the hospital's looking at a crisis that's not going to go away by sprinkling a little pixie dust on it."

"I certainly don't envy her position. I get the feeling Oster's more accustomed to dealing with problems where negative publicity isn't a possibility." Jack spotted Althea heading back toward them. While she was still out of earshot, he added, "It would be nice someday to consult at a hospital where the politics weren't as thick as an ocean fog."

Chapter 13

After spending the afternoon reviewing the latest lab and x-ray results of the leukemic malnutrition patients, Jack and Madison took a break from the hospital. Instead of going for a run, they decided to take advantage of the loaner bikes provided by the hospital. They had just completed the entire five-mile course and were returning the bikes to the rack when Jack's phone rang.

A knowing look appeared on his face. "It's Althea."

"Right on time," she said with a muted chuckle." I guess her meeting with Lennon must be over."

"Hello." Jack listened for a couple of minutes and then said, "Of course. Actually, we felt like we needed a break and just finished up a bike ride." Another few seconds passed, and Jack said, "That will be fine. We'll see you in a few minutes." He ended the call and tucked his phone away. "Althea said she needed our help, and if possible, she'd like to talk to us in her office ASAP."

"About Lennon?" Jack nodded. "That should be an interesting conversation."

"I told her we'd be right over."

"Sorry, buddy. I promised Leah Dunne I'd come back and speak with her. Why don't you speak with Althea and fill me in later? I'm confident you can handle this one alone."

At first, Jack grinned on the inside, but after a few seconds, it blossomed into a full-on smirk.

"You've never been one for dicey political situations," he told her.

"I'll take that as a compliment. I went to medical school to become a doctor and practice medicine, not to spend my time tiptoeing through politically sensitive minefields."

With a bit of a sigh, he said, "There are times when I wish I'd made the same choice." They finished putting the bikes back in the rack. "I'll give you a call as soon as I leave Althea's office."

Chapter 14

"Thanks for coming over on the spur of the moment," Althea said, leading Jack to a smartly decorated alcove where they each took a seat in matching high-backed upholstered club chairs.

"No problem. Madison asked me to convey her apologies for not being here. She promised Leah Dunne she'd stop in and didn't want to disappoint her. I'll brief her on our meeting later."

Fiddling with her wedding band, Althea eased back in her chair. From the solemn expression that crept to her face, he sensed her conversation with Lennon hadn't resolved matters.

"About an hour ago, I met with Lennon regarding her mutating virus theory. I know you haven't had the opportunity to get to know her, but in spite of what you witnessed this morning, she's a talented physician who's passionate about her work—sometimes to a fault, as far as her behavior's concerned." She paused for a few seconds before going on. "This is it in a nutshell. Based on recent research Lennon's come across, she's absolutely convinced her viral theory's correct."

With his interest piqued, Jack asked. "What's the nature of the research?"

"It was work done by a Dr. Karina Austin. She's a pediatric infectious disease specialist with a PhD in virology who just happens to have a special research interest in leukemia. The research was done right here at Oster in collaboration with one our senior scientists. Lennon claims Dr. Austin used highly detailed genetic profiles she created to predict the likelihood a particular leukemia patient would become infected by a specific rapidly mutating virus."

Jack said, "It's an interesting theory, but even if it's true, it's not definitive proof that leukemic malnutrition is being caused by a virus."

"It gets more interesting. Lennon told me that every child we've admitted with leukemic malnutrition appeared on one specific list Austin compiled. She also informed me that she studied the research in detail and insists it was carried out with flawless scientific technique, and we shouldn't hesitate to accept it as one hundred percent accurate." Pressing her palms together, Althea continued in an edgy voice, "My problem is that I simply can't accept this...this list as the holy grail and dismiss all other possible causes of LM. It would mean devoting all of our time and resources to Lennon's viral theory...and, well, I'm simply not prepared to do that."

"Nobody would blame you for that."

"I'm glad you feel that way, but just to be sure what would you say to you and Madison having a look at Dr. Austin's research and offering me an opinion as to its quality and the likelihood Lennon's medically justified in feeling so strongly about its accuracy?"

Jack assumed before he set foot in Althea's office that he might be asked to do something a little on the irregular side, although he'd hoped it might be less politically tricky than swimming across a river overflowing with ravenous crocodiles.

"Surely you have numerous highly qualified physicians and scientists here who could offer you an authoritative opinion on the quality of the research. Madison and I are invited consultants. The last thing we want to do is offend any of Oster's regular medical staff."

"If I ask one of our own...well, it will undoubtedly stir up a hornet's nest of controversy. I'm sure Lennon would immediately move center stage and rail that I'd ordered an insulting departure from our normal procedures."

"But ultimately, you cast the deciding vote."

She stood up and walked over to an impeccably designed floor-to-ceiling dark wood bookcase. Each of its shelves was filled with medical tomes, patient files, and scientific journals.

"You're absolutely correct. I do have the deciding vote, but my concern is that things are stressful enough around here without adding a turf war to the mix. If you and Madison evaluate Austin's work, nobody else needs to know about it except the three of us. Since I'm the one in the wheelhouse, the board of trustees naturally expects me to plan the best way forward. I need your opinion, Jack. And I need it as soon as you can get it to me. I don't know any other way of putting it."

Jack had played chess competitively when he was in college. He knew checkmate when he saw it.

"Madison and I will get started on it tomorrow."

In a voice that echoed her relief, she stated, "I can't tell you how much I appreciate this. Now, before you get started, I suggest you speak with Dr. Kendric Nash. He's an MD, but he spends almost all of his time heading up our research program. I'll give him a call to make sure you and Madison get everything you need."

"Sounds good."

"Perfect."

Althea came out from behind her desk and escorted Jack through the inner office and down the corridor to the elevator.

"Madison and I will give you a call tomorrow afternoon to update you on our progress."

"That's one phone call I'm very much looking forward to receiving."

Jack stepped off the elevator at the lobby level and started toward the exit. He was still mulling over Althea's proposal when it occurred to him that Madison might not approve of this back-door request. As he approached the hospital, he decided the best way to handle the situation was to hope Madison took things in stride but to be prepared to convince her of the importance of supporting Althea if she didn't.

Chapter 15

As soon as the automatic doors to the ICU swung open, Jack spotted Madison standing at the core desk.

"How's Leah Dunne doing?" he asked.

"Not great. In addition to everything else that's going on, she told me she had a horrendous experience in her local emergency room the night Charlee got sick. Apparently, the physician on duty was a total jerk. He accused her of child abuse and then reported her to Children's Services. She was understandably devastated. She asked Althea to get involved to see if she could help and she of course agreed."

"I don't know too much about these things, but I suspect asking Althea for assistance was the right move."

"Let's hope so. How did your meeting go?"

After Jack shared the details of Althea's request, a dubious look came to her face.

"My guess is that keeping our involvement in this secret mission confidential will be about as possible as sneaking the dawn past a rooster. Before this is over, there are going to be a lot of bruised toes from where we stepped on them, especially Lennon's. She's going to have a hissy fit when she finds out about this."

"I wish I could say I'm certain you're wrong, but I don't see what choice we have. Anyway, Althea wants us to speak with Dr. Kendric Nash before we get started on the review. He runs the research program."

"Sounds like a good idea."

Finger combing his hair briefly, he said, "On the way over here, I was thinking about the best way we should handle this thing."

"I feel an attack of angina coming on," she said, folding her arms across her chest.

"Since you have a lot more experience with clinical research than I do, I was thinking it might be better if you meet with Dr. Nash tomorrow morning while I go to the hospital. I'll make rounds and meet up with you later. That way, we can have a look at her research together."

With an acerbic smile, she said, "Sounds great."

"I sense a little sarcasm in your voice."

"I already agreed, Jack. My father taught me the first rule of salesmanship: as soon as you have a signed order in hand—leave."

Jack realized Madison was less than thrilled about complying with Althea's request, but if there was one thing he had learned about her, it was that, absent an overwhelming objection to a proposal, she was likely to go along if only to keep the peace.

"That's good advice. I have an idea. How about calling it a day and finding a nice, quiet, romantic place for dinner?"

"Fine, on one condition."

"Shoot."

"We call a moratorium on all discussions related to leukemic malnutrition or Oster politics until tomorrow."

"I agree," he said sending a mock salute her way as they strolled toward the exit.

Chapter 16

After a bit of discussion, Madison and Jack decided on a nearby family-style Italian restaurant for dinner. With Frank Sinatra crooning Christmas favorites in the background, they nursed a couple of glasses of classic Chianti and split a large grilled antipasto plate. Enjoying a leisurely meal, they mostly talked about the trip to Australia they'd been contemplating for quite some time. They had been seated for almost two hours when they finally signaled their chatty server to bring them the check.

When they arrived at the guesthouse, Jack went into the living room where he grabbed his latest *New York Times* Sunday crossword puzzle and fell into a leather recliner.

"I'm going to jump into the shower," Madison said from the bedroom doorway.

After working on his puzzle for twenty minutes with marginal progress, he tossed it back on the coffee table and went into the bedroom to get his laptop. The sound of the water running was almost eclipsed by Madison's rendition of one of her favorite Alicia Keys songs. Jack grinned while applauding in his mind her decision to devote her life to medicine and not the performing arts.

He strolled back into the living room and stretched out on the couch. Moose jumped up, curled up at his feet, and laid his slobbery jowls on Jack's ankles. Adjusting a velvety throw pillow under his head, he closed his eyes. He hoped a brilliant revelation unmasking the cause of leukemic malnutrition would suddenly pop into his head, but after a few minutes of heavy thought with no flash of genius, he sat up and sighed forcefully.

Just as he did, the land phone rang.

"Jack Wyatt."

"Good evening, Doctor. This is the hospital operator. I'm terribly sorry to disturb you, but I have a physician on the line who wishes to speak with you. With all the publicity we've been getting, we're receiving a lot of calls like this. The administration asked us to screen them carefully before putting any of them through. I'm sorry, Dr. Wyatt, but he's a physician and a very persistent young man."

"Did he tell you why he wanted to speak with me?"

"Oh, yes. He said he had critically important information about leukemic malnutrition and that you were the only person he'd speak to."

Jack gazed up at the white popcorn ceiling briefly. "It's okay. Go ahead and put him through."

"Thank you, Doctor. Please hold for Dr. Kubicek."

Chapter 17

"This is Jack Wyatt. How may I help you?"

"Dr. Wyatt, thank you for taking my call. My name's Hayden Kubicek. I'm a physician. I apologize for disturbing you like this, but I have critically important information regarding leukemic malnutrition that I'm anxious to share with you."

Understandably skeptical, Jack said, "If you don't mind me asking, Dr. Kubicek, what's the nature of this information?"

"I'd rather not discuss the specifics on the phone. The purpose of my call is to set up a time we can meet in person."

Jack rubbed the back of his neck. "I'm sure you can understand how busy we are with this problem, Dr. Kubicek. The number of calls we're receiving from concerned physicians such as yourself offering to join our team has been remarkable. Unfortunately, we simply can't—"

"I've no interest in joining your team, Dr. Wyatt. I'm calling you because I'm certain I know the cause of leukemic malnutrition. I'm convinced, once I show you the scientific evidence I've accumulated, you'll agree with me."

"Certainly, you must be—"

"You can rest assured the information I have is accurate and will save you and the other physicians you're working with hundreds of hours of building bridges that will take you nowhere."

Jack was struck by Kubicek's calm, self-assured manner, and the conviction in his voice prompted him to dig a little deeper.

"I'm sure you're aware that some of the brightest minds in the country are right here at Oster. They have every conceivable resource at their fingertips and, to a person, are working around the clock trying to solve this problem."

"And how are they doing so far?"

Ignoring the question, Jack said, "I assume you haven't examined a single one of these patients, nor have you reviewed any of their medical records."

"And you'd be quite correct in that assumption."

"Which begs the question: why would you have any specific knowledge or special insight into this illness?"

"The manner in which I acquired the knowledge is hardly the point. All I can tell you is that I have irrefutable medical proof as to the cause of leukemic malnutrition." Jack thumbed a new crop of chin stubble. He was just about to respond when Kubicek stated, "If you decide not to meet with me, I fear all the children you're presently treating plus many more who have yet to be admitted will suffer a fatal outcome."

"That's quite a prediction," Jack said, realizing it would be futile to ask Kubicek to back up his fervent claim. "If you don't mind me asking, what's your specialty?"

"I'm a second-year family medicine resident."

Dumbfounded by Kubicek's answer, Jack almost dropped the phone. He assumed he was speaking to a highly experienced hematologist or some other pediatric super sub-specialist, not some rookie whose medical degree was still wet with undried ink.

"I'm not trying to sound skeptical or unappreciative, but—"

"Dr. Wyatt, if you're wondering if I'm some sort of crackpot, I assure you I'm not. You have the reputation of being an outstanding clinician. I'm praying your intuition is equally as sharp. All I'm asking is that you invest thirty minutes of your time."

As was the case with the GNS outbreak and other enigmatic

cases Jack had consulted on over the years, he had been approached by many well-intentioned physicians who felt they possessed unique knowledge that could save the day. After a while, he was able to spot them coming a mile down the road. But something told Jack that he'd be making a mistake if he counted Kubicek among them, and for reasons he couldn't get his head around, he was inclined to take the meeting.

"I've only been at Oster for a short period of time, Dr. Kubicek. To my knowledge, my being here hasn't been reported in the media. If you don't mind me asking, how did you know I was here?"

"I know several people at Oster. Your presence there is hardly a matter of national security."

"I understand you'd prefer not to discuss the specifics of your theory, but would you at least share with me if you believe a virus is the cause of leukemic malnutrition?"

"Leukemic malnutrition is not a viral illness," he answered with impunity. "If it will help you make a decision, I believe I may know where to start looking for the cure."

"Excuse me, Dr. Kubicek. You've already asserted you know the cause of leukemic malnutrition. Are you now saying you know how to cure it?"

"What I'm saying is that, based on the information I've gathered, I've come across a concept that could very easily turn out to be an important clue leading to a cure."

"Why me?"

"Excuse me."

"There are countless people and agencies you could be calling right now instead of me."

"I've discovered the cause of leukemic malnutrition, the specifics of which must be presented to the medical community by a physician with an impeccable reputation and unshakable credibility; that would be you, Dr. Wyatt. And for reasons I'd rather not get into now, this information should come from somebody who has no formal relationship with Oster Children's."

"If I agree to meet with you, I'd like to invite another physician to sit in. Dr. Madison Shaw and I were asked to come to Oster together, and I think it's essential she attend."

"I remember Dr. Shaw from the GNS outbreak, but I'm not sure I can agree."

"This is a deal-buster for me. Either she sits in, or there's no meeting. The choice is yours."

"Okay, Dr. Wyatt. We'll do it your way."

"When would you like to meet?"

"I have to tie some loose ends, which includes a short trip to Cleveland. Would you be able to meet next Tuesday morning at ten at Oster?"

"We'll meet you at the faculty guesthouse. It's here on the main campus."

"Thank you for taking the time to speak with me. I look forward to meeting with you and Dr. Shaw."

With Moose on his heels, Jack walked over to his computer case and removed his laptop. He tapped in Kubicek's name, and after a few minutes of querying various sites, he was able to confirm that he was a second-year family practice resident at Flower Hospital in Toledo.

He was just about to go back into the bedroom when Madison came through the door. She was dressed in a blue terry cloth robe and was briskly drying her hair with a fluffy white bath towel.

"I heard you on the phone. Who were you talking to?"

"A family practice resident from Toledo by the name of Hayden Kubicek. He claims he knows what's causing leukemic malnutrition."

She stopped rubbing her hair and looked at him skeptically.

"Considering the illness has some of the sharpest medical minds in the country completely stumped, that's a pretty arrogant claim... and why would a family practice resident know anything about leukemic malnutrition?"

"I asked him that very question. He told me he preferred not to share the specifics with me on the phone. He only wants to discuss it face to face. He was very convincing. I checked him out online, and he is who he says he is."

"How did you persuade yourself of that?"

"Pardon?"

"If you found him online, so could anybody. All you really know is there's a resident by the name of Kubicek working in Toledo. How do you know he wasn't some reporter posing as this doctor hoping to get a story?"

"I don't, but I'm willing to take that chance."

"Are you telling me you agreed to meet with him?"

"I did, and I volunteered you as well. We're going to meet with him next Tuesday morning."

"You can't be serious."

"Don't I sound serious? Look, if we meet with him and he turns out to be a head case, we can politely get rid of him." He shrugged his shoulders and added, "The worst thing that can happen is we've wasted an hour of our time."

"This must be your lucky week. Dr. Kubicek's the second doctor you've come across who's convinced they can unlock the mystery of leukemic malnutrition."

"Which reminds me, I asked him if his theory had anything to do with a virus, and he assured me it didn't. It was the only thing he shared with me."

"I guess we'll just have to wait until next week to find out if this Dr. Kubicek is on the level or not," she said, sitting on the side of the couch putting her contact lenses in unaware that Moose was at her feet chewing on the handle of her hairbrush. Hoping she wouldn't notice, Jack swooped in from behind her, snatched it from Moose's mouth, and put it on the table.

———

SIXTY MILES AWAY, Hayden Kubicek sat in his apartment adrift in thought about his conversation with Jack Wyatt. Being a strong believer in the old wisdom that you only have one chance to make a first impression, he was well aware that a detailed preparation was his best strategy to avoid fumbling the meeting. Leaving Drs. Wyatt and Shaw unconvinced would buy him a polite but unceremonious escort to the front door.

He could feel the stress playing havoc with his gut but found a measure of solace in thinking about his weekend plans. Once a year, he and five of his closest friends from Oberlin College met for a mini-reunion. He couldn't recall ever volunteering, but from the get-go, he had been the one in charge of making all the arrangements.

The high point of the weekend was always the same—their participation in the *Tough Mudder Challenge*, this year to be held in Lexington, Ohio. The event, which was definitely not for the faint of heart, was an eleven-mile obstacle course whose sole purpose was to test the competitors' physical prowess and mental tenacity. Among the demanding tests, the participants were required to scale a variety of daunting walls, plunge themselves into ice water pools, belly across heavy mud fields, and endure electric shocks. Six years had passed since their graduation, but they still considered themselves to be top jocks.

Suddenly remembering he had plans to meet with a group of his fellow residents from the hospital for drinks, Hayden threw on a pair of jeans and a faded midnight-blue Toledo Mud Hens sweatshirt. Grabbing for his wallet, he glanced at the clock on his nightstand.

"Late as usual," he muttered, as he hurried out of his room and made his way to the front door.

Distracted by being late and still pondering his conversation with Dr. Wyatt, Hayden backed his ten-year-old hatchback out of the driveway, oblivious to the white panel truck parked across the street. He drove off, never noticing the truck had eased away from the curb and that the woman driving was cautious not to follow too closely.

Chapter 18

Even though she walked at a good clip, it took Madison twenty minutes to reach Oster's research facility. The building was an eight-story structure, the creation of a Dutch surreal architect whose goal was to make it the crowning achievement of her career. The manner in which she'd blended the qualities of glass and marble in a modernistic style was convincing evidence she'd accomplished her goal.

Exiting the elevator on the fifth floor, she followed a winding corridor to the office of Dr. Kendric Nash. The door was open, and she spotted a plump man staring at his computer monitor. Madison tapped lightly on the door. Nash pushed his reading glasses toward the tip of his nose, swung his gaze in her direction, and then heartily waved her forward. With a welcoming smile, he came to his feet and met her in the middle of his office. She was quick to notice his full head of unkempt silvery hair and dense walrus mustache that reminded her of her favorite uncle.

"You must be Madison. Welcome," he said in a robust but scratchy voice. "Please, have a seat. Althea told me you'd be paying me a visit this morning."

"It's a pleasure to meet you, Dr. Nash," she said, taking a quick look around and instantly surmising that, if the administration offered physicians funds to refurbish their offices, he'd never taken them up on their offer. The space was generous enough, but the decor cried out for everything from new built-ins to a plusher grade of carpet.

"I insist you call me Kendric," he said, straightening his striped bow tie. "I'm so delighted you're here. Althea told me all about Lennon's theory regarding the cause of leukemic malnutrition. It's certainly very interesting." Madison was saved from responding when he suddenly slapped his thighs with purpose. "So tell me, how can I help you and Jack?"

"I was hoping we could talk a little about Dr. Austin's work."

"I'll be happy to share with you what I know." He flattened his hands on his leather desk pad like an excited teenager about to disclose a juicy piece of gossip. His expression changed in a way that made her wonder if something else had just popped into his mind. "Would you like some tea first? It's from the Orient, and it's excellent."

"No...no, thank you," she said, remembering a time several years ago when she'd experimented with different Far Eastern blends. Kendric struck her as a bit flighty and over-animated. As long as she could remember, she'd relied on first impressions— perhaps too much. "How did Dr. Austin come to do research here at Oster?"

"She called one day and asked if she could collaborate with us on a project. As I recall, she held both an MD and a PhD, and required access to the records of a large number of leukemia patients for her research. We asked her a number of questions about her project; her answers were appropriate, and since we've had a long-standing policy of encouraging young researchers, I approved her request."

"How long was she here?"

"All of her work was done virtually, so she was never actually on campus. We gave her access to all of our patient records and other resources with the understanding she'd work under our direct supervision."

"Do you know where Dr. Austin was working while she was collaborating with your team?"

He gazed upward and began softly humming a tune. "You know, I don't recall."

Kendric reached behind him to the credenza and tenderly slid a hand-carved meerschaum pipe from a large antique wooden rack. Madison's father was a pipe smoker, and she remembered vividly the distinctive aroma that wafted through the house on most Sunday afternoons. Placing the tip in his mouth, he held the barrel cupped in his hand. He didn't reach for a match, nor was there a tobacco canister in sight. She assumed the pipe was more of a comfort than anything else.

"Do you know if Dr. Austin ever finished the project?"

"As I recall, she completed the first phase of it but stopped there. I assume it was a time issue, but I'm not entirely sure."

"I did a search earlier this morning. I can't find that she has ever published her research."

"I don't believe she ever submitted a manuscript to be considered for publication. Again, I don't know why, but to her credit, she did compile data that may prove very helpful in finding the cause of leukemic malnutrition." Pausing for a moment, he added with a wink, "But I think you already know that, and that's part of the reason you're sitting across from me."

"How familiar are you with the details of her research?"

"I only have an idea of the basics. Through genetic analysis and other criteria, she developed a system to predict which of our leukemia patients would be prone to becoming infected by a specific strain of a rapidly mutating virus." He moved his pipe from one side of his mouth to the other. "As you know, after Lennon reviewed her work, she was convinced that, since almost all of the leukemic malnutrition patients appeared on only one of Dr. Austin's lists, it's highly suggestive that a rapidly mutating virus is the cause of leukemic malnutrition."

"It's just a list. Maybe the whole thing is simply a coincidence."

"Anything's possible, but that would be quite a coincidence," Kendric said. "Have you personally spoken to Dr. Austin about any of this?"

"No, but I assume Lennon has."

"The person you really need to speak with is Dr. Haas, but I'm afraid he's out of town on vacation."

"Dr. Haas?"

"Yes, Abel Haas. He was the senior scientist I assigned to mentor and oversee Dr. Austin's research. They worked closely together, and I'm sure he'd be in a much better position to answer your questions than I."

"I'll give him a call. I'm sure, under the circumstances, he won't mind."

"You can try, but I doubt you'll be able to reach him. When he's on vacation, he's completely unreachable. He's always insisted on that. I've known Abel for almost twenty years, and if there's one thing I've learned about him, it's that he's full of eccentricities. But I'll tell you this: he's one heck of a researcher, and I decided years ago his scientific talents far outweighed his little peccadillos."

Madison came to her feet and extended her hand. "I've already taken up too much of your time. It was a pleasure meeting you, and I thank you for your help."

"The pleasure was all mine," he said, reaching for his phone and tapping the intercom button. "Fay, can you please come in here?"

A moment later, a dowdy woman with unbalanced facial features and a cool tone to her complexion walked through the door. Her overstated perfume wafted through the air.

"Dr. Shaw, this is Fay. She's probably the world's greatest personal assistant and laboratory administrator. I don't know what we'd do around here without her."

With raised eyebrows and a minor scowl, she said, "Dr. Nash exaggerates to excess."

"It's nice to meet you," Madison said.

"Dr. Shaw would like to have a look at Dr. Austin's research.

Would you please make sure she has access to our computer system and anything else she might need?" Coming out from behind his desk, he said, "The next time you come over, please bring Jack. I'd love to meet him."

"I'm sure he'd be pleased to meet you as well."

Fay pointed the way, and Madison escorted her out of Dr. Nash's office.

"Your boss is quite a character," she said when they reached her work area.

"The first time people meet him, they're usually stumped trying to figure out where he hides all that genius. But I assure you, he's a brilliant man who's done more to put Oster on the map as a center of excellence in cancer care and research than any doctor on our staff. He's also one of the nicest people you'll ever meet, so don't let his bumbling Lieutenant Columbo routine fool you for a second."

Fay invited Madison around to her side of the desk and then walked her through the process of reviewing research projects. She set up credentials for Madison and Jack to be able to access the data from their own computers.

"This seems pretty straightforward. I think I'm all set."

"If you need anything at all, just give me a call."

Madison rode the elevator down to the lobby, exited the building, and started back toward the hospital. She took a moment to gaze overhead at the dreary charcoal-gray sky that stretched as far as she could see. A rogue gust of frosty wind slipped across her shoulders, prompting her to hurry along.

She reached for her phone.

"Hi, Jack. I just finished meeting with Dr. Nash. I'll be back in the hospital in a few minutes. How about briefing me on the patients and then an early lunch before we have a look at Dr. Austin's research?"

"Sounds good. I'll meet you on the unit."

Another harsh gust of wind slammed into her side, forcing her to lean into it to keep herself moving forward. Preoccupied in thought, she pressed on, admitting to herself that when Jack had first told her about Althea's request for help she'd been skeptical about getting involved. But now, and for reasons she couldn't quite get her head around, she was more than a little curious about what Dr. Austin's research might reveal.

Chapter 19

Lisbet Collymore had been the nurse caring for Sam Shively since shift change at four p.m. From the moment she'd received the report from the day nurse, Sam had required her full attention. Lisbet had come to Oster five years earlier, had immediately been identified as a rising star, and had advanced quickly through the ranks to become an assistant nurse manager. On the tallish side with smooth facial skin and velvet brown eyes, she always maintained a calm demeanor and was a born problem-solver.

Sam had been battling leukemia for five years, having been in and out of remission four times. Having recently attained his fourteenth birthday and worn out from his long ordeal, he had become withdrawn and considerably less cooperative than most of the other leukemia patients. Lisbet had cared for him many times and was sure from an emotional standpoint he was nearing the end of his rope.

In spite of trying several different medications to sedate him, he continued to experience alternating periods of restless sleep and agitation coupled with disorientation. As was the case with the other children, his overall condition was made worse by continuing weight loss. Lisbet felt a welcome wave of relief when he finally dropped off into a more peaceful sleep. She had no illusions it would last very long, but she hoped she'd have enough time to complete her charting. It was eight p.m.

Her plan came to an abrupt end when the high-pitched shrill of the first alarm pierced the air. Her gaze flashed to the cardiac monitor. When she saw the flatline tracing, she raced to the bedside. Her mind flooded with possibilities as she went through her mental checklist, trying to figure out what was happening. Considering that less than a minute earlier his heart rate and blood pressure were completely normal, she prayed the problem was a technical one involving the alarm itself and not a sudden adverse medical event that had befallen her patient. But when her eyes fell on his ashen complexion and the bluish discoloration of his lips, she knew her prayers had gone unanswered and that Sam was in trouble.

Yanking his cover back, Lisbet exposed his chest and confirmed her worst fear—it wasn't moving. In the flash of an eye, she slapped the code blue button and fitted an oxygen mask on his face. She rechecked the heart monitor and felt for a femoral pulse. There was none. He was in full cardiac arrest. Just as two nurses and a respiratory therapist charged into the room, Lisbet began chest compressions. Right behind them was Dr. Aiden Rogers, the ICU specialist on call.

"Somebody talk to me," he ordered, taking up a position directly behind Sam. "C'mon people, I'm waiting." Rogers had only been on staff for a little over a year. He tended to be disorganized and to forget his manners in emergency situations, but he remained supremely confident in his abilities. The more senior nurses advised the less seasoned ones to keep their suggestions to themselves when he was attending to a patient. Lisbet had one disagreement with him regarding a patient care issue that had ended with him telling her that, when he wanted her opinion, he'd be pleased to give it to her.

"His vital signs have been stable all night," she reported, continuing to do chest compressions. "He just suddenly arrested."

"Nothing happens suddenly. You weren't paying attention. Has he received any medications in the last half an hour?"

"No."

"You missed something," Rogers stated, turning to the respiratory therapist. "Let's get a tube in him and get a ventilator in here." He then shifted his attention back to Lisbet. "Give him an amp of epi and draw up 150 milligrams of amiodarone and infuse it over ten minutes. Anything abnormal in his ten p.m. lab work?"

"Nothing that I remember, but I'll recheck them—"

"C'mon, I need straight answers right now—not when you get around to it. This is a code blue, and he's your only patient, Lisbet. You should have this information at your fingertips. We don't have time for you to look up the answers to everything I ask you."

"Dr. Rogers," she began in an even tone. "There was nothing abnormal in his lab studies. He's been restless but stable since the shift began. There were no changes in his condition that would explain a cardiac arrest."

Rogers's face tightened into a rigid stare. "The facts seem to tell a different story."

"Tube's in," the respiratory therapist announced to the group, as she securely taped it to prevent it from slipping out of Sam's windpipe. She then attached a breathing bag to the tube, and with each squeeze of her hand, she filled his lungs with an oxygen rich breath. Nothing the team tried worked. His heart remained in complete arrest.

"Keep the chest compressions going and give him another amp of epinephrine," Rogers ordered.

Jenna Keith, the nurse manager, positioned herself beside Sam's IV pump. The pharmacist handed her the two medications Rogers had ordered. She wasted no time injecting both of them into the line. "Meds are in," she announced.

Rogers took a step back and scrutinized the monitor for a minute.

"Nothing," he said. "Give him 40 units of vasopressin."

"It's getting a lot more difficult to ventilate him," the respiratory therapist said, squeezing the bag harder with each breath to deliver the same amount of air. "His lungs are getting tight. They must be filling up with fluid."

"I'm aware of that. Just keep bagging him, but hold the chest compressions," he said, as he placed his stethoscope on Sam's chest. "Let's get another IV in him and call for a stat chest x-ray. I also want a complete new set of labs, including ABGs." He pointed to the monitor. "Nothing. He's still flatline."

For the next fifteen minutes, the team did everything possible to jolt Sam's heart back to life. But their efforts were completely in vain. Lisbet feared whatever thread of life he was clinging to was quickly unraveling.

It was at that moment that the respiratory therapist called out, "He's back. We've got a rhythm."

"His blood pressure's coming up," Jenna added, matching her colleague's enthusiasm with a fist pump.

Everybody stopped what they were doing and kept their eyes glued to the monitors. Rogers folded his arms across his chest and said nothing. An infectious smile spread through the room as Sam's cardiac function continued to improve.

After another ten minutes of observation, Rogers pulled off his gloves and tossed them to the floor.

"I thought for sure we'd lost him. Better lucky than good," he said with a straight face as his eyes locked on Lisbet. Strolling to the other side of the room, he picked up one of the cardiac tracing strips and looked at it briefly. Even though she was speaking with one of the other nurses, he motioned to Lisbet. She groaned inwardly but cautioned herself to remain professional. She reluctantly crossed the room and joined him.

"The oxygen content of his blood was pretty low during most of the code," he stated.

"I was just discussing that with Paula."

"It's impossible to know if he suffered any brain damage. I'm going to arrange for the neurologists to see him. I'll put the order in the chart in a few minutes. Right now, I'm going to speak with the parents." His tone of voice was even, and he seemed under control. Lisbet wondered if it were remotely possible he regretted his behavior. Whether he did or not was a moot point, because she doubted his ego would permit an apology. She shook her head and watched him exit the room. Too emotionally spent from the code blue to dwell on Dr. Rogers's unprofessional behavior any longer, she made her way to the bedside. Sliding her stethoscope off her neck, she listened to Sam's heart for a full minute. It was strong and regular.

Looking up, she checked the monitors. For the moment, everything looked good. She turned around, drew a cleansing breath, and scanned the room. The floor was littered with all manner of empty boxes and used medical supplies. Without giving it a second thought, she began picking them up and disposing of them in a large plastic bag. She'd been working for about five minutes when Jenna strolled over.

"I'm sorry about the way Rogers spoke to you. He can be a pompous jerk sometimes."

"Sometimes? You're very generous." She grinned, demonstrating no outward signs he'd rattled her in the slightest.

"He's still new and…well, the excitement of a code blue has a way of bringing out the worst in rookie physicians."

"If it's experience we're talking about, I agree—the guy's as green as Ireland. Maybe if he realized it, it would help him be more professional." She paused and then in a single breath asked, "Do you think our new nurses would get the same pass the doctors do if they behaved in the same unprofessional manner Rogers does?" She held up her hand. "It was a rhetorical question, and I should probably be more charitable. Perhaps a conversation about Dr. Rogers's behavior is best left for another time."

"I'll look forward to that chat," Jenna said with a wink. "I'd better give Dr. Kavanaugh a call. If she finds out about this from somebody else, she'll have my butt in her briefcase."

After making sure Sam remained stable and finishing her code blue charting, Lisbet asked one of the other nurses to cover for her for a few minutes to give her the opportunity to speak with Sam's parents. She had come to know them well, finding them more patient and understanding than many of the other parents.

She left the room and almost immediately saw them standing outside the parent lounge. They had their arms around each other and were both sobbing. Feeling the despair of the moment, Lisbet did everything in her power to hold herself together.

Sam's future was in serious doubt. She knew that. Continuing toward Sam's parents, she prayed she'd somehow find the words that might in some small way ease their suffering.

Chapter 20

After spending the entire afternoon completing a detailed review of Dr. Austin's research, Jack and Madison exited the library and started back toward the guesthouse. As they strolled down a tree-lined walkway, a cloud-covered dusk was settling in over the campus. Before they had started their analysis of Austin's work, they had agreed not to discuss their impressions of its quality and importance until they had finished the review.

"You go first," Jack said.

"I've got mixed feelings. It's certainly a very straightforward study, and I think it would stand up to scientific scrutiny with respect to the way it was done." After pausing briefly to sidestep a small pile of wet leaves, she continued. "That being said, I can't say her conclusions are convincing enough that I'd be comfortable advising the focus group to blindly accept Lennon's contention that Dr. Austin's research is the beacon lighting the way to curing leukemic malnutrition." When Jack didn't immediately respond, she asked, "What do you think?"

"For the most part I agree with you, but it's hard to dismiss the fact that she did compile a list of leukemia patients who are now suffering from LM before anybody ever heard of the illness. I have a problem writing that off to pure coincidence. The question is, what's the best way to share this with Althea without sounding like we're dodging her question?"

"I don't know, but you're going to get your chance in about half a minute," she said with a faint wag of her finger at the woman carrying an umbrella who was walking straight toward them. When Jack lifted his eyes, Althea was already waving at them.

"I assume you heard about Sam Shively?" she asked.

Madison nodded once in her direction. "We had a look at him this morning. He had a pretty stable night. Hopefully he didn't suffer any neurologic damage."

"We're all praying for that," she said. "I heard you were in the library. I was just on my way over there to track you down. How's the review of Dr. Austin's research going?"

"We finished up a few minutes ago," Madison said.

"Don't keep me in suspense. What do you think?"

"We're in agreement that it was a nicely done study," Jack answered.

"That's nice to hear but are her conclusions well-founded enough to justify completely shifting gears and following Lennon's pleas to devote all of our resources to looking for some mystery virus?"

"We'd say no," Jack was quick to offer. "We're unconvinced there's enough substance to the work to justify Austin's scientific conclusions, especially as they relate to leukemic malnutrition."

"Is there anything further you need to do?"

Madison said, "We'd like to withhold any final conclusions until we've had a chance to speak with Dr. Austin directly. We feel her input would be helpful."

Althea tapped her index finger against her cheek. "I think that's a good suggestion. I just hope it won't take too long to reach her. I've got Lennon circling like some famished bird of prey."

"We have a question," Madison began. "Since Dr. Austin's research was never published, how did Lennon even know about it?"

"Dr. Austin was working with us on this project. Since we don't keep things like that a secret, I can only speculate somebody in the lab must have mentioned it to her."

"Any further word when Dr. Haas will be back?" Madison asked.

"The same question occurred to me, so I checked with his assistant." She shook her head. "He hasn't heard a word."

"I wish I could schedule my vacations with no end date," Jack said.

"Dr. Haas has made some incredible research contributions," Althea stated. "Kendric Nash tends to indulge him, and to be honest with you, I kind of look the other way myself. He's unquestionably one of Oster's most outstanding assets."

"Madison and I will contact you as soon as we speak with Dr. Austin."

"I look forward to that. I'll try to keep Lennon at bay until then, but I don't think I'll be able to keep my finger in the dike for too long. Now, if you'll excuse me, I think I'll go visit a few of the parents. I haven't spent much time on the unit today, and after what happened last night, I'm sure there's no shortage of anxious family members who could benefit from an encouraging word. Are you two headed back to the hospital?"

"Actually, Jack promised to take me into Defiance to do some Christmas shopping and grab an early dinner." Having no recollection of any such promise, Jack looked at Madison askance.

"Enjoy yourselves. I'll see you tomorrow morning," Althea said as she walked away.

"I don't recall making that promise," Jack mentioned.

They started back toward the guesthouse.

"C'mon, you'll enjoy yourself. You need to get your mind off medicine for a few hours."

Jack was surprised Madison had suggested the trip into Defiance, but more than anything, he was beyond pleased she felt up to going.

Chapter 21

It was eight a.m., and Jack and Madison had just walked onto the LM unit when they noticed Althea approaching, accompanied by a woman. When they were a few steps closer, Madison recognized her immediately.

"I'm glad I ran into you," Althea said. "There's somebody I'd like to introduce you both to." Before Althea could continue, Madison gave Dr. Gabriela Addesso, the director of the Ohio Department of Health and the principle adviser to Governor Sorenson on healthcare issues, a quick hug. Althea folded her arms in front of her and said with a grin, "I guess the introduction won't be necessary after all. Obviously you two already know each other."

"Madison and I serve on a couple of the state's children's advocacy committees together. And last year we worked together on a puzzling nest of infant meningitis cases in Southern Ohio." Gabriela turned to Jack. "And how are you, Dr. Wyatt? The dean of the med school tells me you've been working your butt off."

"Which is entirely your fault, Dr. Addesso, because you were the one mainly responsible for getting the funding we needed to open the Elusive Diagnoses Center at the university."

Althea said, "The governor has personally expressed to me his grave concerns regarding leukemic malnutrition. He and I thought it would be a good idea moving forward to have Gabriela join us from time to time, not only to allow us to keep her briefed on our progress, but also to get her input."

"As Althea just mentioned, the governor is deeply concerned about the crisis you're facing here at Oster. He's authorized me to assist you in every way I can. He's also asked me to keep him in the loop, so you'll probably be seeing me around from time to time. I'll do my best to stay in the shadows, but if I become a bit of a pest, please forgive me."

"I hate to break this little reunion up, but Gabriela has a meeting with the entire board in a few minutes, so I'm afraid we'll have to get going." Althea shifted her gaze to Jack and Madison. "Would you mind if I join you two on rounds after I escort Gabriela to the board room?"

"We'd welcome it," Jack said.

"Have you rounded on Kip Dale yet?"

"No, but we were planning on seeing him in a little while," Madison said.

"How about I join you in his room in about ten minutes? I'm sure his father will be there and I'd like to introduce you to him."

"Ten minutes it is," she said.

"I certainly appreciate both of you taking the time to meet with me," Gabriela said, shaking each of their hands before strolling toward the exit with Althea.

"Are you surprised to see Gabriela here?" Madison asked.

"A little, maybe. What about you?"

"Actually, I'm surprised it's taken this long," she told him. "C'mon, let's get started on rounds. From what the nurses told me on the phone this morning, it sounds like a lot of the kids had another rough night."

As they started down the hall, Jack couldn't help but wonder how much longer the situation at Oster Children's Hospital could be considered contained before hopelessness gave way to panic and panic gave way to all the wheels falling off the wagon at the same time.

Chapter 22

As Althea had requested, Madison and Jack's first stop was Kip Dale's room. It would be the first time they'd rounded on him. When they entered the room, Jack spotted a heavily built man sitting in a club chair with his legs outstretched and crossed at the ankles. His creased brow and haggard eyes betrayed his fatigue. From the way he wore his black hair cropped high and tight, Jack suspected he was ex-military.

As soon as his eyes fell on his visitors, Frank Dale stood up and moved toward the center of the room. Just as he did, Althea came through the door.

"Frank, I'd like to introduce you to Drs. Shaw and Wyatt. They've recently joined our team. I've been spending some time introducing them to the parents."

Frank extended his hand first to Madison, then to Jack.

"I think I speak for all the parents when I say we're extremely happy you agreed to come to Oster and lend a hand."

People who knew Frank Dale would say he was well suited to his chosen profession. Thorough and insightful by nature, he was an accomplished problem-solver who accepted little at face value. After leaving the Coast Guard, he spent five years as an investigator in the

Ohio State Inspector General's office. At night, he attended law school. The moment he had his degree, he'd resigned his position. Having no interest in practicing law or remaining in public service, he tried his hand in the private sector.

"Kip was diagnosed with leukemia two years ago and has been a model patient since day one," Althea said.

"Seventeen and a half months ago, to be exact," Frank said. "The day we found out he had cancer is not one I'm ever likely to forget. It was one week before his varsity baseball season started. He'd been getting into shape for almost six months. In addition to being in the top ten in his class, he's probably the best pitcher who ever played for Wright High School. The baseball coach from Ohio University told us he'd be a shoe-in for a full ride." He paused as his face flushed with pride. "When our family doctor told him he had leukemia, Kip was more upset by the news he'd be missing his senior season than the tough treatment he'd have to go through to get better. To this day, all he ever talks about is someday pitching in the majors." The last of Frank's words caught in his throat, prompting him to retreat into silence.

"He's certainly been a trooper in every sense of the word," Althea was quick to inject, as she laid a reassuring hand on Frank's shoulder. "I know you've already answered a lot of questions from some of our other physicians, but Dr. Shaw and Dr. Wyatt would like to sit down and talk with you about Kip's illness."

"Whenever you say. I'll do anything it takes, if it gets us even one baby step closer to beating this thing." Frank picked up Kip's baseball glove from the end of his bed. Slipping it on, he made a fist and began molding the leather pocket just the way Kip liked it. "There are probably a lot of similarities in what we do. I own a firm that investigates high-end insurance fraud. I spend most of my days searching for clues and asking people questions, trying to fit a bunch of small pieces together, hoping to solve the mystery."

"Sounds pretty interesting," Madison said.

"Not always. Unfortunately, a lot of the individuals I deal with have a shaky relationship with the truth. It can get pretty discouraging seeing people at their worst as often as I do." His cheeks billowed with a mouthful of air. Blowing it out, he offered, "I'm happy to talk now, if this is a good time for you."

"If you'd be more comfortable, we can wait until Mom's available to join us," Madison suggested.

"My wife suffers from severe depression, Dr. Shaw. About a month ago, she talked about committing suicide." With his gaze cast downward, he added, "The only option I had was to admit her for inpatient treatment." After a difficult silence, he continued, "She's showing some signs of improvement, but for the foreseeable future, it's just Kip and me."

"Frank's been a true pillar of strength," Althea said. "I've got some other parents who are waiting to speak with me. I'll be on my way and give you folks a chance to speak."

Jack and Madison spent the next half hour interviewing Frank, covering every detail of Kip's illness. His recollections were clear and comprehensive. What he disclosed closely mirrored the information they had obtained from the other parents they'd interviewed.

"Has any of this helped?" he asked.

"Kip's symptoms seem to be similar to the other patients," Madison said. "As we mentioned, what we're searching for is some common factor that will point the way to the cause of the illness."

With skepticism in his voice, he said, "From the looks on your faces, I'd say I haven't provided you with the essential piece of information you're looking for."

"We're still very early into the process. Hopefully, in time, hidden somewhere in all the information we'll be gathering, we'll find the common link we're looking for."

Frank nodded. "I understand."

"It's our plan to see Kip every morning. I'm sure we'll have more questions for you as we move forward."

Frank flattened his lips together and nodded once.

For now, Jack realized there was nothing more to be said. He was certain he and Madison would be facing many more difficult conversations in the days to come. Trying to strike a balance between optimism and honesty when talking with the patients' families was going to be a challenge.

Jack had always been a stark realist when it came to the practice of medicine. He'd known from the first time he'd spoken to Althea in his pro shop that finding the cause of leukemic malnutrition was going to be a formidable challenge. He knew that expecting a sudden flash of brilliance that would miraculously reveal the cure for leukemic malnutrition would be beyond naïve.

Chapter 23

Flanked by his college buddies and hundreds of other pumped-up participants, Dr. Hayden Kubicek stood poised at the starting line of the *Tough Mudder Challenge*. A rogue gust of wind brushed his shoulders, prompting him to look overhead at the steel-blue, cloudless sky. Three of his friends had consumed an injudicious amount of beer and tequila at dinner the night before and stood beside Hayden with peaked expressions and crimson-tainted eyes. Their partying to excess was something Hayden could never understand, but it brought a grin to his face. All year, they talked about crushing their personal best performance, but then, without fail, they drank themselves into a stupor and showed up for the event so hungover they could barely hold their heads up.

For the first time in days, Hayden had managed to relax a little, and he actually looked forward to the competition. The event started on time, and before the first hour passed, the competitors were widely spaced. Hayden and Rick DeMartino, a lawyer and Hayden's roommate during his senior year, stayed in the middle of the pack, while their impaired friends brought up the rear. They'd completed the first three miles of the course when they reached the Berlin Wall. It was a nine-foot-high wooden barricade constructed to look like its namesake. Almost everyone required a boost from a fellow participant to successfully make it over. With Hayden's help, Rick had already negotiated the wall and told him he'd meet him at the next obstacle.

A few seconds later, a solo competitor jogged up and joined Hayden.

"Need some help?" the athletic-appearing young woman asked. He could hardly believe she wasn't out of breath, and there wasn't a drop of perspiration on her face. He was envious of her conditioning to say the least.

"You bet," he answered between short gasps. He looked behind her and asked, "Going it alone?"

"I started with three of my friends, but they're pretty far back. Too much clubbing and not enough training."

He laughed. "A couple of the guys I'm with suffer from the same misguided thinking." He extended his hand. Taking note of the black and red music note tattoo she had on the side of her neck, he said, "My name's Hayden."

"Carla." She pointed to the wall, stepped in front of him, and interlocked her fingers into a makeshift stirrup. "C'mon, Hayden. We're losing daylight."

"Ladies first," he told her.

She wagged her finger at him and with a playful smirk said, "Not on your chauvinist life. This is a gender-neutral event. You were here first, which means you go over first."

"Fair enough," Hayden said, as he moved back from the wall. After a final gulp of air, he sprinted forward and vaulted toward the wall. Carla captured his front foot in her cradled hands, helping to propel him upward, where he grabbed hold of one of the climbing ropes. As he pulled himself up, he felt a mild stick on the back of his calf. It wasn't enough of a distraction to make him look over his shoulder, and he continued his hand-over-hand assent of the wall. Even with gloves, his hands ached, and the muscles of his arms tightened in an unexpected spasm.

When he finally reached the top, he threw his leg over. Before descending the opposite side, he looked back. To his surprise, Carla was jogging off in the opposite direction. He assumed nobody was there to assist her or she was going to short-circuit the course and head off to a different obstacle. Either way, his mind shifted back to the task at hand, which was to navigate his way down the other side of the wall.

Once he was firmly on the ground, he waited for a minute or so, just in case she changed her mind and returned to the wall. When she didn't appear, he shook his head and pressed on. It was only a few hundred yards to the next obstacle, which was a series of rings suspended over a sloppy mud field. He began a slow jog to catch up to Rick.

After about fifty yards, he felt a sudden twinge in the center of his chest. If it were under his rib cage, he would have likened it to a typical stitch from running too hard, but Hayden was in good shape and accustomed to moderate cardiovascular workouts. The wrenching pain struck him again. He rubbed his chest a couple of times, but the strange discomfort persisted. When he finally reached the mud field, he was wheezing. Bending forward, he placed his hands on his thighs.

"You look like shit," Rick told him. He placed a hand on his shoulder. "Let's take a break. It's not like either of us is going to win this thing."

"Hell no," Hayden managed between labored breaths. He looked toward the rings stretched out in front of him. There were about twenty people waiting their turn to grab on and make their way to the other side of the muddy swamp. Although he wasn't about to admit it to Rick, he was thankful for the extra couple of minutes of rest.

It was when he took a few steps forward that he noticed the unsteadiness and that the waves of pain were now fanning out from his chest and shooting down his spine. Feeling the heat of the sun on the side of his face, he assumed it was the rising temperature that was affecting him. He tried shaking his head to relieve the dizziness, but it only made his equilibrium worse. Struggling to ignore the wobbliness, he managed to work his way forward in the line.

"Are you sure you're ready?" Rick asked.

Looking away, he stole a final drink of air and answered, "You first."

Rick grabbed the first ring and started out over the mud field. Squinting from the sun, Hayden struggled to focus on the closest ring. Using feel more than vision, he located it and grabbed on. The soggy terrain before him blurred and then suddenly became laced with reddish-orange swirls of concentrated light.

Sapped of strength and now drawing on his dwindling reserves, Hayden somehow managed to reach the second ring. But he progressed no farther. Suddenly, all his sensory functions became upended. His fingers began to uncurl, leaving him suspended like a side of beef in a meat locker. A few seconds later, his grasp on the ring failed, sending him flailing toward the mucky ground below. Unconscious when he impacted the mud, his knees instantly buckled, leaving him face down and motionless.

A competitor falling into the mud was a common occurrence, and at first, none of the competitors around him paid much attention. But Hayden wasn't moving. It was the man on the rings behind him waiting for him to come to his feet who first realized something was wrong. He released his grip, and landed a few feet away. Grabbing Hayden under his arms, he pulled his partially submerged face out of the mud. He was built like a linebacker, and it took him only a few moments of backpedaling to drag him out of the mud pit and onto a dry patch of land.

The inherent risks of the *Tough Mudder Challenge* demanded that emergency medical services be immediately available. It didn't take long for two of the event's safety officers to converge on the scene. They did a quick check of Hayden's pulse and breathing rate. After swapping an ominous look, one of them yanked a walkie-talkie from his belt and called for urgent medical assistance.

Five minutes later, Andy Foster, a senior paramedic and his partner arrived by golf cart and rushed to Hayden's side.

"I can't get a pulse," Foster said. "Let's get him tubed and start chest compressions."

His partner looked up at the event official. "Tell them to send for an ambulance right now."

By this time, a small crowd of crane-necked participants formed a circle around Hayden. There was an inherent risk to running in the *Tough Mudder*, and everybody knew it, but serious injuries were few and far between. Participants fainted from exhaustion, got sick and dehydrated, and suffered a wide variety of orthopedic injuries, but a full-blown cardiac arrest was a rare occurrence.

"Tube's in," Foster said, giving him ten consecutive breaths before stopping to see if Hayden would start breathing on his own. When his chest didn't move, he said, "Nothing. He's got nothing," he repeated, placing a tourniquet on Hayden's upper arm and starting an IV line. In the meantime, his partner kept going with the chest compressions. Continuing CPR, they injected a flurry of IV medications.

"I still can't feel a pulse," Foster's partner announced, as he moved his fingertips up and down Hayden's neck between compressions, trying to feel the pulse of his carotid artery. He placed his stethoscope squarely over Hayden's heart. After a few moments, he again checked the portable cardiac monitor. "There's no activity."

"Ambulance is on its way," the safety officer announced.

Foster raised his eyes to the bystanders. "Anybody here with this guy? Does anybody know him?"

"I do," Rick said.

"Does he have any chronic illnesses?"

"No. He's totally healthy."

"How about medications? Is he taking any?"

"Not that I'm aware of."

"Do you know if he took any performance enhancers before starting?"

"No way," Rick responded.

Without holding out much hope of success, Foster and his partner continued CPR, but it was to no avail.

"Doesn't make sense," Foster said, more to himself than his partner. "He's a young healthy guy. We should've gotten some cardiac response." He shifted positions, removed a penlight from his pocket, and shined it into each of Hayden's eyes. He rocked back and put his hands on his thighs. "His pupils are fixed and dilated. He's had it."

"What the hell happened to this guy?"

"I don't know, but be careful where you step. There may be a king cobra around." By this time, a second paramedic team had arrived on the scene. "There's nothing more we can do here," Foster told them. "Let's get him loaded and transported to County ASAP."

The two teams worked together to strap Hayden onto the stretcher and wheel him to the ambulance. Even before the howl of the siren faded, the crowd began to break up. Foster and his partner began to gather up their supplies.

"Maybe they'll be able to do something for him in the ER," his partner said.

"Other than call for a priest, I doubt it."

Unfortunately, Foster had it right. Thirty minutes after he was wheeled into the emergency room of Richland County Medical Center, Dr. Sarah Heinlein, senior physician in attendance, suspended further efforts at resuscitation and pronounced Dr. Hayden Kubicek dead.

Chapter 24

As somebody who had never been sympathetic to those who suffered from phobias, Abel Haas never quite understood his own trepidation of flying. He traveled by air when necessary, but if there was an alternative way to get where he was going, he jumped at the chance. It was no different on this particular day. The wide-body he'd just flown in from Chicago to Paris taxied to its assigned gate at Charles de Gaulle Airport. As was usually the case, he had been saucer-eyed and white-knuckled for the entire flight. To his delight, he was able to clear customs and immigration with no delay.

He exited the terminal into an overcast and unseasonably chilly afternoon. Haas had first visited Paris as a graduate student in biochemistry. Before the week was out, he had fallen in love with the iconic allure of the city. When he had boarded his flight back to the United States, he'd promised himself that someday he'd own an apartment overlooking Parc Montsouris. Ten years later, he fulfilled that pledge when he purchased a furnished studio with a majestic view of the east side of the park. In the years that followed, he had visited Paris every six months. Everything about his life in Ohio that he loathed was instantly eclipsed by his love of this city. His colleagues at Oster had the idea that he was a world traveler, spending his vacation time all over Europe and the Far East, but the simple truth was that he rarely ventured beyond the Paris city limits.

It was ten minutes past two when his cab turned off Boulevard Jourdan and pulled up in front of his building. Because he kept sufficient clothing in his apartment to deal with Paris's schizophrenic weather, he'd brought only a small leather carry-on. He exited the late-model Citroen, and with a light mist falling on his face, he strolled around to the driver's side window.

A slender man holding an umbrella, a cigarette dangling from the corner of his mouth, approached. Tipping his umbrella back from his face, the bearded man cast a glance Haas's way and strolled past. As he did, the dense column of smoke from his unfiltered Gauloises filled his nostrils. Between coughs, he handed the driver a fifty-euro note. He barely had time to pull his hand back before the cab bolted from the curb.

When Haas turned to walk into his building, he noticed a small white SUV parked across the street. The two poker-faced men dressed in dark blazers who were leaning against the side of the vehicle abruptly averted their eyes. Noticing the engine was running, he hiked his carry-on higher on his shoulder, entered the building, and took the elevator up to the fourth floor. Once inside his studio, he walked over to the only window that overlooked the front of the building. The minivan was still there, but the two men were now seated inside.

Being totally exhausted from his long day of travel, he convinced himself not to overreact to the presence of the men. With a light shrug of his shoulders, he flopped down on his bed. Expecting to see the SUV gone when he awakened, he thought about his favorite brasserie and the prospect of enjoying a salade verte and a double order of escargot for dinner. A minute later, he was asleep.

When he awakened, it was six thirty. Feeling the usual effects of an overnight flight, he pushed himself out of bed. The first thing he did was make his way to the window. Without turning on any lights, he eased the curtain back a couple of inches. His gut tightened when he saw the same two men standing in front of the SUV. What he'd believed was probably an overactive imagination when he'd arrived was suddenly his worst nightmare come true.

Hurrying to his closet, he reached up to the highest shelf and brought down a larger carry-on than the one he'd arrived with. Ten minutes later, he was packed and making tracks down the rear corridor to the back stairs. He exited the building and, under the blanket of darkness, continued east behind three apartment buildings. By the time he emerged on the boulevard, he was sucking in one frightened breath after another. Scanning the area, he surmised he was well out of sight of the two men and only a short walk to the Porte d'Orleans metro station.

From there, he traveled to the Gare du Nord, where he purchased a first-class ticket and boarded the next Eurostar to London. It wasn't until the train was approaching the English Channel that Haas was able to take his first relaxed breath.

Chapter 25

Anticipating their meeting with Hayden Kubicek, Madison and Jack arrived at the hospital early to make rounds and give themselves extra time to evaluate Sam's progress. To their delight, he continued to make slow improvement. Having emerged from his coma, the consulting neurologist was cautiously optimistic that, if he recovered from LM, he would do so without significant neurological damage.

They walked through the front door of the guesthouse at nine thirty and made their way to the kitchen, where Jack poured them each a mug of coffee before joining Madison at the table.

While he was adding his customary dram of whole milk, he inquired, "Any luck locating Dr. Austin's contact information?"

"Nope, but I can't say I've had much time to try. I was hoping to give it more attention tomorrow."

"If she worked on a research project with the hospital, shouldn't they have her CV on file?"

"One would think, but when I checked the research protocol, her CV wasn't there."

"That's a little strange," he said. "If you get tied up tomorrow, let me know, and I'll give it a shot."

Their conversation had moved to the new admissions overnight when the doorbell rang. It was five minutes before ten.

"That must be him," Jack said, coming to his feet and dumping what little coffee remained in his mug into the sink.

"He's punctual. I'll give him that."

When Jack opened the front door, he was immediately stunned by the appearance of Dr. Kubicek. He was pigeon-breasted man with tired eyes and an oblong shaped face. The years had thinned out the skin on his face, revealing dozens of minute, tortuous blood vessels that framed out his pointed nose. With one hand, he supported his excess weight with a four-stand cane; in the other, he held a manila folder.

With a mixture of uncertainty and confusion, Jack pushed a cordial smile to his face. Because Hayden had told him he was two years out of medical school, Jack was understandably expecting to be shaking hands with somebody considerably younger.

"Dr. Wyatt?" he asked with a warm tone to his voice, as he looked past Jack into the foyer.

"Yes...and you must be Dr. Kubicek. Please come in," he said.

"Thank you."

Jack looked at his guest with continued confusion as he used his cane to navigate the two steps into the entranceway. After a brief but strained silence, he couldn't help himself.

"Please forgive me for asking, but I seem to recall you mentioning that you were a..."

"A family practice resident?" With lips drawn into a fixed line, Jack nodded. "Let me help you out of this awkward situation. I'm Dr. Peter Kubicek. I'm Hayden's father. I'm not a physician. My doctorate's in metallurgical engineering." He paused while he pulled off his leather gloves. As he was slipping them into the pockets of his parka, Madison strolled up and joined them.

"This is Dr. Peter Kubicek. He's Hayden's father."

"I'm Madison Shaw," she said, as she reached out, shook his hand, and then helped him hang up his coat. "Why don't we sit at the dining room table?" she suggested, pointing the way. Peter's steps were cautious and deliberate. Seeing he was relying heavily on his cane, Jack stayed shoulder to shoulder with him as they advanced into the dining room. "We just made some coffee, Dr. Kubicek. May I offer you some?"

"It's Peter, and thank you. It smells wonderful."

Jack walked over to the marble-topped credenza, poured a cup of French roast, and set it down in front of Peter, who wasted no time raising it to his narrow lips and taking an audible couple of sips.

"What time should we expect your son?" Jack asked, electing not to mention that Hayden had failed to tell him he had invited his father to sit in.

Peter's face stiffened, and he hunched forward in his chair. "I'm sorry to tell you that my son died last week while participating in an athletic event."

"My goodness," Madison said in just above a hush, raising her hand to her mouth. "We're terribly sorry to hear that."

"Hayden was in good physical shape. His death was completely unexpected and came as a devastating shock to my wife and me."

"Dr. Kubicek, we very much appreciate you coming today," Jack said. "But under the circumstances, we would of course understand if you'd prefer to reschedule our meeting for—"

"My son was not one to diminish the importance of things, Dr. Wyatt. He didn't share a great deal of details with me, other than to say that he'd come across crucial information about leukemic malnutrition and that he'd arranged an important meeting with you and Dr. Shaw to discuss it. Hayden was levelheaded, bright, and in no way prone to over-exaggeration. I have no reason to believe he viewed this meeting as anything other than urgent."

He stopped and slid the folder he had brought with him across the table.

"I found this file on Hayden's desk when I was going through his personal effects. It has your names and today's date written on it. I can only assume he had every intention of bringing it with him and sharing the contents with you."

Jack picked up the file and was quick to note how thin it was. He considered opening it immediately, but dismissed the notion to avoid diverting his attention from Peter while he was talking.

"Yesterday, I took the liberty of having a brief look at the file." With a shake of his head, he added, "I couldn't make heads nor tails of it."

Madison inquired, "Did Hayden mention where or how he'd acquired his knowledge of leukemic malnutrition?"

"I'm afraid not, Dr. Shaw."

"Did your son have some connection to Oster?"

With a slow nod of his head, he answered, "Several months ago, my wife and I lost our youngest son, Max, to leukemia. He'd received all of his care right here at Oster. The boys were as close as any two brothers could be. Hayden made several trips a month to Defiance to visit Max. His treatment was going well until a few months ago when he suddenly developed a serious illness that none of the doctors had ever seen before. In addition to having no idea what was causing it, they didn't have the first clue how to treat it." Peter guarded his silence for a few moments before adding, "It took less than a week for the disease to ravage Max and take him from us."

Struck speechless from the unimaginable thought of losing two children within months of each other, Jack struggled to find any words that might assuage Peter's grief.

"I'm so sorry. Hayden never mentioned anything about his brother," Jack said, wondering if whatever he believed he knew about leukemic malnutrition might in some way be tied in to Max's death.

"After we lost Max, Hayden told my wife and me that he had major concerns about the circumstances surrounding his death. He said there were far too many unexplained medical events and unanswered questions. He made repeated inquiries of the physicians and administrators, but his pleas for information fell on deaf ears. Eventually, he came to believe Oster had constructed a well-orchestrated conspiracy of silence to cover something up."

"What were some of the strange events that concerned Hayden?" Madison asked.

"As I mentioned, he didn't go into a lot of detail, but I remember him saying that he was especially concerned about something that happened the morning Max passed away. Apparently, when he returned to his room, he encountered a rather nervous-appearing physician who was making notes at the bedside."

"Did he ever find out who he was or what he was doing there?" Jack asked.

"I think he may have found out his identity, but I don't think he ever discovered what he was doing in Max's room."

Peter stopped and briefly stirred his coffee. "If you're interested in finding out the man's name, you might want to speak with Robyn. She's one of the nurses on the leukemia unit. She took care of Max more than any of the other nurses and was with him when he passed away. Hayden mentioned he spoke to her about the man."

"Did your son ever say if somebody had helped him acquire the information about leukemic malnutrition?" Madison asked.

"Not specifically, but I think it's possible."

Jack placed his hand on the file. "Can you think of anything else your son might have said that could help us? Irrespective of how unimportant it might have seemed to you at the time, we'd like to hear about it."

"I'm afraid I've given you all the information I have." He regarded Jack and Madison through weary eyes and then reached for his cane. "I can appreciate how busy you two must be. Hopefully, the contents of the file will shed some light on things. So, unless you have any further questions, I should be getting back to Toledo."

Jack and Madison stood up and accompanied him to the front door. They continued their conversation while he zipped his coat and slid his gloves on.

"We'll walk you to your car," Madison offered, putting her hand on his arm and escorting him outside and down the stone pathway. It was a windless morning with stacked gray clouds adding to an already dreary skyscape.

"Thank you again for making the trip," Jack said when they reached Peter's car. "It was a pleasure meeting you. If you think of anything else that might help us, please don't hesitate to call."

"Of course. And if you have any questions after you've had a look at the contents of Hayden's file, please call." He slowly maneuvered into the front seat of his car. Before closing the door, he said, "My wife and I are too old and in far too much emotional pain to continue where Hayden left off. But please, don't believe for a second that we have any intention of abandoning the matter if somehow new information comes to light."

"We understand, and thank you for making the trip," Madison said.

Peter pulled the door closed and lowered his widow.

"If Max was truly the victim of a rare, overwhelming illness, we'll find a way of accepting it. But if there are facts that have been intentionally concealed from us or manipulated in any way, that's an entirely different matter." A look of resolve solidified on his face, and his voice became grave. "We understand the truth isn't always easy to come by, but we're willing to wait as long as it takes. I don't claim I'm possessed of the wisdom of the ages, but I do believe two things. I'm convinced that there are those at Oster who continue to intentionally conceal information about Max's death. I also believe if you can discover what Hayden knew about leukemic malnutrition you'll be able to cure this terrible disease."

Peter raised his window, started the engine, and pulled away from the curb. Jack and Madison watched as he disappeared down the street.

"What do you think?" he asked.

"I'm not sure, but for a parent who's lost two sons over the course of a few months, he struck me as calm and rational. My gut feeling is not to dismiss his or Hayden's concerns. It's just possible they're correct in their suspicions that Oster hasn't been entirely forthcoming regarding Max's passing."

"That sounds like a not-so-lightly veiled accusation."

"I'm not trying to sound like a conspiracist, but it's not as if things like this haven't happened before. There have been some pretty prestigious hospitals who have chosen to use alternative truths to explain away an embarrassing or possibly litigious medical outcome," she said, taking him by the arm. "C'mon, let's take a look at the file and see what Hayden was so anxious to show us."

Chapter 26

The Oster Children's Hospital guesthouse had been specifically designed to accommodate visiting professors, physicians, and other academicians. The den, which was fashioned in the style of a nineteenth century English library, was the centerpiece of the house. It boasted an ornate L-shaped oak bookcase that stretched to the ceiling and was meticulously crowned with a handcrafted mahogany molding. The matching library ladder with its highly polished brass wheels and rails ran the entire length of the bookcase. Jack pulled up a chair and joined Madison at the antique kidney-shaped desk.

"Okay, keep your fingers crossed," he said as he opened the file. "Hopefully, whatever's in here will open a door or two." Jack removed the items from the folder. His skepticism when he'd first accepted the file from Peter was confirmed when he saw its contents consisted of six pages secured together by a small paperclip.

He swung a pessimistic look in Madison's direction.

"Hard to imagine this will turn out to be a treasure trove of information," she said.

Jack shuffled through the pages. "These are all photocopies—nothing original here. This keeps getting worse."

Madison reached for the pages and laid them out on the leather desk pad in an orderly arrangement. They each took a few minutes to have a cursory look at them.

"So, it appears there are two separate items here," Madison said. "One's a copy of an article from an old medical journal, and the other looks like four photocopied pages from a scientific log describing some type of medical research."

They gathered the pages, held them up, and took a few minutes to read them.

"This looks like well-organized research, but from the vocabulary and content, I'd guess this work was done at least fifty years ago," Jack said.

"All the entries were made with a fountain pen," she said, pulling one of the pages a little closer. "Look at the painstaking organization of the graphs and tables and the flawless handwriting. I'd love to see what the original log looks like. These descriptions may be old, but it appears to be elegant scientific work for its time."

"The scientific description isn't detailed enough to pinpoint exactly what they were working on. But if I had to venture a guess, I'd say they were comparing groups of chemical substances…maybe plasma proteins or complex enzymes."

Madison pointed to a small notation in the bottom right corner of each page. "These are obviously random page numbers. One seventy-four is the highest one. This proves they have to be part of a much larger log or journal."

Jack turned sideways in his chair. "Which naturally begs two rather important questions: Did Hayden have the entire journal? And if he did, was it the holy grail of information he relied upon to claim he'd discovered the cause of leukemic malnutrition? He told me on the phone he was in possession of an extensive body of medical information that led him to his theory."

"I'd hardly call four non-consecutive pages extensive. I'd bet anything he had the entire journal."

"If you're right, why did he make photocopies to show us? Why wasn't he planning on bringing the entire journal with him?"

"I don't know, but from what little we know about him, I suspect he had a method to his madness," she said. "Maybe he assumed these photocopies were proof enough of what he had, and he wanted to see our reaction before he laid all his cards on the table."

Coming to his feet, Jack strolled over to the bookcase and absently ran his fingertips down the spines of the books. A minute later, he returned to the desk and picked up the two-page medical article.

"Let's shift gears a sec and take a closer look at this."

As they had done with the photocopies, they took a few minutes to review the article. It was a straightforward summary presented at a medical conference on the topic of proteins. The last page was a photo of three serious-looking men and a woman in white coats seated at a long table. The caption read: Conference Directors: Doctors Melbourne, Hartmann, Gillman, and Obenhauer."

"Wait a sec. I just found the publication date: May 18, 1958." Madison's forehead wrinkled as she held up the last page of the article, pointing to the small print in the right lower corner. "What in the world could an article containing medical information that's been outdated for decades have to do with Hayden's insistence that he'd discovered the cause of leukemic malnutrition, and why would he want to bring it to our meeting?"

Jack leaned back and interlocked his fingers behind his neck.

"Let's be logical about this. I don't think Hayden stumbled across this old medical article or the research journal in some old book store or nostalgia shop. Nor do I believe he did extensive research and came upon this information on his own." Pausing briefly, he added in a point-blank manner, "I think he had help, and it would sure be nice if we could figure out who that person was."

"I agree, but finding that individual could turn out to be quite the undertaking."

"Maybe…but maybe not," Jack offered. "Hayden was a doctor. By the time Max died, I bet he'd formed relationships with a lot of the Oster physicians and nurses. Remember what Peter told us? He said Hayden knocked on a lot of doors at Oster and made no secret of the fact that he wanted straight answers to some tough questions regarding how Max died—answers that might have proven embarrassing to Oster." Jack pressed his palms together and added, "It's just possible he eventually got lucky and found somebody willing to help him."

"Supposing you're right, and Hayden did have his *deep throat*. That might explain a lot of things, but it's still a long shot at best, Jack."

"A lot of important discoveries began as a long shot, but maybe it's a long shot worth pursuing. We can start with a simple phone call to Robyn and ask her who the mystery doctor was in Max's room the morning he died."

"Even if she knows, she may not want to get involved."

Nodding with purpose, he said, "When I was a teenager going through my awkward stage, my mother used to ask me, *What's the worst thing that can happen if you ask a girl out on a date?*" He paused, raised an enlightened finger, and added, "She can say no."

"That's very metaphorical, Jack," she said, with a mock applause. "Go ahead and make the call to Robyn."

Chapter 27

"Hi, Robyn. This is Dr. Wyatt calling. I'd like to ask you a question, if I may."

"Sure."

"Dr. Shaw and I are looking into some of the circumstances surrounding Max Kubicek's death. We just met with Peter Kubicek, who suggested we give you a call. He mentioned you and Hayden became well acquainted during Max's illness."

"Yes, we did."

"We're sorry you lost such a good friend."

"I still can't believe he's gone. From the first day I met him, I knew he had everything it takes to be a great doctor."

"I don't know if Hayden mentioned it to you, but he was very concerned about a man he saw in Max's room the morning he passed away. Dr. Shaw and I are looking into the possibility that the illness that took his life might have been an earlier form of leukemic malnutrition," Jack explained. "We'd really like to speak to whomever it was in Max's room. I hope I'm not putting you in an awkward position, but this could turn out to be something important. Do you happen to know who it was?"

"His name's Abel Haas. He's a highly regarded researcher."

"Do you have a guess as to why he was in Max's room? We were thinking that perhaps it had something to do with a research study he was enrolled in."

"I'm not sure, although I do remember Hayden telling me that Max wasn't part of any studies that Dr. Haas was running."

Jack had other questions that he was tempted to pose, but since he'd already found out what he wanted to know, he chose to tap on the brakes for now.

"Thanks, Robyn. You've been a big help."

"I hope the information helps," she said, before adding in a hesitant voice, "Dr. Wyatt, I'd appreciate it if you could keep this conversation between you and me. The administration can be a little squirrely sometimes about what they frown upon."

An easy smile appeared on his face. "I was just about to make the same request of you."

"It's a deal. If there's any other information I can help you with, please call me."

"Thanks again."

After Jack hung up, he spent some time on his laptop researching Abel Haas. He was just finishing up when Madison strolled into the room holding a large sugar cookie. Snapping it in two, she handed him his fair share.

"What did Robyn have to say?"

"As it turns out, she did know who was in Max's room."

"That's a stroke of good luck. Who was it?"

"His name's Haas. I've just been reading about him. He's a senior researcher and one of Oster's most prestigious scientists. He has an MD and a PhD in molecular genetics and has published a couple hundred scientific papers and several book chapters on leukemia. He's also responsible for bringing in a lot of grant money from the NIH."

"Did she have any idea why he was in Max's room?"

"Not really."

"In my experience, researchers have no reason to be in a patient's room." Madison was just about to take another bite of her cookie when she suddenly stopped and lowered it from her lips. "What did you say his name was again?"

"Haas."

"Abel Haas?" she asked with a creased brow. Jack nodded. "Was Robyn sure?"

"Positive, why do you ask?"

"When I met with Kendric Nash, he told me when Oster agreed to collaborate with Dr. Austin on her viral research they assigned one of their senior scientists to supervise and mentor her. That senior scientist was Dr. Abel Haas. Nash advised me to speak with him when he got back from vacation if we had any questions about Austin's research. Evidently, he's unreachable when he's out of town."

"Did you try anyway?"

"Of course, but his assistant told me the same thing—when he's out of town, he doesn't even take his cell phone. She said she couldn't reach him even if she wanted to."

"When's he supposed to be back?"

"Also a well-guarded secret. I suppose Haas being Austin's supervisor and also being in Max's room the morning he died could be nothing more than a coincidence."

"I guess we'll have to wait until he gets back to find out."

Jack's eyes dropped away, and in a voice dusted with uncertainty, he stated, "I can't remember ever feeling this baffled by a disease. At the rate these kids are being admitted and the speed at which this disease is progressing…well, we'd better come up with something pretty damn soon, or we may be looking at the worst childhood health problem this country has faced since polio."

Chapter 28

The late afternoon brought with it a perfect day— clear skies and no wind. The moment Madison turned the corner and started down the paved path leading to the tennis courts, she spotted Jack standing on the baseline reaching into a shopping cart half filled with practice balls. It was almost four o'clock. She opened the chain-link fence and walked over to him.

"How are you doing?" she asked.

"By the uncertain tone in your voice, I assume you're guessing I spoke with Nicole."

"You mentioned this morning you were planning on calling her. How did it go?"

Jack's head bobbed to one side. With a frown, he said, "I'd say it was a civil conversation."

"For a divorced couple, civil is fine. Whenever I speak to Scott, the phone turns to ice and fire."

"Scott's a jerk, plus you guys didn't have any kids, which makes a huge difference."

"Which begs the question: is Nicole still planning on sending Annis to Columbus for her birthday next month?"

"I asked her that and she claims it's still a go," he answered.

"That sounds great. Why the long face?"

"Because I've seen too many of these plans go up in smoke."

"Don't you think things have been a lot better since they moved back from France and are living here now?"

"Philadelphia's a lot better than Amiens—I'll give you that."

"C'mon, Jack. Do we really need to have the glass half-full talk again? I've seen you and Annis together. You guys are great and she adores you. Before you know it you'll be taking her on great daddy-daughter trips to look at colleges."

He blew out a lazy breath and the first hint of a smile settled on his face. "I'd like that."

"Stop worrying. We'll get her a really special gift and plan a terrific weekend for her in Columbus. It'll turn out great. I promise."

"I hope so," he said placing his tennis racquet on top of the tennis balls. "So, tell me, what brings you over here? I thought we were going to meet later back at the guesthouse."

"Just thought I'd check to see if your change in atmosphere idea is working. Have you come up with anything inspirational on leukemic malnutrition?"

"I'm afraid not. When I got here, I cleared my mind of any preconceived theories or hunches that were swirling around up there and went all the way back to square one. So far, no flashes of genius. I'm at the same dead end I've been at ever since we got here." He shook his head in frustration. "I can't remember the last time I said this, but I think I'm ready to wave the white flag."

"It's not like you to sound so discouraged. We just haven't turned over enough stones yet."

"I've turned over so many stones, my fingers are starting to blister. I've dealt with a lot of elusive cases over the years, and even though they were all diagnostic mysteries, I always felt like eventually we'd figure out a successful treatment. But this one...it's in a league of its own." He shook his head briefly. "These kids are really suffering. Forget about a cure for right now. I'd settle for just coming up with a way to give them a thimbleful of relief. I almost wish we'd been a thousand miles away when Althea showed up at the tennis club."

"What's with you? You're probably the biggest closet competitor I've ever met. It's you versus the disease…like you've gone into the Roman Colosseum swinging a gladiator's sword."

He reached over, grabbed a few of the tennis balls and began tossing them back into the cart. He dropped his voice a little, forced a grin to his lips, and said, "Don't worry. I know what I need to do. I'm just venting a little."

"I'm okay with that, but there are a lot of people looking to you for a solution. So if you get another sudden urge to vent—make sure you do it somewhere where nobody can hear you except me." She put her arm around his shoulder and gave him a little hug.

Reaching for another tennis ball from the basket, he tossed it over his head, and served it into the empty court.

"I assume you didn't come all the way over here to listen to me grumble about our progress or watch me practice my pathetic serve. What's going on?"

"I'm afraid tracking down Dr. Austin has turned out to be a lot more difficult than we initially anticipated. I've been at it all afternoon and haven't even come close to finding her. I've checked every search engine known to mankind and went through the Directory of Medical Specialists – another dead end."

Jack leaned his racquet against the shopping cart. "Maybe she got married and changed her name, or became ill… or worse. It's also possible she gave up clinical medicine and is doing something else."

"All excellent possibilities, unfortunately private investigation wasn't part of my medical school curriculum."

"With everything else going on, I don't know how much sense it makes to spend any more time on this. I'll give it a shot tonight, but I can't imagine I'll have any more luck than you have. We'll just have to chalk it up to another dead end."

From her immediate silence and the dubious expression on her face, Jack suspected she wasn't ready to wave the white flag just yet.

"I have a thought, but it's a little out of the box, and I'm not sure you're going to like it."

"In that case, maybe we should sit down." Jack gestured toward a forest green bench that sat in front of a chain-link fence. He set his racket on the cart, and they walked over. When he was done brushing off the bench, they sat down, and he readied himself for Madison's brainstorm. "Let's hear it," he said, closing his eyes and turning his face toward the sun.

"I think we should ask Frank Dale to help us."

Jack's eyes popped open. He stared at Madison as if she'd just fallen on her head and suffered a concussion.

"Need I remind you that Frank Dale's one of our patient's fathers? Don't you think it's a tad inappropriate and unprofessional to attempt to involve him in any of this?"

"I don't know. Are we still in agreement that finding Dr. Austin's a matter of extreme importance? Think about it. He's an experienced investigator who told us he'd do anything to help. I know he's going through a lot right now, but Kip's holding his own, and I'm sure if we explained to him how important this is, he'd give our request serious consideration."

"I don't doubt his willingness to help. What I'm questioning is how smart it is to ask him."

"Don't overthink this, Jack, and don't forget all of this was your idea. Althea's been calling us three times a day. She's getting a little impatient, which means the governor is also. We need a shortcut to finding Dr. Austin."

Jack massaged the back of his neck for a few moments before responding. "I hear you, but I still think involving the parent of one of our patients flies in the face of conventional wisdom."

"Listen, buddy. I'm as much for following the rules as anybody, but we're in the middle of a crisis here, and I think we passed the conventional wisdom exit about fifty miles back. Try looking at it as if we're not stepping across the line—we're just moving it a little."

After twisting his purple sweatband around his wrist for a few seconds, he slipped it off and exhaled deeply. "So you'd like my approval."

"Not necessarily. I'd just like you to go with me when I ask Frank."

Jack couldn't stop the amused smile he felt sneaking over his face. When he didn't say anything, she walked over to the shopping cart, returned with his racket, and tossed it to him.

He plucked at the strings briefly and said, "Okay, you win. Let's head back to the guesthouse. I'll grab a shower, and we'll go speak to him, but this is a first for me."

Madison came to her feet. "Me too. But sometimes you just have to hold your nose and jump."

As they started across the campus, Jack changed the conversation to more innocuous topics. But trapped in the front of his mind was the ever-present fear that the first meaningful clue to solving leukemic malnutrition was still nowhere in sight.

Chapter 29

An hour after they walked off the tennis court, Jack and Madison were standing in Kip's room. He was lying on his back staring at the ceiling with his eyes fixed in a half-open position. His lower face was made swollen by an accumulation of charcoal-colored fluid that had pooled under the skin. Between moments of being motionless, he would grind his teeth. At the same time, the muscles of his upper torso would contract spastically for a few seconds before returning to a normal state. He had lost eleven pounds since the day he was admitted.

Just at that moment, Frank emerged from the parent suite.

"This is your second time here today. I hope this doesn't mean you have bad news for me."

"Actually, Kip's holding his own," Madison said. "His condition is serious but stable." Noticing that Frank was now regarding her through inquisitive eyes, she was quick to add, "We'd like to talk to you about a…a nonmedical problem we're facing that we're hoping you may be able to help us with. Is now a good time?"

"Now's fine."

"The other day, you said if there was anything you could do to help us find a treatment for leukemic malnutrition, we should ask."

"And I meant every word of it," he said, without so much as a casual flinch.

"When we first spoke, you mentioned in passing that your company does high-end insurance investigations." He nodded. "There's some critically important information that Dr. Wyatt and I need. We've tried, but we simply don't have the time or the expertise to track it down ourselves."

Hoping to get some idea of how he was reacting to all of this, Madison stopped momentarily and probed his eyes, but his poker-face revealed nothing. "We don't mean to impose, but under the circumstances, we're hoping you'll agree to help us."

"Are you saying this information could potentially help Kip and the other children?"

"We think it's a possibility."

Frank's lips pulled back into a slight smile. With a slight shrug of his shoulders, he inquired, "What do you need to know?"

An immediate groundswell of relief penetrated every cell of her body. "We've been trying to track down a physician. We suspect she has important information about LM. The problem is, we can't seem to locate her."

"Does she live in the United States?"

"We think so."

"Do you know if she's still practicing medicine?"

"We assume she is, but we have no way of being sure," she answered.

"Why do you think you're having such a problem finding her, Dr. Shaw?"

"If we knew the answer to that, Mr. Dale, we wouldn't be here seeking your help."

"Frank. Please, call me Frank. I know physicians are a pretty formal group, but in my world, everybody's on a first-name basis." He looked at each of them in turn. "I'd be happy to help. Give me all the information you have on her, and I'll get started on it tonight. Finding her shouldn't take more than a day or two."

Madison instantly handed him the notes listing all the key information and dead ends she'd encountered.

"We'd appreciate it if you'd keep this matter between the three of us," Jack said. "As I'm sure you can imagine, we don't ask family members for favors like this every day and…well, even though we're facing extremely urgent and unusual circumstances, there may be those who simply wouldn't understand."

"No explanation necessary, Doc. Discretion's the coin of the realm in my business."

"We appreciate your willingness to help us," he said.

"It's strange. You'd think that one terrible disease in a child's life would be enough. How did these poor kids wind up with two?" He extended his hand to each of them. "I'll be in touch with you as soon as I have the information…and thank you both. One of the hardest things about this…this ordeal has been dealing with my feelings of helplessness. Having a chance to make a contribution…well, maybe it's just the medicine I need."

"Let's all keep our fingers crossed," Madison said. "We'll see you tomorrow morning on rounds."

When they left the room and started down the hall, Jack didn't utter a word. Intent on containing her grin, Madison guarded her silence as well. But as they approached the nursing station, she chuckled proudly and flicked his arm in celebration.

Chapter 30

Jack and Madison started the morning per their now established routine. After a three-mile jog, they got dressed and took a leisurely walk to the hospital. Following a brief stop at the Buckeye Brew for a couple of cappuccinos, they went straight upstairs to the LM unit to begin rounds.

Like Charlee, most of the children had lost their eyesight and were suffering terribly from advancing starvation and sleep deprivation. Their parents were emotionally drained and for the most part at the end of their collective ropes.

Every intervention the doctors had attempted hoping to reverse the effects of LM had failed. Arriving at the precise combination of drugs to keep them sedated was an ever-increasing problem. The nursing staff was rapidly approaching the maximum number of patients they could care for and were on the cusp of exhaustion and begging for more help. During the past twenty-four hours alone, seven new patients had been admitted, bringing the total number of cases to forty-three. Ten children had suffered respiratory failure and were on a ventilator. The one saving grace was that there still had been no deaths.

Nationally, the media was becoming more invested in the

strange disease that was plaguing Oster Children's Hospital. The number of television spots and newspaper articles devoted to the story were going up exponentially every day. The hospital administration was relentless in hounding the physicians to provide them with any information they could release to the media that could be construed as optimistic.

"Let's start with Charlee," Madison suggested, gesturing down the corridor. Jack nodded, and they made the short walk to her room.

"How's she doing?" Madison asked Leah as she met them in the middle of the room.

"About the same," she answered in a monotone, moving to the bedside and gingerly tucking Charlee's pillow a little farther under her head. "A bunch of the parents got together this morning. I guess you'd call it an impromptu support group meeting. You'd need a chainsaw to cut the pessimism. Everybody feels like we're in a nose-dive with not much chance of pulling out of it." While she dabbed Charlee's cheeks with a powder-blue tissue, she asked, "Are all the doctors still stumped?"

"I'm afraid we still haven't determined the cause of the disease," Madison answered.

"Are you any closer?"

"That's hard to say."

"That's what I thought," Leah said, tossing the tissue in a wastebasket.

They spent the next fifteen minutes briefing Leah on Charlee's status, trying whenever they could to inject some hope into an otherwise gloomy situation. Madison knew their words were falling on deaf ears. She assumed Jack had gotten the same impression.

"We'll be back late this afternoon to give you another update," was all Madison could manage.

Without lifting her tear-soaked eyes, Leah uttered, "I'll be right here."

Chapter 31

As soon as they were out in the hall, Madison stopped Jack in his tracks and said, "I want to talk to you about something's that been on my mind since yesterday. I was going to wait until this afternoon to give me a chance to think about it a little more, but I've changed my mind. I'd like to bounce it off you now."

"Sure," he said, gesturing to the staff lounge at the end of the corridor. They made the short walk, entered the nicely appointed break room, and sat down in a pair of matching club chairs under a bay widow that overlooked the front of the hospital. There was nobody else in the lounge. "What's on your mind?" he asked.

"Since our meeting with Peter Kubicek, we've spent almost all of our time focused on the research journal and very little on the medical article."

"That's probably because we have no idea what the two could possibly have in common."

"But Hayden Kubicek did, and it's a pretty good bet he was going to share that information with us during our meeting. Whatever it is that links the journal to the article, we have to figure it out."

"Any ideas?"

"As a matter of fact, I do and I think it may be the link between the two things we've been looking for," she said, filled with uncertainty of how Jack would response to her hunch."

"Shoot."

"I think it may be possible that one of the four panelists in the photograph was the author of the research journal."

Jack inhaled a healthy gulp of air. "Have you been reading tea leaves, or do you have something a little more scientific to back up that wild theory?"

"It's not a theory. It's just a hunch, but my hunches are usually pretty good, and I think it's worth pursuing. I called the medical library and spoke with the librarian. He offered to help me see if we can find out anything about the doctors in the photo. We're getting together later today." It was frequently hard for her to tell what Jack's take on things was, but at the moment she felt he was intrigued with her theory.

"You didn't mention anything earlier."

"If I came up with anything, I was going to tell you afterward."

"I see."

"I was thinking of starting with Dr. Hartmann."

"How come?"

Sweeping a few stubborn hairs from her forehead, she answered, "Because I think the handwriting in Hayden's journal is a woman's."

"How did you talk yourself into that?"

"Let's just call it another hunch."

"Don't you think it's kind of a big leap, going from some doctor appearing in a photo to her being the author of the journal?" he asked.

"One of my favorite pediatric professors once told me that sometimes you have to ignore probability and percentages and just assume everything's fifty-fifty, which means either she is or is not the author."

"Supposing she is, how does that help us?"

"I don't know, but let's not get ahead of ourselves."

Jack said, "As you mentioned the other day, we're not private investigators. We need to keep a reasonable balance between patient care and non-patient care challenges."

"There are dozens of excellent doctors taking care of these kids. We were asked to help figure out the cause and hopefully the cure for this illness. We have to do whatever it takes." She checked her watch. "I'm going to go over to the library now. Maybe the librarian can meet with me sooner."

"I'll finish up rounds. Call me when you're done. I'll brief you on how the patients are doing, and you can tell me about what you find."

"Okay, but I may be a while."

"Not a problem, just find me when you're done."

Jack watched her make her way to the exit. Although he was highly skeptical of her theory, he knew enough about Madison's brainpower and approach to problem-solving not to dismiss out of hand any idea that might pop into her head.

Chapter 32

Jack finished reviewing the chart of his last patient at a few minutes after five. Having an hour before he planned on heading home to meet Madison, he left the hospital, walked around to the south side of the building, and found a seat on one of the black wrought-iron benches in the Hollister Family Tranquility Park. The planners of Oster Children's had the forethought to realize that a generous number of areas for parents to reduce their levels of stress was essential. After a sufficient number of philanthropic dollars were allocated for the purpose, several parent lounges, a chapel, and two lush green spaces were included in the original construction plans.

Gazing out over several acres of woodlands, he became lost in thought.

"You look almost too relaxed to disturb," Madison said.

He swung his eyes in her direction. "The last I heard from you, you said you were going to meet me at the guesthouse at six."

"I finished in the library earlier than I expected and was anxious to tell you what I discovered about Dr. Hartmann."

"How did you know I was here?"

"Because it's a beautiful sunset, and you're a creature of habit who happens to enjoy watching pretty sunsets.

Jack tapped on the seat next to him. "From that look on your face and the fact that you spent all day in the library instead of just the morning, you'd better be overflowing with information. Don't keep me in suspense."

"Dr. Anna Hartmann was a full professor at Cornell University for just over forty years. She retired in 1996 and died in 2009. From what I discovered, it seems like she had a very impressive academic career, which she spent entirely in Ithaca."

"What did she specialize in?"

"Neurology."

"That's interesting, but I'm not sure…" He paused, looked at her quizzically, and said, "Wait a sec. The last time I checked, Cornell's medical school was in Manhattan."

"But their College of Veterinary Medicine is in Ithaca."

"Excuse me?"

"It seems Dr. Hartmann was a veterinary neurologist."

"Are you sure you have the correct Dr. Hartmann?"

"I found a picture of her online in one of the vet school yearbooks and matched it up with the photo in the journal article. There's no mistake; it's her."

"What about the other three doctors in the photo?"

"They were dead ends. One died soon after the conference. One left academic medicine, moved to North Dakota, and had a small practice until his death about a decade ago. And the last taught at Cornell for another ten years or so and then moved overseas. Beyond that, we couldn't find out much information about him."

"It sounds like you hit the jackpot."

"It was one of the more tedious days I've had in a long while, but I think it paid off."

"I still don't quite get why Hayden would be interested in a scientific article describing a seminar run by veterinarians?"

"Nor do I, but we've both already agreed he didn't strike us as the type prone to wild goose chases," she said. "I think this may be more about Dr. Hartmann's career than some conference she attended."

"I hate to mention this, but just because you found out about the lives of the people in the photo doesn't mean any of them was the author of the research journal."

Madison grinned. "We were almost finished looking into her career when we came across something very interesting. It seems Cornell's vet school has a quarterly alumni publication. In 1965, she was honored by one of the national veterinary societies. Afterward, she wrote a letter to the president of the society thanking him, which was published in the alumni magazine." She paused, unable to contain a grin. "The letter was handwritten."

"You're kidding."

With a slow shake of her head, she said, "I compared the handwriting in the letter to one of the research journal pages. I'm no expert, but they sure looked identical to me."

Sucking in a deep breath, Jack's mind began to spin like the gears of a fine Swiss watch.

"I imagine we can locate a handwriting expert just to make sure," he said.

"I was thinking the same thing."

He stood up and faced her. "So, let's recap what we have: we're dealing with a bizarre, never-before-seen disease, which only affects children with leukemia. All of these kids have received their entire treatment right here at Oster. And finally, whatever this disease is, it may have some strange connection to veterinary medicine."

"Are you getting the same feeling I am?" she asked.

"Like we're finally starting to peel this onion back?"

"I couldn't have put it better myself."

Chapter 33

After another restless night, Jack pounded his pillow, rolled over, and checked the time. It was five a.m. Not wanting to disturb Madison, he slipped out of bed, dressed, and enjoyed a brisk walk to the hospital. The first thing he checked when he arrived was the overnight admissions. To his consternation, but not much to his surprise, six new cases of leukemic malnutrition had been added to Oster's census.

Before seeing his first patient, he decided to head to the staff lounge to grab a cup of coffee. The moment he pushed open the door, his nostrils filled with the unmistakable scent of stale coffee. Like most breakrooms, the coffeemaker ran continuously, warming a pot of coffee that was generally older than yesterday's newspaper. Plucking a Styrofoam cup from the top shelf of the cupboard, he filled it halfway. He made sure to add two packets of sugar and ample cream. Even so, he cringed as the first sip of the tar-colored brew passed his lips.

While he was staring at a wall-mounted television that had been there so long none of the staff could recall who had gifted it, his mind drifted to what Madison had discovered about Dr. Hartmann. Even though he'd had most of last night to mull it over, he was still baffled as to why Hayden would place such importance on a rather mundane and outdated article on protein metabolism.

He was also stumped by how a disease with a strange array of neurologic symptoms and untreatable starvation would only attack children with leukemia. The only thing he was convinced of was that there had to be a common thread to explain the strange phenomenon.

While he was still adrift in thought, Skye Linderman, one of the assistant nurse managers, came through the door. Because of the many hours Jack had spent in the leukemic malnutrition unit, he had met most of the nursing staff. From the first time he'd spoken with Skye, she struck him as bright, resourceful, and not one to leave much unsaid. Even though she didn't fit the mold of a polished diplomat, she was held in high esteem by the entire staff because of her skill and uncompromising work ethic.

"How's it going, Dr. Wyatt?" she asked in a hopeful voice, as she headed for the refrigerator. "Any good news for us at all?"

"I wish I could say there was, but we're still kind of gathering information and sorting out the possibilities."

She removed a carton of strawberry yogurt—her preferred morning snack—peeled off the top, and sat down in a large rattan rocking chair. Stirring the contents with purpose, she said, "I know I'm not telling you anything you don't already know, but these poor kids are getting worse right in front of our eyes. What's more frustrating is that none of us has the first clue how to make them more comfortable."

She held up her spoon, wiggled it for emphasis, and continued speaking between quick mouthfuls. "When we first heard Lennon had figured out what was making them so sick, we assumed a cure was right around the corner, and we were ecstatic," she told him as the stony frown on her face broadened. "I guess we were way too optimistic, way too soon. Now, we'd settle for anything that would help these poor kids sleep better. I think their insomnia is a lot worse than their agitation. What's really strange about all this is that it's completely different from what we're used to seeing."

"In what way?" he asked, more than a little intrigued by her comment.

"Normally, when our patients are as sick as these kids are, all they want to do is sleep. That's not the case this time. Since we admitted our first LM patient, I've taken care of quite a few of them. Not a single one has been able to get more than an hour of restful sleep. And now, it seems like some of them are actually starting to hallucinate. Like I said, none of us have ever seen anything like this before." Skye finished the last mouthful of yogurt and tossed the container in the trash. "If we could only figure out some way to deal with their insomnia and night terrors." She pushed her palms together as if in a desperate plea and then started toward the door. "Thanks for listening, Dr. Wyatt. I'll see you on rounds."

Jack shared Skye's frustration, but all he could manage was a polite smile. Not being able to stomach any more of the coffee and hoping to relieve some of the tension in his back, he sat down in a lumpy club chair. Absently twisting his watch band, he continued to think about what Skye had told him, especially the way she'd characterized the patients' distress as insomnia—not agitation. It was easy to think of the two as the same problem, but Jack was experienced enough to know they weren't necessarily the same.

He leaned back and closed his eyes. The more he thought about the importance of insomnia as a symptom, the more the dots began to slowly line up. And then, coming to him almost in the form of a revelation, everything suddenly crystallized. His eyes snapped open, and he could feel his face flush. Two facts melded together and moved to the front of his mind: *the children's insomnia, and a veterinarian who specialized in neurologic diseases.*

"How could I've been so slow on the uptake?" he muttered, squeezing his hands into fists, bleaching his knuckles white. With the first breath he took, he came out of his chair; with the second, he was on his way to Charlee Dunne's room.

⊏⊐

THE DOOR to the parent suite was open, and Jack could see Leah was asleep in a fully reclined lounge chair. Hoping not to disturb her, he quietly made his way to Charlee's bedside. With heightened senses, he spent the first minute studying her face. He continued his examination by placing his fingertips along her facial muscles and gently palpating them.

Another ten minutes passed, and he was finished with his examination. Feeling as if he were no longer staring into an abyss of confusion and uncertainty, his pulse finally slowed and he allowed himself the time to benefit from a few cleansing breaths and a mental pat on the back.

He swung his gaze back to Leah. She was still asleep. He headed for the door. The first thing he did when he stepped into the hall was reach for his phone to call Madison.

"Hi, Jack. What time did you leave the guesthouse? Did you get any sleep at all?"

"Are you in the hospital yet?"

"I'm walking over now. What's up?"

"As soon as you get here, come up to the unit. I want to talk to you about something."

"I was going to stop in Radiology first."

"That can wait. Come straight here."

"What's going on? You sound a little on the excited side."

"I passed excited ten minutes ago on my way to elation. I'll meet you outside the LM unit."

Part II

Chapter 34

Every few seconds, Jack's eyes darted to the elevators. At the same time, he paraded back and forth as if he were sweating out the beginning of an IRS audit. Finally, the doors to the middle car rolled open. The moment Madison stepped out, he ushered her down the hall into a small alcove that housed a bank of vending machines.

"What the hell's going on, Jack?"

"What do you remember about *prion diseases?*"

"Excuse me?" she said, looking at him as if he were suffering the effects of a concussion. "You called me here stat to ask me that?"

"Prion diseases," he repeated. "Tell me what you recall about them?"

"You mean like mad cow disease?"

"Yes, like mad cow disease."

"I'm a perinatologist, Jack, which makes me a little rusty on the topic of prion infections."

Holding his silence, he looked at her with an impatient frown.

"You're serious?"

"As an IRS audit."

"Okay. As I recall, the term prion comes from a combination of the words protein and infection. It's a very serious disorder caused by abnormally shaped toxic proteins that accumulate in the brain and eventually destroy the tissue."

"It appears your memory's better than you thought."

Taking a step backward, she continued, "I realize we're getting a little desperate for answers, but are you seriously trying to tell me you think these kids have mad cow disease?"

"No, because humans don't get mad cow disease. Only animals do, but they do get a variation of it plus other types of prion diseases that closely resemble it."

"Jack, I really think you should stop and—"

"Just hear me out. What I'm about to tell you is theoretical, but I think we need to at least consider the possibility."

"Go ahead."

"There's a whole family of prion diseases. Some occur in humans, while others infect animals. Altogether, there're probably only about ten of them known to modern medicine. They all have two things in common—they're incredibly rare, and as you just mentioned, they all attack the brain. The one that people are most familiar with is mad cow disease, which animals get from eating rotten meat infected with the poisonous protein. Once these toxic proteins enter the bloodstream, they rapidly reproduce and accumulate in the brain. As they continue to build up, the patient develops a bizarre set of symptoms."

Jack slowed down and inhaled a deliberate breath as he waited for her response. He couldn't help but notice the skeptical look that had taken shape on her face.

"We've spent a lot of hours taking a detailed medical history from each of the families. I don't recall any of them mentioning anything about their kids attending a picnic and eating rotten meat."

Overlooking her mild cynicism, he said, "Eating decayed meat is only one way of becoming infected. Prions can also be transmitted by a blood transfusion, by contaminated medical instruments or tainted medications. They can even be inhaled."

"Which begs the question: other than a strange cluster of symptoms, what proof do you have that leukemic malnutrition might be a prion disease?"

"One of the prion diseases humans get is called fatal familial insomnia. It's rare, but I've seen a few cases in my career. The patients have vivid dreams, muscle spasms, and severe weight loss. They progress from restless sleep to hallucinations and eventually to severe insomnia." He stopped, waiting for Madison to say something. When she didn't, he asked, "Does any of this sound vaguely familiar?"

"Okay, I'll admit those symptoms are similar to the ones we're seeing, but the disease you just described is a familial one, which means it's inherited. People who are destined to get it are born with it. It's part of their DNA, and it's passed from one generation to the next. We both know that can't possibly be the case with leukemic malnutrition."

"I'm not suggesting these kids have fatal familial insomnia. I'm saying it's possible they have a prion disease that closely resembles it. One of the other prions that infects animals gives them rapid weight loss and fitful behavior. Some even grind their teeth down to a nub." He cleared his throat and cautiously added, "I don't have all the answers, Madison, but if these kids are suffering from a prion disease, I'm pretty sure it's one that's never been seen before."

Madison leaned back against one of the vending machines.

"Forget about the specifics of how they got the disease for a moment, or why they're the only ones in the country who have it, and tell me how you're going to prove these children are suffering from a prion disease. Because, as I recall, the gold standard for making the diagnosis is a brain biopsy."

"It probably still is, but the last decade or so has seen a dramatic improvement in our ability to diagnose prion diseases. We're now using blood tests, analysis of spinal fluid, and MRIs of the brain to help make the diagnosis," he said, encouraged she hadn't completely dismissed his theory. "Leo Chester is a colleague of mine in Columbus. He's had a long-standing interest in this area and heads up an outstanding prion research lab at the university. It's one of the few cutting-edge centers in the country. For the last few years, they've been looking at new diagnostic techniques, especially blood tests. I'm hoping if we send him blood samples from a few of our leukemic malnutrition patients he'll be able to analyze them for us. What do you think?"

"I don't think we're in a position to rule out any possible causes...no matter how unlikely they might sound. Are you going to discuss any of this with Althea?"

"Not yet. I want to speak to Leo first."

"You know, Jack, your prion theory is a double-edged sword. On the one hand, it would be a monumental breakthrough if we discover the cause of leukemic malnutrition; on the other...well, we both know prion diseases are all uniformly fatal."

Reaching for his phone to call Leo Chester, Jack responded by raising crossed fingers. "I'm aware of that, but you're the one who told me the other day to find my optimistic side."

"Translate."

"If leukemic malnutrition does turn out to be a new strain of prion disease, maybe it'll also turn out to be the first one that's curable, which means we'll just have to work our derrieres off until we find that cure."

Chapter 35

Tapping his foot impatiently, Jack was one ring away from Leo Chester's voicemail when his good friend and colleague picked up the call.

"Hey, Jack. How are things going at Oster?"

"Until now, not great. But we may finally be on to something, and I need your help, buddy."

"What can I do?"

"We have reason to suspect that leukemic malnutrition may be a previously unrecognized prion disease."

There was a predictable silence, and Jack could only imagine the stunned look on Leo's face.

"I'm not trying to trample on your theory, but from what I know about leukemic malnutrition, it doesn't seem like the patient's age or the rapid course of the illness fits the typical pattern of what we normally see with prion infections."

"I know, but the patients' symptoms are highly suggestive of one. And even though it's not exactly like other prion infections, I feel strongly we have to rule it out."

"Tell me how I can help."

"What's the present state-of-the-art approach to blood testing for a prion illness?"

"We've come a long way since the original work in 2017," Leo responded. "The technique we've perfected in our lab is among the most sophisticated assays available anywhere."

"I was hoping you'd say that. How would you feel about analyzing a few tubes of blood for us?"

"We'll be happy to give it our best shot, Jack, but I can't promise we'll be able to tell you with absolute certainty if the blood's positive for a prion infection, especially if it's a strain that's never been seen before."

"We're up against a wall here, Leo—and on that wall, there's large ticking time bomb hanging over our heads. Anything you can do to help us will be greatly appreciated."

"Can you get the blood samples to me today?"

"I'll have them couriered down to your lab this afternoon. Do you have any idea how long it will it take you to run the assays?"

"Probably a day…maybe two, but don't hold me to it."

"Thanks, Leo."

"Listen, Jack. We've known each other a long time, and I'm more than familiar with your remarkable skills as a diagnostician. It's not very often you're wrong, but I hope to god this is one time that you are."

"I'd be lying if I told you the same thing hasn't crossed my mind."

"I'll get our techs to pull a double shift. We'll work around the clock on your samples. The moment I have something, I'll call you."

"Calling you a life-saver may turn out be more accurate than either of us can imagine." As Jack slipped his phone back into his pocket, his eyes met Madison's.

"I'm afraid there's nothing else we can do except sit and wait. I'll give Althea a call and let her know what's going on. I'm pretty sure she'll want us to keep all of this tightly under wraps until we have an answer from Leo."

They came to their feet and headed toward the door.

"You know, Jack, something tells me you're not the only one who suspected leukemic malnutrition was a prion disease."

"You must be reading my mind. I'm guessing the material in Anna Hartmann's journal led Dr. Hayden Kubicek right to the same diagnosis."

"The only hole in the theory is that the existence of prions wasn't established until the 1960s. The photocopies of the journal pages Peter Kubicek gave us were surely compiled several decades earlier than that."

"It's possible Dr. Hartmann discovered toxic proteins before the 1960s, but since her work was never published, her abnormal proteins remained unnamed and unknown to medical science until the 1960s," Jack postulated. They walked toward the exit. "It's interesting that Hayden had no access to any of the hospital records of our patients, nor was he able to examine any of them, yet he was convinced he'd discovered the cause of LM…and maybe the cure. Even with Dr. Hartmann's journal, nobody's that smart."

"So what are you saying, Jack?"

With his head bent forward he answered, "I'm saying Hayden had help."

Chapter 36

It was a sun-drenched morning, prompting Jack and Madison to sit out on the back porch and enjoy a light breakfast.

The blood samples they had sent to Leo had arrived in Columbus at just after three the previous afternoon. Considering it had been less than a day, it wasn't surprising they hadn't heard back from him as of yet. Even so, with each passing hour, their anxiety intensified and their patience thinned.

By the time they had showered and dressed, it was eight thirty. Their first stop when they arrived on the LM unit was Kip Dale's room. The door to the parent suite was ajar, and although they couldn't see Frank, they assumed he was asleep. Jack moved to Kip's bedside. Increasing pressure from behind his eyes forced them to bulge, while at the same time his lids blinked like the shutter on a high-speed camera. He hadn't responded to any questions for the past two days.

"How's he doing?" came a voice from the other side of the room.

"He's holding his own," Jack said. "It doesn't look like there have been any major changes overnight."

"I guess at this point it's encouraging to hear his condition hasn't worsened," Frank said in an unconvincing tone of voice. "Tell me, Dr. Wyatt, have you ever been faced with a case that, no matter how hard you racked your brain, you just couldn't figure it out?"

"I'm afraid so."

"I probably shouldn't have asked you that. I guess the answer's obvious."

They each took a seat around the small table where Jack and Madison spent the next few minutes reviewing the most current clinical information with Frank. He put on a brave front, remaining stone-faced and agreeable, but it was plain to see his true emotional state wasn't far from rock bottom.

"Do you have any questions for us?" Madison asked.

"No, I think I've got a pretty good picture of Kip's condition," he said, as he walked back into the parent suite and returned with a green file folder in his hand. "I have some information I'd like to share with you about Dr. Austin. Is now a good time?"

"Now would be fine," Madison answered. "We're still very anxious to speak with her."

"I wouldn't get my hopes up too high," Frank warned, as he removed the pages from the folder, prompting Jack and Madison to trade a hesitant look.

"Let me tell you what we've been able to discover about Dr. Karina Austin. She's never been issued a birth certificate, driver's license, passport, or visa of any type. There's no record of a marriage certificate or a medical license issued to her in any state. To the best of our knowledge, no governmental entity has ever issued a death certificate in her name. She has no academic records, nor has she ever owned property anywhere in the United States. She's never been in the military or worked for any governmental organization or agency that we can determine. And finally, she has no social security number, nor has she ever filed a tax return." Closing the file, he scrubbed a hand over his face. "I wish I had better news for you."

"I'm confused," Jack said. "She's a licensed physician. There has to be some record of her. I mean, it sounds like you're describing somebody who's dropped off the face of the earth."

"Or worse," he stated flatly.

"Excuse me?" Madison said.

"We don't use bargain-basement websites where you pay fifty dollars to get some vague background information on somebody. Our resources are highly sophisticated and accurate. In my business, there's no room for errors. Millions of dollars and sometimes people's freedom from incarceration depend upon it."

"I guess I feel a little vindicated, but it's still hard to believe, because we know for a fact that Dr. Haas collaborated with Dr. Austin on her research project," she said.

"Actually, the only thing you know for a fact is that Dr. Haas worked with somebody who claimed she was Dr. Austin." After a strained silence, he added, "You have to consider the possibility that the woman was an imposter."

Jack drew back. "An imposter? Why in the world would anybody want to pose as a research doctor?"

With a patient grin, Frank answered, "As much as I'd like to answer that, I'm an investigator, not a psychiatrist. My job's to sift through a quagmire of facts, which are oftentimes more fantasy and dishonesty than anything else, and come up with the truth. I concern myself with the *what* of things, not the *why*. But if it makes you feel any better, there have probably been master imposters around almost since the dawn of mankind."

Jack's mind filled with uncertainty, but the one thing he was confident of was that Frank Dale was a skillful investigator.

"I assume from what you're saying that there's no reason for you to keep looking?" Jack asked.

"I can keep searching, but if I were asked my opinion under oath in court tomorrow, I'd swear no person by the name of Dr. Karina Austin who is a qualified physician and medical researcher exists."

"I don't know what to say," she stated.

"After you've had the opportunity to think things over, if you feel it might help, the three of us can sit down again and go over all of this information in detail." Frank replaced the material in the file folder and walked over to Kip's bed. He leaned forward and kissed his son on the forehead.

"Thank you for going to such lengths to help," Jack said.

"I can't speak for the practice of medicine, but sometimes, in my business, no information is a lot better than thinking you've come across a key piece of information and finding out later you were wrong." He tossed a shrug in their direction and asked, "When do you think you may be in to see Kip again?"

"Early tomorrow," Madison assured him.

Frank walked them to the door. "I'm sorry the information on Dr. Austin wasn't what you'd hoped for, but if you need help on anything else, please just let me know, and I'll be happy to help."

The moment they stepped out into the hall, Madison said, "Well, that's the last thing I was expecting to hear. I guess things just got a lot more confusing. We better get hold of Althea ASAP."

"It's a funny thing," Jack said, as they made their way back toward the core desk. "All of the elusive cases I've been involved with over the years were always about piecing together a bunch of puzzling medical facts to eventually figure out what was causing, and how to treat, a serious illness. But that's not the case this time, because we're dealing with all of these collateral, nonclinical issues that have come together to form this...this massive Gordian knot that's only confusing things more."

Chapter 37

Jack had just finished morning rounds and was waiting for Madison to return from a meeting with the blood bank leadership when his phone rang.

It was Leo.

"Good morning," Jack said, as he looked around the staff lounge to make sure he was alone. He couldn't help but wonder if Leo was simply calling with an update or had some conclusive news for him.

"Sorry about the delay in getting back to you, but I promise you we've been working on the samples since the moment we received them. I'm not sure if this is what you were hoping to hear, but every one of the blood samples you sent us is heavily infected with a prion."

More as a reflex than anything else, Jack asked, "How certain are you?"

"It's a hundred percent and, as you suspected, it's a strain we've never seen before, which I guess makes sense when you consider there's never been a prion that's caused a mini-epidemic in children. What are you going to do, pal?" Jack did his best to focus on his conversation with Leo, but his mind was exploding like a fireworks display over Washington D.C. on July Fourth.

"Excuse me, Leo?"

"What's your plan, Jack?"

"I guess that has just become the question of the day. Madison and I are here as consultants only, so it will be up to the medical staff, but it would seem the obvious next move is to start looking for a cure."

"It's a prion infection, Jack and as much as I don't want to sound like the Grim Reaper...well, I think you understand what I mean. We'll keep working on the sample to see if there's anything more we can find out. You've drifted into unchartered territory, my friend. I don't mean to sound boastful, but I think I know as much about prion diseases as anybody, and I don't have the first clue how a group of children suffering from leukemia could have all become infected with the same prion at about the same time. I think we both know the most obvious answer lies somewhere in the hospital."

"I was just thinking the same thing, and a good place to start is with a review of every transfusion these kids have received."

"I know I don't have to say this, but those kids are sitting on a time bomb. I don't think we can rely on our existing information on known prion diseases as a predictor of how long these kids have before..."

"I know, Leo. You're preaching to the choir. After I have a chance to digest all of this, I'll get back to you. I think, with the information you just gave me, you and I are going to be best buddies for the next few days."

"Whatever I can do to help—just pick up your phone."

"Oh, Leo... as much as it's possible, can we try and keep a lid on this?"

"I'll do my damnedest. I'll speak to my staff and make sure they understand this is a HIPAA compliance issue and that the information stays in our lab."

"Thanks again."

As soon as Jack was off the phone, Madison strolled into the lounge. It didn't take him long to brief her.

"I think the first thing we should do is set up a meeting with Althea," she said. "We'll be getting into some complicated medical and political issues, and I don't think we can take this thing any further without her input."

"I'll give her a call in a few minutes," he said, coming to his feet. "I need a little time to think this through."

"I'm going to take a look at a couple of patients. Come find me after you've made the call."

Jack couldn't deny finding gratification in uncovering the cause of leukemic malnutrition, but it was bittersweet. The thought of taking a victory lap or basking in the achievement in some other way never crossed his mind. Now that making the diagnosis was behind them, the team's focus had to shift at once to finding a cure. He was a neurologist and well versed in prion diseases, and he had a pretty good idea of what they'd be up against. Being the first physicians to find an effective treatment for a disease that modern medicine considered incurable would be a formidable challenge. He prayed it wouldn't turn out to be a bridge too far.

He brought up Althea's phone number and waited for an answer. Their conversation was short but to the point. Jack requested they get together to discuss an important new development. Althea informed him she was in Cincinnati but would be back in her office by late afternoon. As soon as she was able she'd call him back with an exact time for the meeting.

Struggling to remain as optimistic as he was able in a sea of uncertainty, he slipped his phone into his pocket and walked off to see if he could find Madison. As much as he tried, all he could think about was the uncertainty of what the future held for a group of innocent and imperiled children who had already suffered enough for one lifetime.

Chapter 38

As soon as Jack left the lounge, he spotted Madison outside the procedure room speaking on her phone. When he was a few feet away from joining her, there was a sudden commotion outside of Charlee's room. Without saying anything, they exchanged ominous looks and hurried down the hall. When they were a few feet away, Elliot Marsh, the physician on call, approached with his stethoscope unevenly hanging over his left shoulder. His bloodshot eyes and disheveled hair betrayed too many sleep-deprived nights. He motioned to them and then ushered them to a quieter and more private area.

"I'm afraid Charlee's taken another turn for the worse," he said, blowing out a long, discouraged breath. "About an hour ago, her respiratory status suddenly worsened. We didn't have to put her on a ventilator, but she's requiring a lot of oxygen by mask. Her vital signs are okay, and for the moment, she's stable, but I have no idea which way this thing's going to go. It's possible we'll have to put her on a ventilator before shift change." With pursed lips, he hesitated for a moment before adding, "I'm sorry. I know she's special to both of you."

Jack waited for Madison to respond. When she didn't, he assumed she was taking a few moments to collect herself.

"Thanks," Jack told him. "Is Mom in the room?"

"She's there."

"How's she doing?"

"Not great, I'm afraid," Marsh answered, "Just to be on the safe side, we're going to move Charlee to one of the critical care beds. Let me know if you need anything."

When they walked into Charlee's room, they found Leah sitting in a wooden chair with her eyes transfixed on the bed. Her face was expressionless, and the soft tissues below her eyes were heavily swollen and furrowed by a constant flood of tears. Jack took a few seconds to check Charlee's monitors.

"The beginning of the end," she whispered to them.

"We don't know that. It's just as likely this is nothing more than a temporary setback," Madison said. "Her vital signs are fine and this may just be a—"

"She can barely breathe on her own, and she's so out of it I don't think she even recognizes my voice." Pausing to sweep some tears from her cheeks, she went on. "How much worse can things possibly get? I think I'm finally starting to accept that there's nothing anybody can do to help her." She held up her hand. "I know how hard you and all her other doctors are fighting to find a treatment, but I'm starting to believe whatever it is that Charlee has…well, it's incurable."

"Remember what you told me about Charlee's barrel racing and how much grit she has when she competes?" Madison asked.

A smile appeared on her face. "I remember. Everybody who knows her would say the same thing."

"Just hang on to that thought," Madison said, realizing how mentally winded Leah was.

It was at that moment that the transport team came through the door, ready to move Charlee to her new room. Leah went to the bedside to help.

"We'll stop back later," Jack promised.

They stepped out into the hall. They hadn't taken more than a few steps before Madison took Jack by the arm.

"How about taking a walk over to the medical library and back?"

"Now?"

"It should only take us about twenty minutes, and we both could use some fresh air."

"Are you feeling okay?" he asked with a bit of urgency to his voice.

"I'm fine, Jack. I promise."

With a sideways glance, he nodded. "Sure. Let's go," he said, sneaking another look at her. He was fairly certain Madison was telling the truth, but he'd long been a believer in the doctrine of *trust but verify*, and with that in mind, he'd be keeping a particularly close eye on her for the rest of the day.

Chapter 39

It was an unseasonably warm, cloudless morning, just blustery enough to make the walk across the campus to the library and back a refreshing stroll.

Madison was the first to speak. "I keep going back to what Hayden told you on the phone about having an idea for how to treat leukemic malnutrition. We both agree that had to have come from Dr. Hartmann's journal."

"So, it would seem."

"Unless you see a path forward that I don't, our only option is to locate the entire journal and hope we can pinpoint the same clue Hayden did."

Jack said, "When I called Peter he told me he looked everywhere for the journal and couldn't locate it. That's going to make finding it quite a chore. The possibilities are infinite as to where it could be."

"Maybe not," she said.

"Excuse me?"

"You told me Hayden mentioned to you on the phone that he was planning on going to Cleveland for a day trip before our meeting. When we met with Peter, he also mentioned it."

"I'm not quite sure I see where you're—"

"You also told me that when you researched Hayden on the internet, you found out he went to med school at Case Western." Madison coughed a couple of times and slowed her pace.

Jack noticed but for the moment didn't say anything.

"Hayden was smart and apparently very thorough. If he decided to put the journal somewhere to protect it, I suspect he would've chosen the place very carefully." With a gleam of accomplishment in her eye, Madison continued, "The Dittrick Museum of Medical History."

"Excuse me?"

"It's part of Case Western Reserve University. Every medical student and resident who's ever trained at Case is familiar with it. It's well known in the medical community for its impressive collection of medical artifacts, devices, photographs, and other items related to the history of medicine."

"You trained in Florida. How do you happen to know all this?"

"When I was a senior med student, I did a three-month elective rotation in cardiology at Case Western. I've been through the Dittrick Museum a few times." She crossed her fingers and held them up for Jack to see. "I think there's a chance Hayden went to Cleveland to leave Dr. Hartmann's journal under the watchful eye of the Dittrick."

"That's an interesting theory, but as we've both said, we're not even sure Hayden had her original journal. For all we know, every page he had may have been a photocopy."

"I can't tell you why, but I don't think that's the case. I'm not implying that Hayden went on a quest to locate the journal, but somehow it came into his possession, and somebody briefed him as to its possible significance."

He let out a breath that seemed to come from the bottom of his feet. "Even if what you say is so, logic would dictate that he probably had some other reason for going to Cleveland."

"C'mon, Jack. With everything going on in his life? I hardly think a pleasure trip to the Rock & Roll Hall of Fame would've topped his bucket list," she said, as a sudden expression of hesitancy landed on her face. "There's something else. I don't believe Hayden telling you about his trip to Cleveland was an innocuous comment —I think he wanted you to know."

"Then why didn't he just come out and tell me?"

"Because he was smarter than that. I'm sure he planned on keeping all the details of what he'd discovered to himself until after he met with us. I also think he may have had reason to fear for his personal safety."

"Are you suggesting that Hayden Kubicek died of anything except natural causes."

"My mind's open to the possibility." She slowed her pace and put a hand on his shoulder. "What do you think about making a trip to the museum and seeing what we can find out? Even if it turns out to be a dead end, all it has cost us is a little time."

Jack blew out a quick mouthful of air and then nodded. "I'm okay with the idea, but let's be smart about this. The last thing we want to do is come across as a couple of insane conspiracists. If any rational person finds out what's on our minds, they'll have somebody drop a net over our heads."

"Are you going to share any of this to Althea?"

"We're meeting with her at five to brief her on the report from Leo's lab. I'm not sure who else will be there. Maybe, if we can get her alone, we can bounce the idea off her. She knows everybody in Ohio and should be able to grease the skids for us with the curator of the museum."

Madison was pleased that Jack was going along with her suggestion to visit the museum without too much kicking or screaming. She agreed with him that it was unlikely the Dittrick had Dr. Hartmann's journal, but as a place to begin their search, it seemed like a good choice.

Chapter 40

Jack and Madison arrived at Althea's office a few minutes early. On their way over, they had taken ample time to discuss their strategy for the meeting.

"We're sorry about asking you to see us on such short notice," Jack said as she escorted them across the hall into a nicely appointed wood-paneled conference room.

"When you called, the concern in your voice was anything but subtle. I'm anxious to hear what you two have discovered."

Jack wasn't surprised when he saw two men seated at the glass racetrack-shaped table. He recognized Dr. Kendric Nash but was unfamiliar with the man seated next to him. They both came to their feet.

"Jack, Madison—you already know Kendric, but I'd like you to meet Robert Oster. He's not only an outstanding pediatric immunologist, but he also is serving as the interim chair of our board of trustees. He's intentionally maintained a low profile, but I assure you, he's been very much involved in all matters relating to the outbreak of leukemic malnutrition."

"Althea's too kind. It's a great pleasure to meet you both,"

Robert said with a becoming smile, as he shook each of their hands. He was large in stature, a bit stiffed-jawed, and had a solid neck, giving him more an appearance of a lumberjack than the esteemed chair of the board of a children's hospital. "I should have done so sooner, but I thank you both for agreeing to consult on these cases."

Madison said, "I assume you having the same last name as the hospital is not some strange coincidence."

Jack cringed inwardly, thinking to himself that she might have waited a few minutes before broaching that topic. From the grin on Robert's face, he was pleased to see he wasn't put off by her brashness.

"When my uncle retired, my family felt it was important for one of us continue to maintain a strong presence on the Children's Hospital Board, and...well, I was *voluntold* that someone would be me. So here I am, splitting my time between my two passions—pediatric immunology and this remarkable children's hospital."

"Robert's been an incredible leader," Althea stated. "We've accomplished great things since he assumed the role of chair."

"Do you see what I mean about her effusive nature?" Robert asked with a wink. "Althea told us that you two believe you've come across key information regarding leukemic malnutrition."

Jack tapped his fingertips together a few times, stole a peek Madison's way, and slid forward in his chair.

"Madison and I have strong reason to believe that leukemic malnutrition is a previously unrecognized prion disease." He stopped, setting his eyes on the quizzical looks that promptly appeared on their faces.

After clearing his throat, Jack spent the next few minutes explaining how they'd arrived at their conclusion, being certain to emphasize that Leo's laboratory had provided indisputable proof that leukemic malnutrition was a prion infection.

Nervously fidgeting with his bow tie, Kendric asked, "Do you have any idea how these children could have possibly contracted this infection?"

"Our best guess is that it was hospital acquired," Madison

responded. "Discovering the specific method of transmission could be an important step in leading us to a treatment."

Robert said, "I'm hardly an expert in this area, but to my knowledge, there are no effective treatments for prion diseases. Eventually, they're all fatal."

"Unfortunately, you're correct, but since this appears to be a new strain, we're praying we'll be able to find some way to treat it," Jack explained. "We understand we're up against tough odds, but it's the only hope we have of saving these children."

With interlocked fingers Althea leaned in over the table. "Any idea why it's infecting only our leukemia patients?"

"Obviously, that's a key question. As of right now, we don't have an answer, but you have to consider that Jack and I just received the information from the lab, which means the entire team's going to be facing plenty of challenging questions."

Althea stated, "So, you can't say with any assurance that the disease won't spread to other cancer patients or how many new cases we might see."

"I'm afraid we can't," Jack said.

"You mentioned the cause might be a hospital-acquired infection. Are you talking about a hospital error of some kind, or is it more likely this infection was unforeseeable and beyond our control?" Robert inquired calmly.

It wasn't hard for Jack to see where his concern was coming from. "We can't rule out anything at this point."

"Where does this new information leave us with regard to Lennon Armbrister's viral theory?" Kendric inquired. "From what I understand, her hypothesis has merit, but in light of this new information, I assume we'll be dismissing it and concentrating all of our efforts on treating the prion infection."

"That's what we would strongly recommend," Jack said,

"Turning our attention away from Lennon's theory may be blessing in disguise," Althea said. "Jack and Madison have justifiable concerns regarding the legitimacy of Dr. Austin's research."

"That's disappointing to hear," Robert said. "Was that research done here at Oster?"

"In part. It was a collaborative effort," Kendric answered.

Robert scanned the group. "Even though it may be a moot point as far as treating leukemic malnutrition is concerned, if the work was done here and fell short of our quality expectations, I'd like to hear about it."

Madison took the lead. "In trying to better understand and verify her work, Jack and I attempted to reach out to Dr. Austin. We did everything in our power to locate her, but when we couldn't, we arranged for professional help."

"What kind of help?" Kendric asked in a hesitant voice.

"A private investigator of sorts," Jack answered, with no intention of naming Frank Dale unless he was specifically asked. "We've been informed by the investigator that, in spite of an exhaustive effort, he was unable to locate or verify that any physician by the name of Karina Austin exists. He concluded the person claiming to be her was an imposter."

"I beg your pardon," Kendric was quick to say. "But, I personally assigned Dr. Abel Haas to serve as Dr. Austin's supervisor. I discussed her work with him on more than one occasion. He told me he spoke with her frequently." He waved a dismissive hand through the air. "No disrespect intended to your private investigator, but he could be wrong."

"It's quite possible Dr. Haas did speak with her," Madison said. "The investigator assumed someone who claimed to be Dr. Austin did indeed exist, but she was an imposter."

"That's absurd," Kendric insisted. "There has to be some mistake."

Robert's face tightened with exasperation. "Just how carefully are we vetting researchers who approach us to collaborate?"

Kendric sat straight up and with no hesitation said, "Dr. Austin wasn't our employee, nor are we the FBI. We take the normal precautions to verify any guest researcher's credentials. What we don't do is convene a tribunal every time a promising young investigator asks to work with us. I have no idea of the accuracy of this... this private investigator's report, but I know Dr. Haas's commitment to detail, and I'm sure he was convinced that Dr. Austin's qualifications were impeccable before granting her request to work with us."

"Let's all try to stay calm," Robert suggested. "We're getting off point. Our major focus has to be on caring for our patients—and right now, that means finding an effective treatment for leukemic malnutrition. We'll report the Dr. Austin matter to our security department and let them handle it. If we need to involve the authorities, we'll assist them in every way we can." He paused, and by acclamation, everybody in the room agreed with his plan.

"When do you think we should share Madison's and Jack's prion theory with the focus group and the parents?" Althea asked.

Robert responded first. "I suggest we wait until tomorrow. I'd like a little time to digest all of this." He turned to Althea. "Would you please schedule a meeting of the focus group for first thing in the morning to brief the members on this new information. I'm all for giving the members time to take all of this in, but we need a detailed plan as soon as possible as to how we'll be moving forward."

"I'll take care of it," she said.

"Two final points," Robert began. "I see no reason to share the unpleasant matter of Dr. Austin with the focus group tomorrow. Second, Althea, I'd appreciate it if you'd brief Lennon on all of these recent developments. Please remind her that the matter of Dr. Austin is highly confidential and I'm relying on her professional discretion. I'm sorry to leave this to you; I can't imagine it'll be an easy conversation."

"I'll speak with her this evening."

"Unless there's something else we need to address, I think we can conclude this meeting," Robert said. With that, each of the attendees came to their feet and started toward the door.

Jack asked Althea if he and Madison could have a moment to talk with her about another matter.

"Of course. I'll be back as soon as I walk Kendric and Robert to the elevator. Give me five minutes."

Jack found himself wondering how Oster's board and senior

administrative leadership would manage the firestorm of publicity the announcement of finding the cause of leukemic malnutrition would undoubtedly ignite. Along with the announcement, the issue of how the patients became infected with the prion would undoubtedly be raised by the media.

"You've got that look on your face—what's going on?" Madison inquired.

"I was just thinking about the press conference Oster's sure to call in the next day or two to announce they've found the cause of leukemic malnutrition. I suspect they'll put an interesting slant on the events."

"You can count on it. They never pass on the chance to take a huge bow."

"That's not what I mean. Eventually, the media's going to raise the same concerns Robert did and ask if leukemic malnutrition could be the result of a medical mistake."

"The public relations departments at high-profile hospitals are like politicians," Madison stated. "They're very resourceful at dodging tough questions."

"They can be as inventive as they want, as long as they don't get caught stepping over the integrity line."

"They're too smart for that, but I wouldn't be surprised if they nudged it a little."

Althea returned, and they took a few minutes to brief her on their plan to visit the Dittrick Museum.

Madison looked at her with anticipation. "We were hoping you might be able to facilitate matters for us with somebody at the museum."

"I'll do my best. When were you planning on going?"

"There's no time like the present. We're thinking of going tomorrow."

With a quick tilt of her head, Althea chuckled. "You don't give a girl much time to operate, but I'll see what I can do. I'll arrange a car for you and talk to you in the morning before you leave."

"Thank you," Madison said.

As he and Madison walked down the corridor toward the elevator, Jack was still skeptical a trip to Cleveland would turn up anything. But if by some stroke of luck they did locate the journal, he now found himself wondering if it would be the key they were looking for to unlock the mystery of leukemic malnutrition or if it would turn out to do nothing more than further muddy the waters.

Chapter 41

The Ditrrick Museum of Medical History had become part of Case Western University in 1998, but was originally established in the late 1800s. Because of its vast collection of artifacts, devices, and written records, the museum provided an excellent glimpse into the rich history of medicine. After discussing the matter last evening, Madison said she'd prefer not to make the trip to Cleveland. Instead, she would stay back at Oster to deal with any urgent medical issues that might arise.

Three hours after Jack departed Defiance, the SUV Althea had arranged for him pulled up to the curb in front of the museum. He entered the museum and made his way through the rotunda hall to the information center. A plump man standing behind the desk lifted his eyes. An easy smile came to his face.

"May I help you, sir?" he asked, with a distinct Jamaican accent.

"My name's Jack Wyatt. I have an appointment with Dr. Strauss at ten. I was asked to give her a call when I arrived."

Before the man could respond, a woman with a Mona Lisa smile and long auburn hair walked up.

"Welcome to Cleveland, Dr. Wyatt. I'm Kristin Strauss. I'm the chief curator of the museum."

In spite of what Althea had hinted at, Jack was still a bit surprised by the VIP treatment. He extended his hand to shake hers. Having done his homework the night before, he had learned Dr. Strauss had been hired by the university ten years earlier. She held both a nursing degree and a PhD in library science and had been an influential force in raising the museum's importance in the academic community.

"I appreciate you taking the time to meet with me."

"We understand the magnitude of the problem you're facing at Oster, and I assure you, we'll do anything we can to help." With a polite grin, she added, "It's not often I receive a call from the Ohio Surgeon General to make sure I do everything in my power to assist with a problem."

She pointed across the lobby to a gently spiraled marble staircase with an intricate iron railing. Jack's eye was caught by several large decorative banners that hung from the top of the staircase announcing upcoming events.

"Let's walk," she said to him. "We can talk as I give you the VIP tour."

"I hope you haven't been put in a difficult position regarding museum regulations."

"I think we're way past that," she said with a forgiving smile. As they ascended the stairway, she continued, "We received a gift from Dr. Kubicek about two weeks ago. He requested that it be anonymous. It consisted of three handwritten leather journals. As we do with every donation, we undertook a preliminary examination of the material. We concluded the material dates back to the early 1900s. There's no question the journals are authentic. As to the accuracy of the scientific information they contain or potential impact on the work you're doing at Oster…well, my staff and I will leave those determinations to you and your team."

"I can't tell you what a relief it is for me to hear this." Jack was overjoyed with the news but a little leery about asking his next question. "Would there be some way I might be able to sign out the journals?"

"Other than remaining anonymous, Dr. Kubicek insisted on

only one condition when he gifted the journals to us. He authorized you and only you to take possession of them. The choice to return them to us when you're done with them is entirely up to you."

"Well, being able to take the journals with me will certainly make matters easier."

"I understand that Dr. Kubicek died suddenly, soon after visiting the museum."

"I'm afraid so."

She gestured for him to head down a wide corridor lined with several exhibits of nineteenth century surgical instruments and bloodletting devices. They descended a second staircase and returned to Rotunda Hall. A young lady approached and handed Kristin a white stationery box. She didn't hesitate to pass the box to Jack.

"I wouldn't know how to begin to thank you for your help."

"If these journals contribute in some way to your team finding a cure for leukemic malnutrition, that would be more thanks than any of us here at the museum could ever hope for. Here's my card. I've written my cell phone number on the back. I'm sure you're anxious to get back to Defiance. If there's anything further I can do, please don't hesitate to call."

Jack was still stunned at how smoothly things had gone when he said, "Thank you, again."

He was just about to take his first step toward the exit when Kristin said, "My son was diagnosed with lymphoma six years ago. It was a terrible ordeal for our entire family, but he's been in remission for the past three of those years. I pray those journals contain the information you're looking for. Have a safe trip back, Dr. Wyatt."

Jack exited the building and spotted his driver standing next to the black SUV. As he headed toward the curb, he reached for his phone and called Madison.

"You weren't in there very long. How did it go?"

"You're a genius."

"I hope that means what I think it means."

"I've got the journals."

"Journals? How many are there?"

"Three." The driver moved to the back of the vehicle to assist Jack, but he already had the door open and was climbing in. "I may wind up spending the rest of the day studying them so I'll be at the guesthouse if you need me."

"No problem. I've got plenty to do here in the hospital. Have you told Althea about your good fortune yet?"

"I'll call her on the way back to Defiance. I'm sure she'll want to keep the existence of the journals between the three of us for the time being."

"I'm okay with that. I assume you feel the same way."

"Absolutely."

"Sounds good. I'll see you later."

The classic new-car scent filled his nostrils. As the black SUV poked along through a heavy tangle of downtown traffic, Jack sat back, wondering what secrets the journals might reveal. A part of him didn't want to know, for fear they'd turn out to be a dead end. His mind, beginning to fill with uncertainty, drifted to Hayden. What if he and Madison had been wrong about him? What if he wasn't the levelheaded, bright young man he and his father thought he was? What if he'd stumbled across the journals by chance, and everything he'd concluded about leukemic malnutrition turned out to be a wild figment of his imagination? Jack shuddered to even consider the possibility. A few moments later, he chastised himself for allowing a negative attitude to get the best of him—the same negativity Madison was always bringing to his attention. Placing his hand softly on the box's lid, he shook his head and cautioned himself to see the glass half full.

The traffic jam suddenly unraveled, and the sound of the SUV's engine surged. Clearing his mind of extraneous thoughts, Jack removed the lid and gingerly lifted out three jade-colored leather journals. Each had a ridged spine and was ornamented with gold tooling around the borders. Other than a bold roman numeral indicating their order, there was no title imprinted on any of them. He wasn't an authority, but it didn't take one to see the journals were fragile from age. With an abundance of care, he opened the first one and examined the initial half-dozen pages. The paper was embossed expertly, giving it a smooth and rich texture.

He randomly looked at several pages from various parts of the journal. He found each entry had been made in black ink using a fountain pen bearing a wide nib. Since the handwriting didn't vary, he was convinced Dr. Hartmann was the only author. He read on. There were sections where the ink had faded, but for the most part he found the entries legible.

Each section described a distinct but related scientific experiment. For its time, the detail and scientific method were extraordinary. To his disappointment, nowhere in the journals could he find mention of any other scientists who had participated in the research or where the work had been carried out. The dates of the experiments were also conspicuously absent.

Jack's focus increased as he read one page after another. He was finally brought back to the here and now two and a half hours later when the SUV's front tires thumped over the threshold of the guesthouse driveway.

Five minutes later, he was seated at the dining room table with the three journals, a legal pad, and his cherished fountain pen picking up right where he'd left off.

Chapter 42

By the time Madison finished up at the hospital and returned to the guesthouse, Jack had spent several more hours studying the journals.

"I'm here," she called to him from the foyer, as she kicked her boots off.

"I'm in the kitchen."

Jack was sitting at the table with his eyes buried in the third journal when she strolled in and joined him. He pushed back in his chair and stretched his arms high over his head.

"So I finally get to see them," she said, setting her hands on his shoulders.

"Here they are. Anything happen in the hospital I should know about?"

"I wish I had better news but almost all the kids are worse. I saw Althea briefly.

"Did she have a chance to speak with Lennon?" he asked.

"Yeah. She said she was skeptical at first, but after she assured her that a highly competent laboratory confirmed the presence of a prion infection, she reluctantly caved in and assured Althea she'd do her part in helping to find a treatment."

"Did she tell her about the mysterious Dr. Austin and her so-called research?"

With an unsurprised grin, she responded, "She considered discussing it with her but ultimately decided it would be better to sidestep that landmine for now. I think she felt Lennon had heard enough disconcerting news for one day. She also based her decision on Robert's request that the fewer people who know about Dr. Austin the better."

"What's your gut feeling about how Lennon will conduct herself moving forward?"

"Your guess is as good as mine," Madison said. "She's a tough lady to figure."

"And how did things go at the focus group meeting?"

"It didn't last long, and there was nothing particularly contentious. For the most part, the physicians were convinced that the lab evidence proved conclusively that a prion is responsible for leukemic malnutrition. There were a few nay-sayers in the group, but Althea did a masterful job of bringing them into her camp. By the end of the meeting, the overwhelming feeling was to pivot immediately to finding an effective treatment." Sitting down next to him, she clapped once and said, "Enough of Oster politics. Tell me what you've discovered from the journals so far."

Jack began by telling her they contained well over four hundred pages that described in detail a hundred and sixty related experiments.

"At best, I've done a very superficial review of about half of them," he told her. "There's a lot here and I'm afraid it's going to be slow going."

"So, no major revelations?"

"I'm afraid not. But for its time, the research is certainly elegant. There's no question that it definitely proved the existence of abnormal toxic proteins that damaged the brain. What's of particular interest is that a few of the experiments specifically address the connection between the poisonous proteins and starvation."

"Any clues as to where the research was done?" Madison asked, strolling over to the refrigerator and pulling out a bottle of lime-flavored sparkling water.

"No, but the English is perfect, so that might narrow down the possibilities."

"So from what I'm hearing, it seems a certainty that Hayden developed his prion theory from the material contained in the journals."

"It looks that way, but we need to know more about his connection to Oster."

Madison took the last swig of her drink. "I wonder why the research team never submitted their findings to a scientific journal for publication."

There could be a dozen reasons, and I suspect this won't be the last time we'll be asking ourselves that question. It's possible Dr. Hartmann and her team never appreciated the significance of what they'd stumbled across."

Madison slid the journals toward her and gave Jack a look that clearly communicated his time was up. Rising to his feet, he strolled over to the coffee machine and poured himself his third mug of the French vanilla brew since arriving home. Leaning against the countertop, he nursed it over the next few minutes while Madison took her first peek at the journals.

"They refer to the animal model they infected with the prion as subjects," she stated. "Unless they're more specific in other parts of the journal, I assume they're referring to mice."

"That would be my guess as well."

"Any thoughts as to what facts Hayden came across that made him think he had a clue to a cure?"

Jack squeezed his lips together and forced out a lungful of air with enough force to make his cheeks practically billow.

He answered, "I haven't seen anything yet, but obviously I'm hoping we'll recognize it, if and when we come across it. I'm a little worried."

"Before you go off a cliff with disappointment, remember what you told me: Hayden was a lot more certain about the cause of leukemic malnutrition than he was about a cure. Let's go back to what you said about his possible inside person at Oster. Why do I get the feeling that Abel Haas is number one on your list of possibilities?"

"Because he is…but I'm not exactly sure why."

"Dr. Hartmann's another mystery," Madison said. "It's too bad she's not still alive. She'd probably be a fount of information."

"Unfortunately, I suspect whatever she knew, beyond what's in her journals, she took to the grave with her."

"That doesn't necessarily mean that information's lost forever." Jack bent his head forward and looked at her through the tops of his eyes. Madison sighed. "I've exhausted the resources in the library. I'm just thinking it would be helpful if there were some way we could find out more about Dr. Hartmann's life and career."

Jack leaned back and folded his arms in front of himself. Feeling a nightmare coming on, he said, "I have an idea where you're going with this, Madison, and I'll tell you what I told you the last time you had this brainstorm—it's a bad idea."

"But it worked out fine," she pointed out with a gentle head twist. "Frank was incredibly helpful with the Dr. Austin problem. All I'm suggesting is that we ask him if there are resources we don't have access to that he can check to learn more about Anna Hartmann."

"I'm not so sure he——"

"He doesn't have to get involved beyond that, Jack. You know how anxious he is to help. C'mon, what do you think?"

"I'm not saying it's a bad idea, but let's give it some more thought before we do anything."

"Is that code for we're going to bury my suggestion forever?" Before he could respond, she said, "We don't have a lot of time to be mulling things over, Jack."

He stood up and headed over to the refrigerator. "I'm not rejecting the idea. I'd just like to make sure there's water in this pool before we take a plunge." In search of a tangerine, he opened the door and stuck his head inside. "I'm just suggesting we do our best to maintain a low profile."

"And, I'm in complete agreement with that. Do you want me to speak with him, or do you want to go together?"

"I'm not sure. Let's talk about this later—after dinner," he said, his voice muffled by the side walls of the refrigerator.

Chapter 43

Instead of going out, Jack and Madison had potluck for dinner by cleaning out whatever leftovers remained in the refrigerator. It was a smorgasbord from several different foreign countries and food groups. When they were finished, they went into the living room, built a fire, and took up opposite ends of the couch, ready again to tackle Anna Hartmann's journals. With mellow jazz playing in the background, they paused intermittently to discuss a point of interest one of them had come across.

After an hour, with a lengthy stretch of his arms, Jack said, "How about taking a break?"

"Okay, what do you say we take Moose for a walk?"

"I have a better idea. I was down in the basement yesterday. It's finished and even has a ping-pong table."

A smile appeared on her face as if she were running a shell game.

"Don't do this to yourself, Jack. It was pretty ugly for you the last time we played."

"I've done some practicing since then. My backhand slice will destroy you."

"Let's go," she said, tossing a light shrug. "It's your funeral, buddy."

They descended the steps into the large basement room that had been nicely remodeled using travertine floors and whitewashed brick walls. At the far end, a few feet from the entertainment center and bar, sat a ping-pong table. It took them an hour to play four games to twenty-one. The best Jack did was eleven points in the third game. He pouted most of the time, complaining about his hand cramping and accusing Madison of being lucky. With her competitive juices flowing, his comments fell on deaf ears and she did little to console him until they were finished.

Jack grabbed a couple of bottles of water from the refrigerator and they sat down on a matching pair of tripod barstools. The recreation part of the evening was over and both of their minds turned back to the current problem.

"I've been thinking about Max Kubicek," she began. "We've talked about this before, but do you think it's possible those first three kids could have died from a prion infection?"

"I don't know. I can't say the thought even crossed my mind. Their symptoms were somewhat different from our kids with LM."

"I guess if we're dealing with one new strain of unexplained prion, there could be a second."

"It's an interesting possibility," he said. "It's too bad we don't have blood samples from Max and the other kids. We could send them up to Columbus for Leo's lab to analyze. Without doing that, the only way to prove they died of a prion infection would be to have their bodies exhumed, which would quite likely create a firestorm of problems."

"In Ohio Children's, when a child dies and the cause of death is unclear, we almost always save a couple of tubes of their blood. It's a fairly common practice among a lot of children's hospitals."

Jack's brow instantly wrinkled with intrigue. "If they did hold on to a couple of tubes, and we requested them through official channels...well, I suspect we'd have some pretty dicey questions to answer."

"If there are some, maybe we can get them through unofficial channels."

"Excuse me?"

"Think about it, Jack. It's kind of like the first time we sent samples up to Columbus. Let's assume these tubes of blood do exist, and we can get our hands on one from each child. If they test negative, we don't say anything to anybody. It's like it never happened. On the other hand, if they are positive for a prion infection, I think the powers that be around here will be far more focused on our discovery than the methods we used to get the blood samples." Madison tossed her water bottle in a trash can, and they headed upstairs. "I'll meet you in the den in a couple of minutes."

"Where are you going?" he asked.

"To make a phone call. I'll be right back."

When she returned a few minutes later, she was holding her coat.

"Where are we going?"

"You sit tight. I'll be back in an hour," she told him, as she kissed the top of his head.

"I'm happy to go with you," he said, jumping up and following her down the hall.

"Sorry, buddy. This is a solo mission. Why don't you take that slobber puss you love so much for a nice long walk?"

"C'mon, Madison, are you really going to leave me hanging like this? Where are you going?"

"To meet the person I hope will be my new best friend."

Chapter 44

Madison entered the hospital through the emergency room. Taking the back stairwell, she climbed two flights, which brought her to the waiting room of the outpatient laboratories. Before finding a seat, she took time to gaze at the large vivid murals depicting fairytale characters and children at play. Behind where she was standing stood a snack kiosk and an area filled with video game machines.

She heard the door open and watched as Lennon Armbrister approached. Poker-faced, she was wearing her white coat open over neatly pressed light blue scrubs.

Not quite sure of what her mood might be, Madison walked over to greet her.

"I can't tell you how much I appreciate your help with this."

Lennon held a square shaped specimen container. "I don't get a lot of cloak-and-dagger calls for urgent help at this time of night, so I thought I'd better come running."

"I hope none of this creates a problem for you. I haven't been at Oster long, but I get the feeling the best way to get from one day to the next is to kind of stay in your own lane."

"I've been tiptoeing my way through the Oster's diplomatic

minefield since the first day I arrived here." She gestured to a cushioned bench, and they sat down.

"For the record, the only thing I care about is doing everything in my power to help these kids recover. I realize I was wrong about the cause of LM, and I came dangerously close to sending the focus group in the wrong direction." She cast a slight shrug Madison's way and grinned. "I can be overly obstinate at times. It's a character flaw I've been working on for more years than I care to remember."

She handed Madison the container. "There are three tubes of blood. Each one is clearly labeled with the child's name."

Madison opened the container and checked the freeze pack. It all looked good. "Do you anticipate anybody asking you about this?"

"I signed the samples out to myself," Lennon answered. "My gut feeling is that it won't draw any attention. If I'm wrong, and somebody asks you about it, just tell them I authorized it. If they find that causes a knot in their underwear, tell them they can take the matter up with me directly."

"Do you think that'll make the problem go away?"

"I may have to endure some foot stomping and stern finger wagging, but I'm pretty sure that's as far as it'll go. At the most, it will amount to a minor flesh wound." With a telling grin that widened slowly, Lennon inquired, "You were pretty aloof on the phone regarding your interest in the blood samples. I'm familiar with these three kids and the circumstances surrounding their deaths. I'm also aware we were never able to make a definitive diagnosis or determine an exact cause of death. So do you feel like confirming what I'm already ninety-nine percent sure of regarding what you and Jack are up to?"

On her way over, Madison had wondered how Lennon might react to her request for the blood samples. Her question didn't surprise her…in fact, she had expected it. She thoroughly trusted Lennon, and there was no doubt in her mind she owed her an explanation.

"Do you have a few minutes to talk now?"

"You bet I do."

Madison quickly brought her up to speed on the reasons she and Jack had requested her help in their investigation of Max and the other two children's deaths.

"What's your gut feeling?" Lennon asked.

"I'm trying to ignore my gut feeling and keep my fingers crossed that the cause of death wasn't a prion infection."

"When will you know something?

"We should hear from the lab in a day or two," Madison responded.

"If they confirm that we're dealing with more than one strain of prion infection, I think the major players around here are going to lose it."

"I guess we'll just have to jump off that bridge when we get to it."

They talked for another few minutes before Lennon rose to her feet. "If there's anything more I can do to help, just let me know."

"Thank you again for your help tonight."

As Madison came to her feet, the room suddenly began to spin. She grabbed for the arm of the chair and quickly sat back down. Looking straight ahead, she said nothing.

"Are you okay?"

"I just got dizzy all of a sudden. I'll be okay. I just need a minute."

"Do you mind if I ask you a personal question?" Lennon asked, sitting down next to her.

"Not at all."

"How's your health?" Madison was taken back by the question and hesitated to respond. "I'm an oncologist," Lennon continued. "Sometimes you get a feeling. It's kind of like a sixth sense; skin color, the way people's hair grows back, a bunch of things."

"I was treated for acute myeloblastic leukemia. I finished treatment ten months ago. My last bone marrow and blood tests showed no residual disease."

"That's certainly good news. How many of these episodes of dizziness have you been experiencing?"

"A few a week for about the last month or so."

"No other symptoms?"

"Apart from a little lethargy, I'd say no."

Any chance you could be pregnant?"

"I don't think so," she answered in a monotone. "Everything I've read plus what my oncologist told me doesn't paint a very rosy picture about the likelihood of ever getting pregnant."

"I wouldn't take that as the voice of God. Every oncologist I know including myself has been wrong about that prediction at least once in their career. Does your doctor in Columbus know about your symptoms?"

"I didn't think it was necessary to call her just yet."

"I'm getting the feeling you don't believe you're out of the woods yet."

"I'm not sure any cancer patient ever does," Madison answered with a forced smile, sensing the lightheadedness and nausea starting to fade. "I'm feeling a little better. I appreciate your concern."

Lennon placed her hand on Madison's shoulder. "I have an idea. We're sitting here in the lab. Why don't I grab a couple of tubes and draw some blood? It'll only take a few minutes. As soon as I get the results I'll give you a call. That way you'll know that every-thing's looking okay. Do you have another bone marrow scheduled?"

"Yes, in a couple of months."

"What do you say? The chances are you're fine."

There was a part of Madison that wanted to politely decline Lennon's offer, but she couldn't deny she was having growing concerns there could be something wrong. Assuming her blood tests were normal, it would also be nice to tell Jack that everything was okay.

Madison frowned and said, "I guess you're right— I've been putting it off long enough."

"Good decision. I'll be right back with the supplies. We should have the results in less than an hour."

Waiting for Lennon to return, Madison stared without purpose across the waiting room. She warned herself not to allow her rising anxiety to get the best of her. But as hard as she fought it, the fear that she had relapsed and would require more chemotherapy filled her heart with the kind of deep-seated despair she prayed she'd never feel again.

Chapter 45

As Madison exited the hospital and started back toward the guesthouse, she thought about what Lennon had done to help her and the children suffering from leukemic malnutrition. There could be no question that she had stretched her neck way out.

She filled her lungs with several breaths of the cool evening air. Briefly, she was able to clear her cluttered mind of the barrage of unanswered questions and clinical enigmas she found herself juggling. She checked the time on her phone for the third time. She assumed she'd be hearing from Lennon about her blood tests within the next few minutes.

All of a sudden an idea popped into her head that prompted her to slow her pace to a near standstill. Deciding to let her impetuous side trump her more thoughtful one, she turned around and quick-stepped it to the main entrance of the hospital. Her resolve unshaken, she crossed the lobby and took the elevator up to the leukemic malnutrition unit. Just as she was stepping out of the elevator her phone rang. It was Lennon.

"Everything's completely normal, Madison. There's absolutely nothing to suggest you're suffering a relapse."

Consumed with relief, she was left speechless for a few moments.

"Thanks, Lennon, I…I wouldn't know where to begin to thank you for everything you did tonight."

"Then, don't try. I'm very happy for you. Have a good evening."

"Thanks, again," she said as she hurried down the pathway toward the guesthouse.

The moment she opened the door Jack marched into the entranceway.

With his eyes glued to the container, he said, "Tell me it isn't so. Who was our benefactor?"

"Lennon Armbrister."

"I'd be very interested to know how you managed to pull that off."

"You'll have to wait until morning." She handed him the container and started down the hallway. "Take good care of this. I'm going to bed."

"Are you feeling okay?"

"I'm fine…just a little tired is all."

"I'll put this in the fridge and arrange for the courier service to pick it up first thing in the morning."

"Thanks."

Jack didn't waste any time putting the blood samples in the refrigerator. After double checking to make sure they were secure, he went straight to the bedroom. Madison was already in bed thumbing through her latest copy of Bridge Bulletin magazine.

"Why were you gone so long?" he asked her.

"After Lennon gave me the blood samples, she offered to draw some routine blood tests on me. After that I stopped in to see Frank Dale."

"Wait a sec," he said, rubbing the back of his neck. "Forget about what led to Lennon drawing your blood, and just tell me when you'll have the results?"

"I already do. Everything's completely normal."

Jack leaned over the bed, gently pulled her shoulders forward, and gave her a hug. "That's wonderful news."

"I told you not to worry," she said. "Enough about me— when are you going to ask me about Frank?"

"I feel a freight train coming at me— I'm almost afraid to."

"You worry too much. He was very cooperative."

"I thought we were going to discuss the whole Dr. Hartmann matter before asking Frank for his help."

"I knew you'd see the light and agree it was a good idea. Seeing as how I was right there, I figured I'd save time and go speak with him."

In a voice drizzled with skepticism, Jack asked, "So he's going to check a few databases and things like that? I mean, he wouldn't do anything crazy like go to Ithaca... Would he?" When Madison averted her eyes, Jack pressed the point. "C'mon, Madison. It'll be easier if you just tell me."

"When I posed the problem to him, he said the best way for him to handle something like this would be to go to the vet school and try to speak with people who may have known Dr. Hartmann."

"And, of course, you did everything in your power to dissuade him from doing that."

"I told him it wasn't exactly what you and I had in mind, but since he's the expert on investigations and knows a lot more about these things than we do, he should make that decision."

Jack cast his eyes to ceiling for a few seconds and then let his chin drop to his chest. "This is a nightmare," he muttered.

"We can talk more about it in the morning."

Madison put the magazine up, fisted her pillow into the precise contour she preferred, and then reached up to turn out the light on her side of the bed.

Chapter 46

TWO DAYS LATER

FRANK DALE ARRIVED at the Cornell University College of Veterinary Medicine at just after six p.m. He'd called the day before and informed the dean's office he was a writer working on a piece about the school and would appreciate a meeting with a faculty member who was well versed in its history. The administrative assistant to the dean was able to arrange an appointment with Dr. Constance Veneble, one of the emeritus professors who probably knew more about Cornell's veterinary college than any other living human being. She apologized for the lateness in the day but explained that six p.m. was the only time Dr. Veneble was available.

After a lengthy day of travel, Frank was escorted into a small, brightly lit office, its walls bedecked with silver-framed diplomas and certificates. Dr. Veneble was seated at her desk with her head bent over a large textbook. She was frail in appearance, with thinning silvery-white hair and alert hazel eyes that were framed by wrinkly skin. Frank was surprised by the spry manner in which she came to her feet to shake his hand.

After he introduced himself, she invited him to have a seat across the desk from her.

"Please tell me about the project you're working on. It sounds very interesting."

"It's a profile piece on six distinguished professors who spent their career at Cornell," he explained.

"How did you happen to select Cornell professors? Are you an alumnus?"

"No, but my parents were, and my younger brother graduated from the medical school."

"Which university did you attend?"

"I started at Purdue but then transferred to Ball State."

"Are all of your pieces educational in nature?"

"Not all of them, but I like to write about accomplished individuals."

"Who are the other five?" she asked him.

"I beg your pardon?"

"You said you're writing about six distinguished Cornell professors. I was interested in who the other five are."

Not having anticipated such a barrage of pointed inquiries, Frank found himself momentarily tongue-tied.

"This may sound a little odd," he finally managed, "but I prefer not to discuss my projects in detail until they're completed."

"I was told you're interested in learning more about Dr. Anna Hartmann. How did you happen to select her?"

"I interviewed a number of veterinarians who graduated from Cornell. Her name was mentioned quite a few times."

"By whom? You must have spoken with some very senior grads."

"Some," he answered. "When I telephoned yesterday, I was told if I was interested in writing about Anna Hartmann, you'd be the person to speak to. I took that to mean you must have known her quite well."

"That's correct. I did." She looked at him askance. "What would you like to know?"

"I'd like to learn about her as a person and what, if anything, you know about her life before she came to Cornell, and what distinguished her as an individual."

"I thought you'd be more interested in her professional accomplishments," she said with a wry grin, as she drummed the leather desk mat with fingers made crooked by three decades of arthritis.

"Those are always easy to track down. I'm looking more for the human-interest side of her."

"I imagine you'd prefer it if I spoke honestly."

Puzzled by her comment, Frank answered, "Well, yes. I would."

"In that case, I will if you will."

"Excuse me?"

"Oh, come now, Mr. Dale. Who are you, and what are you really doing here?" She leaned in over her desk and wagged a reproving finger at him. "If you're a freelance writer, I'm the goalie for the Cornell hockey team." Before he was able to counter her not so veiled accusation she raised a halting hand. "Please, Mr. Dale, save your breath. You should have done your homework before you stepped into my office. You didn't ask my permission to use a recording device, you gave me no real background into the project, and you speak with zero passion."

"Maybe I'm not a very passionate writer. Some of us are just trying to make a living,"

"If that's the case, you're the first one I've met. You didn't brag to me about all the magazines that have published your work. And, if you don't mind me saying so, you don't look very much like a writer. I could be wrong about you, but I'd be willing to wager a month's salary that you, sir, are a gold-plated fraud."

"That's quite a statement to make after speaking to somebody for less than ten minutes."

"I'd agree, if I hadn't googled you and been unable to find anything you've ever written. So why don't we start over by you telling me who in perdition you are and what you really want?"

Realizing he was busted, Frank paused briefly to gather his thoughts. He was a man confident in his ability to carry off most charades and fast-talk his way out of any tight situation, but at the moment, his confidence was shaken. She was four moves ahead of him and he never saw it coming. To his surprise, he was more amused by Dr. Veneble than embarrassed by his failed attempt to pass himself off as a writer. He feared he was a nanosecond away from being unceremoniously tossed out of her office.

"I apologize, Dr. Veneble. You're correct. I haven't been completely honest with you."

"Don't stop now, young man."

"I'm an investigator. I don't have much time, and it's of the utmost importance that I learn as much about Anna Hartmann as I can. I apologize for not being truthful, but I think we both know I wouldn't be sitting here right now if I had been up front with the dean's assistant."

"That's a feeble justification for your disingenuous behavior. You sound like one of my students trying to convince me the dog ate her homework."

Frank smiled inwardly. "Are you familiar with the leukemic malnutrition cases being treated at Oster Children's Hospital in Ohio?"

"I'm an educated woman, Mr. Dale. I read the newspaper and I own a television. Of course I'm familiar with the leukemic malnutrition cases at Oster."

"I was asked by certain individuals at Oster to discretely gather as much information about Dr. Hartmann as I could. They believe there may be a connection between research she's done and understanding more about leukemic malnutrition. I have no other information to share with you, other than that my trip here today, from an official standpoint, is off the record."

"If I asked you why, I'm sure you'd tell me you don't know, and I suspect you'd be telling the truth."

He could feel her eyes shifting across his face. Before she could politely decline his request for help, he said, "Even as we speak, Dr. Veneble, my son is lying in Oster's ICU close to death. I'm convinced he's surrounded by some of the brightest physicians in the country. I have a certain skill set, and for reasons I'm not totally clear on, they've asked me for help. They told me there was a possibility that my efforts could be important in finding a cure for leukemic malnutrition. I didn't waste a lot of time asking questions or demanding explanations—I just got my butt on a plane and came up here. I'm begging you. Please help us."

The office went silent. Frank watched as she bit down on her lip. Finally, she said, "Anna Hartmann and I were very close friends. She was a professor here for almost fifty years and was considered to be an outstanding researcher and teacher."

"Did she ever talk to you about her life before she became a vet?"

"She spent her childhood in England. After World War II, she and her family made their way to the United States. She became a citizen, worked hard, and was accepted to vet school." She paused and drummed her leather blotter for a few moments. "I'm sorry, Mr. Dale. I can't imagine anything about Anna's career that could in any way shed light on a possible treatment for leukemic malnutrition."

Frank listened politely. He couldn't be sure, but there was something about her manner that suggested to him that she wasn't being totally forthcoming in her answers.

"Are you aware of anything in her personal or professional life that might in some way have given her knowledge of a disease that didn't even exist during her lifetime?"

"She was an outstanding academic veterinarian who had the courage of her convictions and was completely devoted to her work and to her students. Her research is well known in the scientific community, and I'm unaware of any secrets in that area. From a personal standpoint, she was a person who detested pettiness in any form. She wasn't political in any sense of the word. She led a frugal and very private life."

Frank spent the next twenty minutes asking Dr. Veneble questions across a vast array of topics. Her answers were responsive, but there were no revelations. More than once, something in her words or actions led him to suspect she was holding back.

When he noticed her answers were becoming clipped and that fatigue had crept to her face, he said, "I should be going. You've been very helpful. I can't thank you enough for taking the time to talk with me."

"You'll pardon me for disagreeing, but I don't think I was of much help to you at all, Mr. Dale."

He looked at her and then thumbed the corner of his mouth a few times. It was at that moment he decided to take one more swipe at the piñata.

"May I be blunt, Dr. Veneble?" he asked her.

"I thought that's what you were doing," she was quick to respond.

"I appreciate you trusting me enough to talk to me. I'm not a physician or a veterinarian, so I'm not in a position to know what is and what isn't important from a medical standpoint. What I do know is that a couple of very intelligent physicians are convinced Dr. Hartmann knew something that might hold the key to finding the cure for leukemic malnutrition." Pausing to prevent his voice from fracturing, Frank waited until he collected himself before going on. "So I'm begging you, if you know anything that could possibly help these children, please tell me."

With her eyes locked on Frank, she responded, "Anna Hartmann was a great woman whom I knew for five decades. For most of that time, I suspected her past was crisscrossed with secrets that she clung to dearly." Her face became pinched. "I'm sorry, Mr. Dale, but if there was something in my cherished friend's past that had something to do with this terrible disease, she chose not to share it with me. I'm a person of integrity. If I knew anything that might help those poor children in Ohio, I would tell you."

A brief but awkward silence followed. Dr. Veneble stood up and came out from behind her desk. She walked with a bit of a limp. Jack met her in the middle of the office. She escorted him into her outer office, where three eager students were waiting to meet with her.

"Thank you. Is there anybody else I could speak with who you think might be able to help me?"

"I'm afraid not, Mr. Dale. Have a safe trip back to Oster."

She turned and walked with her students back toward her office.

As she crossed the threshold, she stopped briefly and cast a backward glance his way but guarded her silence. After she closed her door, Frank remained for a couple of minutes, unable to stop wondering if Constance Veneble had indeed been completely forthcoming with him.

Chapter 47

It was nearing seven p.m. when Frank reached the parking lot. As he straightened his ragg-wool beanie and reached for his cell phone to call Jack, thoughts of his meeting with Dr. Veneble continued to occupy his mind. The afternoon shower that had been forecast to last for an hour or two had a mind of its own and persisted as an icy rain.

Hunching his neck into the collar of his coat, he waited for Jack to answer his phone. "Doc, it's Frank. I've just finished meeting with Dr. Veneble. I'm sorry, but I can't say she shared any startling information with me about Dr. Hartmann's life that's likely to lead to anything."

"Not exactly the news I was hoping for."

"I'll fill you in on the details as soon as I get back. There's no way out of Ithaca tonight. I'm on a morning flight, but I won't be back at the hospital until late afternoon. How's Kip?"

"He's about the same, Frank…holding his own."

"Okay, Doc. Thanks for the update," he stated in a monotone.

"I know it's tough, but try and stay positive," he told Frank. "Have a safe flight."

Frank's lightweight jacket wasn't doing much to keep him warm.

He drew in a breath to the base of his lungs as he walked under an anemic floodlight mounted atop a twenty-foot wooden pole. He was about halfway to his rental car when he saw a young woman approaching. She was wearing a lambswool peacoat and talking on her cell phone. Having an idea of the academic demands vet students faced, he assumed she was in for a long night of studying in the library. When she was just about to pass him, she lifted her eyes and smiled. He nodded once and returned her smile.

With the rain stinging his face, he continued walking at a brisk pace. When he finally spotted his rental in the next aisle, he turned and cut across a row of cars. The moment he emerged on the other side, he heard the footsteps of somebody coming up behind him. Swinging his gaze, he recognized the young lady who had walked past him a minute ago. Her eyes were cast downward, and her hands were buried deep in the pockets of her coat. Guessing she had forgotten something and was heading back to her car, he assumed she was having the same battle against the elements that he was.

After a few more seconds passed and he no longer heard her footsteps, he took a casual look behind him. When their eyes met, her becoming smile had vanished. She suddenly picked up her pace and drew her hand out of her right pocket. Frank's mind instantly switched gears as he realized everything about her movements was wrong. When she was ten feet away, she stopped and widened her stance.

The instant he saw the handgun emerge from her pocket, muscle memory from his extensive training in the military and martial arts kicked in. He whirled his shoulders around to reduce her target and lunged at her. He had only covered about half the distance when he saw the gun leveled at his head. Before he could launch his next step, he heard a single muffled thud and again shifted his shoulders and torso, forcing her to re-center her aim. While she swung the working end of the gun around, he took a second huge lunge in her direction. The dimly lit parking lot and sheets of obliquely falling rain favored his chances. She tried to reset the weapon to get off a second shot, but she was too late, and before she could pull the trigger again, he slammed into her abdomen and locked her wrist in his grasp.

Firmly controlling the weapon in his crushing grip, he jerked her arm straight overhead and angled his back into her body. With no hesitation and in one swift and powerful motion, he yanked down on her locked arm. The move was precise, causing her elbow to impact his shoulder with such force that it snapped all three bones of the joint into a bleeding cluster of splintered fragments. Her handgun sailed through the air and came to rest on the ground five feet away.

As if it were a choreographed dance, Frank spun back toward her, launching a strike that drove his elbow deep into the fragile bones of her midface. The fountain of blood that spewed from her fractured nose spattered in every direction. Feeling her go limp, he released his grip and watched her crumple to the ground, where she came to lie on her back in a stuporous state.

The entire encounter was over in ten seconds. His assailant never made a sound. Frank quickly completed a three-hundred-sixty-degree scan of the area to assure himself she didn't have an accomplice lurking behind one of the cars. When he saw nobody else in the area, he kneeled down beside her.

It wasn't long before he heard one muffled moan after another. He considered an attempt at questioning her, but he quickly realized it would be fruitless. Totally befuddled by what had just happened, he took another look around. He was relieved to see nobody in sight. He went through her pockets, hoping to find some clue as to who she was or why she had tried to kill him. To his frustration, but not his surprise, the only things he found were a cell phone, a second magazine, and a car key. There was nothing unusual about her appearance, although he did make note of a red and black musical note tattoo on the side of her neck.

"What the hell?" he finally muttered, as his eyes fell on the gun. Skeptical that he had been the victim of a random mugging, he stood up and walked over to the weapon. He recognized it immediately as a Sig Sauer P226, a highly advanced handgun preferred by the military. It wasn't exactly a weapon used by your run-of-the-mill street thief, he thought to himself. The thought of calling 9-1-1 anonymously and leaving the scene crossed his mind, but he dismissed the notion as soon as he had a look around and saw the three surveillance cameras.

He returned to the woman, whom he guessed to be about thirty years old. From her injuries, he doubted whether she was at risk of losing her life. On the other hand, he also had no concerns she would suddenly jump to her feet and flee the scene of her botched crime. After making the call, he leaned against the nearest car and pondered how to best deal with the authorities. He realized there were a few reasons why she might have attacked him, but as far as his interview with the police, he would paint a picture of a robbery attempt gone bad.

While waiting for the emergency vehicles to arrive, Frank began to consider the possibilities that could have motivated the woman's attempt on his life. As unlikely as it sounded, perhaps he had simply been the random victim of a homicidal maniac. There had been numerous people he had crossed paths with during his career who he'd had a hand in sending to jail. Was it possible that one of them had gathered the courage to make an attempt at extracting her or his revenge? What seemed the least plausible possibility was that he had been professionally targeted because of his interest in Dr. Anna Hartmann.

Frank was alerted to the impending arrival of the emergency vehicles by the wail of their sirens. An Ithaca Police Department cruiser with red and blue flashing lights pulled up. An ambulance pulled up thirty seconds later. Two officers exited their cruiser. One approached him, while the other kneeled next to the young woman. As it turned out, he was detained by the police for thirty minutes. The ordeal wasn't as bad as he expected it would be. He answered their questions directly, and they seemed satisfied with the picture he painted of a bungled robbery.

After checking in to his hotel, he headed to the sports bar off the lobby and ordered a cheeseburger and a draft beer. While he waited for his food, he thought about Jack and Madison and whether he should tell them about the attempt on his life. He had no reason to believe they would have the first clue to explain the peculiar occur-rence. He further reasoned that, since he wasn't certain of his attacker's motive, and they had enough on their minds dealing with leukemic malnutrition without being distracted by strange events at a veterinary college, he'd keep the matter of the assault between him and the Ithaca Police Department.

At 8 a.m. the next morning, Frank boarded the first leg of his flight back to Toledo. His plan was to brief Jack and Madison on his meeting with Dr. Veneble as soon as he arrived in Defiance. He didn't view his trip to Ithaca as a complete dead end. It was true he hadn't uncovered any significant information about Dr. Hartmann, but he remained suspicious that Dr. Veneble was aware of things in Anna Hartmann's past that she was not going to disclose. Whether those facts could have some connection to leukemic malnutrition was anybody's guess.

Chapter 48

Jack and Madison were on their way to meet with the radiologists to go over the morning x-rays when his phone rang.

"It's Leo," he said. Madison pushed her palms together in a mock prayer. Putting his phone on speaker mode, he raised crossed fingers.

"Hi, Jack. We just finished analyzing the three blood samples you sent us. There's no question—they're all heavily infected with a prion."

"Are you able to tell if it's the same strain as the first batch we sent you?"

"I'm almost certain this strain is different." After an awkward pause, Leo added, "Look, Jack. I don't mean to add to your troubles, but I just want to make sure you're aware that nobody in our field has ever seen the two strains of prions you've sent us in either adults or kids. Any idea of what you're going to do from here?"

"I was just asking myself that same question."

"I don't envy your situation. If there's anything else we can do, just let me know."

"I think I can safely say you'll be hearing from us again. Thanks again, Leo."

Trying to manage all the thoughts colliding in his head, Jack slowly replaced his phone in its case.

"Well, I guess we just went from bad to worse," Madison said.

They started back across the bridge that connected the two main patient care pavilions to the outpatient clinic building. It wasn't often Jack found himself with no way to turn when faced with a difficult diagnostic challenge. At the moment, he no longer felt comfortable making that claim. What put him more on edge than anything was that, within a matter of hours, every eye at Oster would be on him and Madison.

"We can't sit on this new information," Jack said. "I'll give Althea a call."

Chapter 49

Four years ago, Eshan Moga had been on vacation with his parents at a beach house on Lake Erie when he'd developed extreme fatigue and shortness of breath. He was eleven years old at the time. After an extensive evaluation, the emergency room physician informed Chandra and Subhash Moga of his strong suspicion that their son was suffering from leukemia. Urgent arrangements were made to transfer him to Oster Children's. His ninth admission to Oster came ten days ago because of rapid weight loss, agitation, and muscle spasms. The diagnosis of leukemic malnutrition was made while he was in the ambulance on his way to Oster.

When Jack walked into Eshan's room, he was greeted by a woman with widely set brown eyes, a small midface, and silky black hair.

"You must be Dr. Wyatt," she said. "I'm Chandra Moga, Eshan's mother. We haven't yet had the chance to meet."

Jack moved toward the middle of the room. "It's a pleasure Mrs. Moga. I met your husband a few days ago when Dr. Shaw and I first made rounds on Eshan."

She walked over to the bedside and pulled Eshan's blanket up a little. "So tell me, Doctor, how is he doing today?"

"I just spent some time reviewing his chart and his most recent x-rays. I'd say his condition is unchanged over the past twenty-four hours. He's holding his own."

Some of the worry seemed to lift from her shoulders. "The nurses are reporting they're having more difficulty sedating him."

"We're aware of that. Now that we know what's causing the disease, our major focus is finding an effective treatment."

"I know many of the parents have resigned themselves to what they consider to be the inevitable, but I refuse to give up. You see, Dr. Wyatt, many years ago my husband had an unexpected recovery from a severe neurological disease."

With his interest piqued, Jack asked, "Would you mind telling me about his illness?"

"Not at all. Subhash comes from a large family in Eastern India that has been plagued for several generations by a strange neurological disease. When my husband was in his mid-twenties, he first noticed difficulty walking. After about a month, he began having subtle speech and memory problems." She sighed and added, "It didn't take long for his symptoms to affect his behavior."

"Were the doctors able to make a definitive diagnosis?"

"No, but that was twenty-five years ago, and most of my husband's family lived in remote areas where medical care was very marginal."

"I've met your husband, Mrs. Moga. He seems perfectly normal to me."

"He is. That's why I feel I've witnessed a miraculous recovery."

Jack was mystified. He cautioned himself about taking a medical oddity and making it into something it wasn't.

"What were the circumstances that led to his recovery?"

"We saw his physician for a routine check of his neurological status when a blood test revealed he was severely anemic. His doctor recommended a transfusion, which he received. About a week later, he was discharged. But even before he got out of the hospital, his symptoms began to disappear. Three months later, he was back to normal, and he's been that way ever since. We left India about three years after that. He saw his doctor regularly before we moved to the

U.S., but other than being overjoyed with his recovery, he had no explanation for it."

"I've been a neurologist for many years, Ms. Moga, and that's among the most extraordinary stories I've ever heard. Your husband's an incredibly fortunate man."

"We agree, and that's why we're just as hopeful that Eshan will fully recover. Too many of the parents have given up. They believe their child's fate is already sealed."

"We're hoping we can change that," Jack said. "Thank you for speaking with me. Are there any questions I can answer about Eshan's condition?"

"No, not at this time," she answered, extending her hand. "It was a pleasure meeting you."

Jack had almost reached the door when he stopped and turned around.

"By any chance, was it somebody in your family who donated the blood for your husband's transfusion?"

"He was one of Subhash's cousins. I remember my mother and father-in-law contacting everybody in the family hoping to find a suitable donor."

"And was his cousin healthy?"

"Oh, yes. Very healthy, Dr. Wyatt."

"Do you happen to remember how old he was?"

"I can't be sure, but I'd say he was in his late teens."

"You wouldn't happen to know if he became ill later in his life?"

"I have no idea."

Jack stood up and extended his hand. "I very much appreciate you taking the time to speak with me, Ms. Moga."

"Of course. Subhash and I know you and the other doctors are doing everything in your power to help all the children. We're very appreciative."

"Thank you." Still thinking about his conversation with Mrs. Moga, Jack started down the hall. Suddenly he realized what had his mind turning cartwheels. "It's not possible," he muttered to himself. He reached for his phone and called Madison. "Are you finished meeting with the nursing leadership?"

"We wrapped up about five minutes ago. You sound worried. What's up?"

"I'm going to head over to the guesthouse. How about meeting me?"

"I thought we were going to go see a few of the patients."

"I just came across something rather interesting I'd like to go over it with you."

"Sure. Give me about fifteen minutes."

Struggling to rein in his excitement, Jack broke into a quick walk. He still couldn't help but wonder if it was really possible the key to treating leukemic malnutrition had been staring him right in the face since the moment he'd first laid eyes on Dr. Hartmann's journals.

Chapter 50

When Jack came through the door, Madison was standing in the entranceway waiting for him.

"You beat me here," he said, hanging his parka up on the highest hook.

"What's going on? You hung up before you told me anything."

"That's because I knew you'd have a million questions, which I wouldn't be able to answer on the phone." He tossed his leather gloves on the glass side table and looked past her.

"Where are the journals, still in the bedroom?"

"On my night table."

"Great," he said, hurrying down the hall with Madison right behind him.

Jack sat on the side of the bed and patted the mattress next to him, inviting her to sit beside him. He selected the third journal, opened it, and lightly thumbed through the latter pages. It took him a couple of minutes to find the experiment he was after.

"Here it is," he said. "I knew I remembered it." Even though he was somewhat familiar with it, he took his time to read the description of the experiment again. When he was finished, he left the open journal on the bed where Madison could see it.

"I knew it," he said, in just above a whisper, as a slender smile came to his face.

"Can you give me some clue as to what's going on?"

"Except for one, every experiment described in the journals involved infecting the mice with one strain of prion." Pointing to the page, he continued, "Take a look at this. It's the only experiment where they gave the mice two strains of prions instead of one."

"I vaguely remember it. I guess I wasn't as impressed with it as you are."

"That's because you weren't with me a half an hour ago when I spoke with Eshan Moga's mother. Take another look at the experiment."

When she was finished, she said, "It's kind of what I remembered."

"They gave the second prion to the mice a few days after the first when the animals were already pretty sick. Left alone, they all would have died. But, the fascinating thing about this experiment is that almost all of the mice recovered. Only about five percent died."

"I understand that, Jack, but it didn't make any sense. Obviously, common sense would dictate if one strain of prion is lethal, two would be just as bad. I naturally assumed she'd simply made an error in reporting her results."

"I don't think so. Dr. Hartmann was far too meticulous in her research techniques to make a careless mistake like that."

"There's been a lot of research done on the topic of prions in the last forty years. Has any other researcher observed the same thing inexplicable result when two strains of prion were used?" she asked.

"The only thing I could find was one obscure reference to the possibility. It was reported by a Russian scientist nineteen years ago. For all intents and purposes, she observed the same thing Anna Hartmann did. She referred to the phenomenon as *prion neutralization.* I can only assume nobody in the scientific community took her research seriously."

"What made you think about all this? What did Eshan's mother tell you?"

Jack took a few minutes to recount his conversation with Chandra regarding her husband's strange symptoms as a young man and his miraculous recovery following a blood transfusion from his cousin.

Madison got off of the bed, sat down on the velvety throw rug next to Moose, and began petting the top of his head.

"So with the father's neurologic symptoms and strong family history, you suspect he was suffering from a prion disease."

"I think it's a real possibility," he said. "I'm going to give the father a call and see what more he knows."

With her neck bent forward, she asked, "So, you're proposing Eshan's father underwent a blood transfusion where the donor also had a prion disease?" Jack nodded. "And that this blood transfusion resulted in prion neutralization, which led directly to Mr. Eshan's complete recovery?"

Jack pushed a quick hand through his hair. "I know it's a stretch, but…"

"A stretch, Jack? That would be like pulling a rubber band from here to Tokyo."

"But you can't tell me it's not remotely possible."

"Actually, I think I can."

"C'mon, Madison. Two scientists made the identical observation. Open your mind a little to the possibility they both could have stumbled onto the same thing. It wouldn't be the first time in the history of medicine that an important discovery was made by serendipity."

"That also completely escaped the attention of the scientific community?"

"We're not sure that's the case. As I said, open your mind a little. Stranger things have happened."

"Okay," she said, purging her lungs of a generous breath. "What do you suggest we do with this information?"

"That's easy. We call Leo. If there's any research on prion neutralization going on that hasn't been published yet, he'll know about it." Tossing a mild shrug her way, he added, "Let's just get his thoughts on the possibility. If he tells me I'm as deranged as you think I am, I'll abandon the whole thing. It's no big deal to call Leo."

With a faint tilt of her head, she stated, "I agree with you."

"So you do think it's possible?"

"No. I think it's no big deal to call Leo."

Jack chuckled. Raising his hands, he briefly positioned them as if he were going to strangle somebody. He then reached for his phone and made the call.

"Hi, Jack. I was wondering when I'd be hearing from you. What's up?"

"Sorry to bug you, but Madison and I need another huge favor. What's your schedule looking like for tomorrow?"

"My afternoon's pretty packed, but I was planning on taking the morning off."

"If we drive down early, can you give us a half hour or so of your time? There've been some developments here at Oster that we're very anxious to get your input on."

"I have a better idea. I'm going flying in the morning. Since, I don't have a particular destination in mind, I'll meet you guys at the airport in Defiance. We can talk there." Jack had almost forgotten Leo had served as a Marine Corps pilot. When he was discharged, he decided on medicine as his next career, but he never lost his love of flying, and to this day, he remained an avid pilot.

"Great. What time?"

"Meet me at CAS Aviation at ten."

"We'll be there," Jack said, sending a thumbs-up Madison's way.

Chapter 51

Jack and Madison had been sitting in the lounge of CAS Aviation for about fifteen minutes when Leo came through the door carrying his flight bag. The same age as Jack, he had smiling blue eyes and a slight ripple to his nose. Never high-minded or calculating, he'd always been a good friend to Jack, willing to roll up his sleeves and help with any tough clinical problem.

"How was your flight?" Madison asked, as he sat down across from them.

"It was okay, but flying's no fun unless somebody's shooting at you," he answered with a wink and a grin before tucking his sunglasses into the inside pocket of his shirt pocket.

"Spoken like a true military pilot," Madison said, thinking of her cousin who flew for the Navy and how many times she'd heard him say the same thing.

Leo reached down and petted Moose's head. "Hey, pal," he said, scratching his ears. He glanced up at Jack while Moose flopped down at his feet. "Do you go anywhere without this pathetic creature?"

"He's my good luck charm."

"Try a rabbit's foot. It's cheaper and drools less."

"I'll have to think about that."

With intrigued eyes, Leo said, "So, tell me about this new information you've come across."

Jack and Madison spent the next few minutes briefing him on what they'd discovered regarding Eshan Moga's strange clinical improvement after receiving a blood transfusion from his cousin.

"In a nutshell, the major research centers with a strong focus on prion infections haven't taken much of an interest in prion neutralization," Leo explained.

"Is there any serious work at all going on in the U.S.?" Madison asked him.

"There is a privately funded research facility in Montana that works on prions exclusively. About two years ago, they began an entry-level study to look into prion neutralization. Six months ago, they reported their early results at our national meeting. Most of us expected to hear that they'd dismissed the possibility of its existence, but that's not exactly what they reported," he explained as he stretched his lanky legs out to their limits. "They didn't jump up and claim they'd made the most important breakthrough in prion research history, but they did say they couldn't rule out the possibility that prion neutralization could take place under the right circumstances."

"Which would be what?" Jack asked.

"Well, the biggest factor is the individual strains that are mixed together."

Jack asked, "Have they started the FDA approval process?"

"They're light-years away from that." he answered, drawing his legs back in. "Why am I getting the feeling you two didn't invite me up here to have a hypothetical conversation about a highly experimental and untested treatment of prion diseases?" When a deafening silence followed, Leo began tapping the corner of his mouth. "I was afraid of that."

"Theoretically speaking," Jack began, "could your laboratory prepare a mixture of the two prion strains that would be suitable for intravenous administration to our leukemic malnutrition patients?"

"I thought that's where you were headed," he answered. "Okay, from a purely theoretical standpoint, it's possible, but without FDA approval, the only way you can give the second prion strain would be under the blanket of humanitarian use."

"We're in a dire situation," Jack stated. "I can't be certain, but I think if the use of prion neutralization is explained carefully, with full disclosure of the risks, the powers that be at Oster would give serious consideration to offering the treatment to the parents, citing humanitarian reasons for justifying its use."

"I wish I could offer an informed opinion on that, but I can't."

"I hate to pin you down, but if Oster agreed to sign off on prion neutralization, and the parents gave their written consent, is there any chance your lab agree to prepare the infusion?"

"I don't know. It's not my decision alone, Jack. I'd have to pitch the idea to our board."

"What's your best guess?" Madison asked.

He edged forward in his chair. "As long as we dot every i and cross every t regarding its use for humanitarian reasons, I think they'd probably give the idea the go-ahead."

"What about the technical aspects of preparing the infusion?" Jack inquired.

"I'd have to get in touch with the folks in Montana, but if memory serves me correctly, the process they used to prepare and administer the second strain of prion wasn't very complicated. Let me know what your administration says. I don't see any reason to approach my people until you give me the word you have the approval from yours."

"It's a deal. "I'll speak to our leadership today. We'll give you a call as soon as we know something." Jack stood up and shook his hand. "Thanks for everything."

Leo reached down and picked up his flight bag "If you guys pull this off, I'll expect you to take me out to the best steak dinner in Columbus."

"You name the restaurant," she said.

Jack and Madison watched as Leo exited the building and crossed the flight line toward his Cirrus SR22.

"How do you feel about all of this?" he asked Madison, as they headed toward the parking lot.

"There's no denying that we're almost out of both time and options. I think we're obligated to present the treatment plan to Althea. Where she chooses to take it from there…well, I have no idea." She held her thought for a moment. "You know what I was thinking about when we were speaking to Leo? Wouldn't it be interesting if the two strains of prions we've isolated at Oster turned out to be the same ones Dr. Hartmann used in her experiment?"

"You must be reading my mind. I was thinking the same thing." Removing the fob from his pocket, he unlocked the van. After Moose hopped in, Jack looked at Madison across the roof. "This is the longest longshot I've ever been involved with."

"Maybe… but it kind of brings to mind what Wayne Gretzky was famous for saying."

"Excuse me?"

"He said you miss a hundred percent of the shots you don't take."

Chapter 52

Jack and Madison exited their van in downtown Defiance and walked across Front Street to the entrance of Old Fort Defiance Park. The historic Revolutionary War site marked the former location of the fort by the same name. The park with its pathways along the Maumee River was considered by most locals to be Defiance's most popular tourist spot. Madison had always been an American history buff and had actually read about the park when she first arrived in Ohio.

As soon as they came through the entrance, they spotted Althea jogging in place. She dropped to a walk, and a guarded smile accompanied her gesture for them to join her.

"Thanks for seeing us on such short notice," Madison said, taking a second look at the Ohio State University hoodie she was wearing.

"You've discovered my secret hideaway. I try to get in an afternoon speed walk a few times a week."

"Your secret is safe with us," Madison assured her with a grin.

"Let's take a stroll," she said, pointing toward one of the paths that followed the River. "You sounded a little urgent on the phone.

This is not exactly my preferred location for holding meetings," which means I'm very anxious to hear what you've discovered."

Madison took the lead. "Several months ago, three patients with leukemia suddenly became seriously ill and died. Max Kubicek was one of them."

"I'm quite familiar with those cases."

"Then you also know the cause of their deaths remains a mystery. After reviewing their cases in detail, Jack and I were suspicious they'd died of a prion infection. The Oster lab had frozen a few tubes of blood from each of them, which we were able to acquire and send to Leo in Columbus. His lab positively verified that the samples contained a prion, but they also confirmed it was a different strain than the one that's causing leukemic malnutrition."

"Good god," she said coming to a stop. "Is it really possible this problem is getting worse? Who else knows about this?"

"I obviously can't speak for the lab personnel, but besides Leo and the three of us, I don't know of anybody else," she answered.

"And I assume you're comfortable that Leo can be…"

"I'm comfortable we can rely on his discretion," Jack assured her.

They began walking again and strolled past a crooked wooden flag pole displaying an American flag.

Jack continued, "As hard as it might be to believe, there may be a silver lining to all of this."

"I admire your optimism. I'd be interested in hearing what that could possibly be."

"We think it's possible that the discovery of the second strain could offer us a clue to a treatment," he said.

They continued at a relaxed pace along the river. Madison was surprised Althea had reacted as calmly as she had to the news, prompting her to wonder what her initial reaction to their proposal would be. They took the next few minutes to explain the details of prion neutralization and its possible use in treating leukemic malnutrition.

"So, this…this prion neutralization theory has never been verified, but a research facility in Montana is presently doing embryonic work on it."

"That's correct," Jack said.

"And I assume the FDA process of approval is nowhere close to even being started."

They each nodded in response to her rhetorical question.

Althea slowed her pace and stopped to lean against a black cannon that overlooked the confluence of the two rivers.

"I'm neither a researcher nor an expert on prions. I'm a simple pediatrician. But the idea of curing a deadly prion infection by mixing it with another strain, which is just as lethal… Well, it strikes me as an idea that's disconnected from rational medical thinking." Her chin dropped and she added, "Are you two asking me to seriously consider approving the use of this dangerous and unproven treatment."

"We're here to share with you that, from an operational standpoint, Leo feels his lab can produce the infusions," Madison said. "The decision to proceed with is entirely up to you and the Oster leadership."

"You're tap dancing. I'm asking you to tell me what you think of the idea."

Madison took a couple of steps closer. "These kids are getting worse by the hour. This would be a hundred-to-one shot but we have nothing else to offer them."

"Well, that was direct," she said. "I hope you both realize that it's quite possible, if we decide to go ahead with this plan, the FDA and the Ohio Medical Board will come after us with pitchforks and lanterns."

Jack offered, "In an otherwise hopeless situation, humanitarian reasons can justify the use of non-approved treatments. It's both ethical and legal."

"I'm aware of the doctrine, and I assumed you would bring it up, but even so, the scale of what you're proposing would be unprecedented."

"What's the alternative?" Jack was quick to ask. "The best minds in this hospital agree that leukemic malnutrition will prove to be fatal in all cases in a relatively short period of time. More importantly, there's absolutely no other treatment option on the horizon. At least from a theoretical standpoint, prion neutralization has a chance."

"I understand we're in dire straits, but we have to be vigilant and not allow ourselves to become the victims of some senseless panic." Althea's shoulders slumped like an exhausted prizefighter. She massaged her brow and let out a heavy sigh of capitulation. "I'm going to set an emergency meeting of both the focus group and the board of trustees. Let's at least see what they think of the idea. I'm going to need your help at both meetings. I'd like to have a go or no-go answer on this within the next twenty-four hours."

"As we mentioned, Leo is standing by. If we get the go-ahead, we'll call him immediately," Madison said.

"Let's confine our description of the treatment to the research being done in Montana, Leo's willingness to help, and the article from the Russian literature. I'd prefer to keep the existence of Dr. Hartmann and the contents of her journals strictly between the three of us for now. If I'm right, this proposal will be contentious enough without throwing that oddity into the mix." She gave the cannon's black muzzle a couple of pats. "I'm going to finish up my walk, do a little more thinking on this matter, and then call Robert. I'll let you know what his reaction is as soon as I speak with him. It's possible he might kill the whole idea right there on the phone, which would obviously mean no meetings will be necessary."

"Is that what you think he'll do?" Madison asked her directly.

"Knowing Robert as well as I do," she said with a wave of her hand. "I don't believe that's what he's going do, and I'll further predict the three of us will be attending an emergency meeting of the entire board before you can say prion neutralization."

Madison held up crossed fingers as the corners of her mouth rounded into a smile.

"By the way, Madison, do you two know who built Old Fort Defiance?"

"It was General 'Mad' Anthony Wayne."

With a note of surprise in her voice, she said, "That's absolutely correct. I only hope when this thing's over my medical colleagues don't assign the same nickname to me."

Chapter 53

The Oster executive auditorium was used exclusively by the hospital trustees and board members for their meetings. It was an ultra-modern space containing plush theater-type seating for sixty people, integrated lighting, and a high-end video conferencing system. When Jack and Madison entered the room, all of the trustees were already seated on the podium. Kendric and Althea sat center stage, directly facing the audience. Jack and Madison settled into a couple of seats that had been reserved for them in the first row. There wasn't an empty seat in the auditorium.

Each of Oster Children's Hospital's five board members served without financial compensation. Being appointed to the board was an honor, and it went without saying that each new member was expected to make a generous yearly contribution to the Oster Family Foundation. The only Oster family member on the board besides Robert was Sarah Oster Everson, his first cousin. She had never demonstrated much of an interest in the family's business interests, but she was passionate about its many philanthropic initiatives. Robert made no secret of the fact that he only intended to serve as chair for another year or two, and it was his strong recommendation that Sarah succeed him.

"I'd like to call the meeting to order," he announced, striking the gavel against the sounding block twice. The side conversations subsided, and the room faded to silence.

"The purpose of tonight's meeting is to discuss a possible treatment for leukemic malnutrition. This illness has unquestionably been the most difficult and challenging problem our hospital has ever faced. It has evoked a tremendous amount of emotion, not only in our patients' families but in the entire Oster staff as well." Robert paused and adjusted his butterfly-style bowtie. "I'd like to make it perfectly clear from the outset that we shall not approve any treatment plan unless it has the unconditional support of our physician leadership. That being said, I'd like to turn the meeting over to our chief of staff, who'll brief us on this innovative treatment."

"Thank you, Dr. Oster," Althea said, pulling her microphone a few inches closer. "As you already know, we have conclusive evidence that the cause of leukemic malnutrition is a previously unrecognized prion disease. We now have good reason to believe that several months ago three of our hospitalized patients died of an infection caused by a different prion strain." As soon as the buzz in the conference room subsided, she continued, "Recently, we've learned that there may be an experimental intravenous infusion that could be an effective treatment for the disease."

As Jack listened to her explain the proposed therapy in detail, he suspected the board members weren't listening to anything they hadn't already been briefed on unofficially. Jack took special note of how cautious Althea was to make it abundantly clear that prion neutralization had never been tested in humans, and if the hospital decided to move forward with the idea, its use would fall under the umbrella of a humanitarian treatment.

"Thank you, Althea" Robert said. "I'd like to take as much time as necessary to offer our board members the opportunity to ask any questions they may have."

Carson Bivens, an industrialist and real estate developer who had business interests in every county in Ohio, was the first member Robert recognized. Bivens, a man who never left anything unsaid, could be difficult and high-minded, but he was usually faster than his fellow board members to move on an issue.

"I'm a numbers person," he stated flatly. "I deal in percentages and carefully calculated chances of success on a daily basis."

To Jack, he almost sounded like he was delivering the opening remarks at his company's annual retreat.

"I see Dr. Kendric Nash is here with us this evening, and I'd like to ask him this: In terms of a percentage, what's the likelihood this double-prion treatment will work?"

"I can't give you a percentage, Mr. Bivens. I wish I could. All I can do is echo Althea's words and say that, from a theoretical standpoint, it's on reasonable scientific ground."

"Is there a chance, Doctor, that this...this infusion could backfire and turn out to be a fatal error?"

"I can't rule out that possibility."

Sarah Oster Everson spoke next. "If I've learned anything during my tenure on the board, it's that keeping anything confidential in a children's hospital is next to impossible. So my question is this: Do we have even an inkling of how the parents are likely to react to this? I mean, if they're opposed to it, I don't think we can take the question any further."

"We have no idea how the proposed therapy will be received," Althea responded. "If we decide to recommend the treatment, all we can do is present the proposal to them in an honest and comprehensive manner. I imagine we'll see a wide range of responses. Ultimately, it's the parents' choice to consent to the treatment or not."

Jane Brewer, the superintendent of Toledo Public Schools, was next to be recognized. A quick study, she had been on the board for ten years and usually was inclined to go with the flow rather than stir the cauldron of controversy.

"Over the years, this hospital has saved the lives of thousands of children, but we've also lost some. We've always accepted that harsh reality but have never undertaken any unproven, possibly even reckless experimental treatments. My concern is that, if we approve the use of this infusion, we may be creating a dangerous precedent for the future. Are we saying that, from now on, every time we're faced with an illness we can't figure out, it's an invitation to experiment with some risky, unproven treatment? I guess what I'm asking is, are we sure there's not some other treatment we could consider before we jump off of this bridge?"

"If there is, we've been unable to find it," Kendric said in a sober voice. "This treatment strategy is not only our best shot—it's our only shot."

Before anybody could respond, there was a sudden commotion in the back of the auditorium.

Jack turned around to see that both rear doors had opened and there was a steady stream of people filing into the auditorium. Grim-faced to a person, they fanned out and lined up against the back wall. The sudden disturbance filled the air with muffled conversations from those already seated.

A hesitant look appeared on Robert's face. As he raised his gavel to restore order to the meeting, Kendric approached and cupped the microphone.

He leaned in and whispered in his ear, "I just want to make sure you're aware, those folks are our patients' parents."

"I'm well aware of that," Robert said to Kendric as he exhaled a substantial breath before restoring order in the room with a triple smack of the gavel. Before he or anybody else could make a comment, a petite woman with auburn-streaked hair and a milky white complexion emerged from the back and positioned herself in front of the group.

Chapter 54

"My name's Ivy Socolow," the woman said. "Please excuse this interruption, but we're here as a unified group and would like to address the board. We've all agreed to wave our parental confidentiality rights so that we might be heard."

After a series of affirmative nods from his fellow board members, Robert said, "Of course, Ms. Socolow. We'd be pleased to listen to whatever you'd like to share with us."

"Thank you. Oster has always been at the forefront when it comes to believing in family-centered care. It's our hope you'll continue to embrace that concept and give weight to our feelings in your decision-making process."

Ivy took another step forward as her voice gained in confidence. "We've all come to accept that, absent a miracle, we're going to lose a child. We also understand that all medical treatment decisions come with no guarantees of success." She fell silent as she reached for the handkerchief her husband held out to her. He moved forward, took her opposite hand, and she continued. "It's our understanding the doctors have found a possible treatment for this horrible disease. We've heard it's highly experimental and very dangerous. We're also aware the purpose of this meeting tonight is to decide whether to recommend it to us or not. We've come here tonight to tell you we don't want to wait any longer for a cure that almost certainly will never come. We all agree this treatment will be our last stand." After a sideways glance at the other parents, she opened a small piece of paper and read it aloud. "We wish to formally inform the Oster Board of Trustees that the undersigned wish to proceed with the treatment presently under consideration as soon as possible. We will give our unconditional written consent to do so." Ivy's hand fell to her side, tightly holding the paper. "We stand unanimous in this decision and thank you for allowing us this time to express our wishes."

With a ghostlike silence hanging over the room, Ivy and her husband took a few steps back to join the other parents. Without entertaining any questions from the board or making further comments, the family members quietly exited the room.

Robert stood up. "I think this would be an excellent time to take a short break."

The remainder of the board members came to their feet and made their way to a small conference room across the hall.

"You don't see that every day," Madison said to Jack. "How long do you think they'll be out for?"

"If my intuition's right, not very long."

Ten minutes later, the board members retook their seats, and Robert reconvened the meeting.

"It is the decision of the Oster Board of Trustees, pending the recommendation of our physician focus group, to invoke humanitarian reasons to justify and authorize the use of a prion neutralization infusion in any patient suffering from leukemic malnutrition where appropriate parental consent has been obtained." He paused briefly to scan the faces of his fellow board members. "With no other items on our agenda, this meeting is adjourned."

Ignoring the clamor and the flurry of hands that immediately filled the air, Robert reached for his gavel and struck it with purpose against the sounding block.

Chapter 55

Jack and Madison were sitting in the lobby coffee shop, each sipping a morning latte and still talking about last night's board meeting when Althea and Robert came through the door and approached the table. It was five minutes past eight.

"We just got out of the meeting with the focus group, and it appears we're good to go," Robert said. "With their support, the board consented to proceed with prion neutralization. It's official."

"Was there any opposition?" Madison asked.

"Nothing we couldn't deal with," Robert said, taking a quick look around. Jack got the impression he was checking to make sure nobody was within earshot. "But the decision to move forward is not without a couple of conditions. The board wants our legal department to create an airtight parental consent. They've also insisted on receiving detailed daily briefings for the first few weeks."

"Since we're good to go, you can give Leo a call," Althea said. "When was the last time you spoke with him?"

"An hour ago. He's already spoken with his people, and as soon as we give him the go-ahead, the lab will start working on the infusions. He estimates they'll need two to three days to prepare ninety-eight doses. As soon as they're ready, Madison and I are planning on going to Columbus and bringing them back ourselves."

"Assuming the infusion is effective, did Leo have an idea how long it would take to see the first signs of recovery?"

"We asked him that, among a lot of other questions," Jack answered. "I'm afraid he doesn't have any answers. He said we'll be flying blind once we start the infusion. Based on what Chandra Moga told us about her husband's experience, the best we can hope for is a few days."

"My apologies but I have to get going," Robert said. "I still have some arrangements to make and some bruised-ego massaging to attend to. Please keep me in the loop."

As soon as Robert and Althea walked away from the table, Jack reached for his phone to call Leo.

"I'm going to head up to the floor," Madison said. "I promised the nurses I'd meet with them as soon as a final decision had been reached."

After she had left for the unit and he had placed the call to Leo, Jack permitted himself a few minutes to sit back and gather his thoughts. To his dismay, he was feeling as if he was shouldering a responsibility roughly equal to the weight of a battleship. He had no doubts, if prion neutralization therapy was a success, the victory would be as grandiose as a ticker-tape parade. He didn't doubt for a moment the entire Oster leadership team would proudly move center stage to take an endless number of bows. But if the infusions failed, it wouldn't take long for the finger of accountability to start pointing in more directions than a field-bred golden retriever at a duck pond.

Chapter 56

For both Madison and Jack, waiting to hear from Leo was nothing short of torture. Every hour dragged by at a glacial pace while they awaited his call. They were both beginning to wonder if his confidence in his ability to prepare the infusion might have been a little overstated. Jack had called him a couple of times for a progress report, but at Madison's behest, he'd reeled in his impatience and stopped calling.

They spent the entire morning and most of the afternoon in the hospital attending to the ever-increasing number of patients being treated for leukemic malnutrition. To the dismay of the physicians and nurses, the children continued to deteriorate. The hospital had made all the arrangements to begin treatment as soon as they heard from Columbus.

Jack and Madison spent a considerable amount of time counseling the parents about the infusion, trying to balance painting a positive picture with being fair about the likelihood of success. Some of the parents remained trapped in despair, some were guarded, while others saw the infusion as the magic bullet they'd been praying for. Frank Dale viewed the choice as an obvious one. He was the first one in line to sign the consent form.

At four p.m., they attended a meeting of the focus group to go over the exact step-by-step protocol for administering the infusion and monitoring the patients afterward. Jack set his phone on silent but kept it firmly in his grip for fear of missing Leo's call. The meeting lasted for two hours, and the group was successful in signing off on a precise treatment plan. After another few minutes of hallway conversations, Madison and Jack left the hospital and headed back to the guesthouse.

They were making their way across campus when Jack's phone rang. He checked the caller ID and briefly puffed his cheeks with a mouthful of air.

"It's Leo," he said with a solemn expression, as he and Madison came to an immediate stop. Pushing the phone against his ear, he listened intently with an unhurried but continuous nod of his head. A minute later, he said, "Thanks, Leo. You've been great. Thanks for everything you've done. I'll speak to you later."

"Shit," Madison muttered. "I had a feeling he wouldn't be able to pull this off. How the hell are we going to tell the parents?"

"We'll simply have to tell them the infusion's ready."

"Excuse me?" She drew her hand to her mouth.

"Leo did it," he told her with eyes that suddenly shone with unbridled joy. "His lab's going to finish up the preparations tonight. He's going to call us back in an hour with the exact pickup time for tomorrow." All at once, he turned, grabbed Madison around her waist, and lifted her two feet off the ground. "He did it. That son of a bitch really did it."

Part III

Chapter 57

The Air National Guard helicopter made a lazy bank to the right as it descended through the scattered gray cloud layer of clouds in preparation for its landing at Oster Children's Hospital. The flight from Columbus had taken fifty-five minutes. The only two passengers aboard were Madison and Jack. Each of them flew the entire way with one hand on the ice chest that held the doses of the prion neutralization infusion.

With the reverberations from the lumbering helicopter's rotor blades chopping the air, the pilot gracefully set the ship down as if it were a butterfly with sore feet. The engine slowed and came to a stop. A couple of minutes later, the door opened, and Jack and Madison were assisted out of the helicopter by one of the flight crew.

There were about a dozen people standing to the side of the platform-style helipad. Jack was relieved to see the area wasn't teeming with media. He knew Oster had gone to extraordinary lengths to keep the details of the infusion under wraps, and he was pleased to see they'd been successful. The first ones to approach were Lisbet and two senior laboratory technicians.

"Please take good care of this," Jack said, handing the ice chest to one of the technicians.

"We got it," she promised.

Althea and Kendric approached and greeted them.

"Did Leo mention any particular precautions or unexpected complications we should be watching out for?" Kendric asked.

"Nothing specific," Jack responded, having no trouble reading how nervous Kendric was.

"The kids aren't doing well," Althea said. "The sooner we get going on this, the better. If we stick to our schedule, we should finish our final briefing at eight and begin administering the infusions right afterward."

"Frank Dale came to us and offered to make Kip the first patient," Kendric said. "As you recall, we all agreed it would be best if we treat one child first and then wait two hours to see if there are any severe reactions."

"Does Frank know about that?" Madison asked.

"We made it clear," Althea assured them, checking her wrist-watch. "I've got to get back to my office. The board members have been lining up outside my door all morning. They're all as nervous as a cat in a room full of rocking chairs." She turned to Kendric, placed a calming hand on his arm, and added, "Take a breath. You look a little panicked."

"In just a few hours, we're going to pump a completely untested and potentially fatal infusion into the bloodstreams of almost a hundred critically ill children. These are kids whose parents look at us as if we can do no harm and are possessed of the wisdom of the ages. So if you're telling me I look a little fearful...well, I sure as hell hope I do."

Chapter 58

Madison was on her way to join Jack in the unit when she saw Leah coming out of the chapel. Her face was fretful. When she looked up and set eyes on Madison, she was only a few feet away.

"Dr. Shaw," she said, pushing an unfinished smile to her face. She looked back briefly at the chapel and added, "I'm not a very religious person, but I didn't see any harm in getting some divine guidance."

"I have an uncle who was career military. He once told me there were no atheists on the battlefield. Any second thoughts about going ahead with the infusion?"

"I signed the consent this morning. I don't know what else to do, but there's still a part of me that's wondering if I've made a terrible mistake. The thought of giving Charlee another deadly prion with the hopes it will make her better is a little hard for me to get my head around." She paused for a few seconds and then asked, "What would you do if you were in my shoes?"

"They taught us in medical school to never answer that question."

"Pretend you were absent that day."

"I'd be the first one in line to sign the consent."

"When you have a critically ill child...after a while, you're so emotionally exhausted you wouldn't recognize the rational thing to do if somebody hung it around your neck with a gold chain on it. I can tell you one thing for certain—I'm scared of doing nothing. Charlee's always been a very determined kid. I'll never forget how her fourth grade teacher put it. She told me Charlee's a child unacquainted with quitting."

"So you're saying..."

"If the decision were hers, she'd want the infusion—so, that's what I'm going to do." Leah reached out, took Madison's hands in hers, and gave them a gentle squeeze. "Thank you for everything. I wish I could better express my deep feelings of gratitude. Sometimes, I'm afraid all of this stress makes me forget my manners. Well, I should be getting back to her. Will I see you later?"

"For certain," she said.

Leah started walking back in the direction of the lobby.

Madison realized that no words of hers were likely to reduce Leah's pain and uncertainty. Feeling as if she were teetering on losing it, she battled back her tears. Understanding she had to do everything in her power to detach herself emotionally, she reached deep inside, put on her best game face, and continued down the hall.

Chapter 59

Almost before Jack and Madison realized it, the start time was upon them. At five minutes after ten, they joined Lennon and Kendric in Kip's room. From the nursing service, Robyn and Lisbet were also present. Because such a large number of patients were scheduled to receive the prion solution after Kip, two additional physicians were on duty and present in the unit. As chief of staff, Althea had appointed Lennon to be the physician in charge of all matters related to the prion neutralization initiative.

Frank moved one of the chairs from the family suite into Kip's room and placed it a few feet from the end of the bed. Jack caught his eye and tossed an encouraging nod his way. He understood that Frank was a man accustomed to operating calmly in pressure situations, but the stress of the moment was mirrored on his face.

"I'm...I'm not the greatest at expressing my feelings," he said. "But I just wanted to thank all of you for doing everything possible to help Kip." Jack appreciated Frank's heartfelt words. It was the first glimmer of optimism he'd sensed from him in days.

"Let's go through the safety checklist one last time," Lennon said.

Robyn picked up the plastic IV bag containing the prion infusion and held it up. "Kip Dale," she said. "Please read me his medical record number."

Lisbet responded, "756A0963," reading the number directly from Kip's ID bracelet.

The nursing "time-out" safety check continued.

"I agree," Robyn said. "Any allergies?"

"None."

"Has Kip experienced any fever spikes in the last six hours?"

"No."

"Vital signs for the same period of time?"

"All within normal limits."

Robyn paused long enough to gaze around the room. "Is there any reason we shouldn't proceed?" When nobody spoke up, she said, "Okay. We're ready."

Jack was accustomed to pressure-filled medical situations, but there was something different about this one—the sheer tension in the room was practically palpable and far exceeded any other patient intervention he could remember.

Robyn and Lisbet completed preparing the IV tubing and other equipment necessary to administer the infusion. Robyn wiped the skin over Kip's port with an iodine prep pad. Just as she was about to insert the needle into the port, she stopped and looked up at the group one final time through cautious eyes.

Lennon told her, "Go ahead. Per the protocol, we're going to run the infusion in over thirty minutes."

Jack looked toward the open door and noticed somebody had placed a crash cart in the hall. The cart was a common site in this setting and contained all the necessary drugs and equipment that would be needed in the event of a code blue, a cardiac arrest. As much as it further unnerved him to see the cart only a few feet away, he realized it was the sensible and appropriate thing to do.

Frank stood up and moved to the bedside. He placed his hand on Kip's shoulder. Lisbet activated the IV pump. Every eye in the room became fixed on the clear plastic IV tubing as the burnt-orange solution flowed along its serpentine course until disappearing into Kip's port and then into his bloodstream.

The room was consumed by a tense silence. All eyes remained glued on Kip. While the others had backed up and stood a few feet from the bed, Robyn and Lisbet hovered over him, checking and rechecking his vital signs, skin color, and breathing pattern. Fifteen minutes later, half the infusion had been administered, and everything was proceeding uneventfully.

Kendric was the first to speak. "So far, so good," he said, crossing his fingers and holding them up. "I suspect if there were going to be any major adverse reactions, we'd have seen some sign of it by now."

Although, Jack lacked Kendric's confidence, he chose to nod politely instead of warning him to take caution in making observations that were both premature and overly optimistic.

It was five minutes later that Jack first noticed the hint of a speckled red rash forming high on Kip's neck and cheekbones. It was subtle, but it was there. He moved forward to have a closer look. Lennon was already at the bedside, prompting him to suspect she'd made the same observation.

It was when he was studying the rash at the bedside that Lisbet suddenly pointed at the cardiac monitor and called out in a frantic voice, "Something's happening. His blood pressure's crashing."

"Get the cart in here, right now," Lennon ordered.

Chapter 60

With a cacophony of alarms vibrating through the air, Lennon called out, "Stop the infusion, right now." Her eyes darted back and forth between the multicolored displays.

"His blood pressure's still dropping—we're down to sixty, and his heart rate's soaring," Robyn said.

"Start a 1000 cc bolus of normal saline," Lennon ordered, while she yanked Kip's blanket down below his waist. His breathing's way too rapid, and he's tachycardic. Has he ever dropped his pressure like this before?"

Robyn shook her head. "No. Never. It's always been rock stable." She pointed at the monitor and added, "His temp's up to thirty-nine."

"Let's start him on a dopamine drip at ten mics," Lennon said.

Jack's eye was caught by Frank pacing in a tight circle on the other side of the room. He decided to hold off speaking to him for a couple of minutes, hoping Kip would rally. Unfortunately, when Jack stole another peek in Frank's direction, he was moving toward him. Jack took a few steps back to meet him in the middle of the room. Madison was right behind him.

"Just how much trouble is he in?" Frank asked in a voice drenched in panic.

Jack was tempted to reassure him that everything was under control and that Kip would make it through this temporary setback unscathed, but his more guarded side prevailed, prompting him to remain cautiously optimistic at the most.

"It's too soon to say. His blood pressure dropped, and he has a fever, but we're working to get him stabilized."

"And…if we can't get his blood pressure back up…then what do we do?"

"For now, we've stopped the prion infusion. That's the most important thing," Madison explained. "This is uncharted territory, Frank. We'll just have to deal with any problems as they occur."

"Do you have an idea when we'll know something for sure?"

"I'd say at least half an hour, to be on the safe side," she answered. "Maybe you should have a seat in the lounge until we get this sorted out."

"I'd rather stay," he said, scrubbing his face for a few seconds before turning and slowly making his way back to the far side of the room, where he fell into a molded-plastic chair.

Seizing her stethoscope from around her neck, Lennon said, "Tell the pharmacy to move their butts—we need that dopamine drip right now." Her words were scarcely out of her mouth when the pharmacist charged through the door holding an IV medication bag.

"Got it," he said, moving toward the IV pump to hook up the medication.

By this time, two additional nurses had come into the room to assist. The optimism in the room that had been inescapable a few minutes earlier had vanished like a flash of summer lightning, leaving in its wake an eerie silence.

"What do you think?" Jack whispered to Madison.

"I'm fighting off a dreaded suspicion that we've given our first and last prion infusion."

Jack didn't respond.

"The saline bolus is half in, and the dopamine's running at ten.

His pressure's up a little to seventy," Lisbet reported. "Do you want any other meds?"

"For now, just the bump the dopamine to fifteen," Lennon said.

"This doesn't look good," Kendric said. "Maybe we should add another blood pressure medication."

"Let's sit tight for another couple of minutes," Lennon responded. "His pressure's holding at seventy, and his oxygenation level's acceptable. I can live with that for now. I'm worried if we give another drug we have no idea how it'll interact with the infusion. I don't want to take the risk of making his condition worse."

Ten minutes later, Kip's blood pressure was still hovering around seventy. His pulse and breathing rate had leveled off and remained in an acceptable range. The rash over his chest, neck, and face was clearly worse. In spite of an endless number of suggestions from a room that was now filled with other physicians and nurses, Lennon held tight to her plan of continuing the medications she'd already ordered and observation. Nothing else. She was a firm believer that there were essentially two types of medical mistakes: *errors of commission*, which were usually more harmful to patients than *errors of omission*. As she'd oftentimes reassured her residents, "It's oftentimes better to do nothing."

"Hang on a sec," Lennon suddenly said in a voice that echoed a mixture of elation and relief. "Look at that—his pressure's eighty-five over forty."

Jack realized one positive change didn't necessarily herald the end of Kip's problems, but at least for the moment, it didn't appear as if his condition was worsening. To everyone present, the chance of a full-blown code blue was rapidly becoming remote.

Kip's blood pressure strengthened to ninety and remained there. Along with the others in the room, Jack and Madison finally started to relax. Just at that moment, Robert appeared in the doorway. Althea instantly walked over to join him. After they had communicated briefly, they made their way to the bedside to speak with Lennon.

"I assume we're not going to restart the infusion right away," Robert said to her.

"Absolutely not."

He took a few steps closer and spoke in just above a hush. "Assuming you're comfortable stepping outside for a few minutes, I suggest we find a quiet place to sit down and discuss our options. We'll have one of the other physicians take over for you while we talk."

"Fine," Lennon said.

The group quietly exited the room and made their way down the hall to a large classroom that was designated as the nursing education center. They pushed a row of steel classroom chairs across the tile floor, rearranging them into a makeshift circle.

When they were all seated, Robert said, "The question before us is the obvious one: Is the reaction Kips experienced just the beginning of more serious complications to come, or is it a one-time event that's resolving on its own while we speak?" After covering his mouth with the back of his hand for a few seconds, he continued. "The answer will obviously dictate if we should administer the remainder of the infusion."

"I think we have some time to make that decision," Lennon said. "It doesn't seem like we're in a life-or-death situation any longer."

"If you're talking about a period of observation, the question is should we wait longer than the two hours we decided on?" Althea asked. "Did Leo say anything about how long the infusion was good for? I mean how much time do we have before it expires?"

"We asked him that," Madison offered. "He said he had no way of knowing for certain, but his best guess was about twelve hours after it's brought to room temperature for infusion."

"Any suggestions?" Robert asked.

Lennon said, "I suggest we keep Kip under close observation for the next two hours. If he remains perfectly stable with no evidence of any further complications, we should meet again and make a final decision on whether to complete the infusion or not."

"Fine," Robert said. "Obviously, we have to speak to Frank to see where he stands. It's possible, after what's happened, he'll opt out of proceeding whether Kip is fine in two hours or not. So unless anybody objects, let's move forward as Lennon suggests." He paused long enough to scan the faces of the others present. With nobody objecting or offering a counterproposal, he said, "It may be a little overwhelming if all of us approach Frank." He looked to Lennon. "Why don't you, Jack, and Madison brief Frank on what we're suggesting? I think he'd be comfortable with that."

"Of course," Lennon said.

Robert was the first to come to his feet. "Okay, that's it then. We'll meet back here in two hours."

Jack admired Robert for the way he was handling the crisis. But even though he projected an air of calmness under fire, Jack suspected he was keenly aware the situation before him was volatile. Jack assumed, if Kip remained stable and Frank approved, Robert was prepared to authorize completing the infusion, but it would be full well in the knowledge that the consequences could still be catastrophic.

Chapter 61

As Robert had suggested, Madison, Jack, and Lennon sat down in the parent lounge with Frank to explain Kip's situation to him in detail. Jack took the lead and began by assuring him that all hope was not lost. It didn't take him long to see that Frank's emotional state was more controlled. Whether it was a more of a pretense than anything else, he convinced Jack he understood the situation much better than he had thirty minutes earlier.

"That's where we stand at the moment," Madison said. "Assuming Kip remains stable, the final decision to complete the infusion or not will be entirely up to you. We'll obviously support any decision you make."

Frank paused before he responded, "I'm getting the feeling you believe the best option is to complete it."

"This is more of a personal choice than one based on the medical facts. We simply don't know enough about the risks versus the benefits of prion neutralization to make a strong recommendation to you."

"I understand."

"You don't have to make a decision right now. As we mentioned, our plan is to hold the infusion for another hour and a half to allow us to keep a careful eye on things," Lennon said. "That gives you a little time to think things over."

"I assume if he experiences another setback, the offer to finish the infusion will no longer be on the table."

"Depending on the specifics, that's probably correct," Jack said.

Frank stood up and took a few paces toward the door, but then stopped.

In a voice rich with resolve, he said, "I don't need any time to think things over. Kip's condition isn't going to worsen in the next couple of hours. It's going to improve because that's who he is." He raised his gaze, nodded once with assurance, and added, "My decision will be to complete the treatment. It's the only chance Kip has. We've never counted ourselves among the faint of heart, and we're not going to start now. I'll see you back here at twelve-thirty."

Frank's eyes remained steadfast for a few seconds before he turned and slowly walked out of the room.

Chapter 62

Returning to Kip's room, Jack and Madison made their way to his bedside. Lennon stopped at the core desk to check on the most recent laboratory results.

Dr. Rogers had begrudgingly agreed to cover for Lennon while she was out of the room.

"How's he doing?" Jack asked.

"I guess he's about the same as when you all paraded out of here," Rogers answered with a condescending smirk. "I have a question, Dr. Wyatt. Did any of you or the focus group members stop to consider that your reckless foray into unproven therapies could cost this young man and countless others their lives?"

The last thing Jack needed at the moment was to enter into a contentious medical debate with somebody who had obviously made up his mind on the topic of prion neutralization. Ever aware he was a guest at Oster, he cautioned himself to remain collegial, even if it meant being civil to a pompous jerk.

"Dr. Rogers, we're going to hope that Kip continues to improve in the next hour or so. If that's the case, we'll consider finishing the infusion. We understand the risks as does his father."

"The evidence I'm looking at is somewhat to the contrary. I

understand that I'm a junior member of the medical staff, but I'm a responsible doctor who took the same oath that you, Lennon, and Dr. Shaw did. I consider myself part of the medical profession, sir—not some irresponsible experimental think tank."

"It would appear the parents don't see the situation the same way you do."

"The parents are a desperate group of people who would follow the advice of anybody who happen to be wearing a white coat."

"You're entitled to your opinion, but perhaps this isn't the ideal time to have—"

"Since I wasn't asked for my opinion, did any of those involved in making this reckless decision stop to even consider the possibility these patients might recover on their own? Millions of people get the flu every year and return to normal health without incident, but a few die. It's the reality of the practice of medicine. We've admitted almost a hundred patients with leukemic malnutrition. Correct me if I'm wrong, but the last time I checked, all of them were still alive. Your team is shooting from the hip, sir. You made a tragic mistake by dismissing the possibility of a spontaneous recovery."

From behind him, Jack heard a familiar voice. "Thank you for covering for me Dr. Rogers. Have there been any changes in Kip's condition?"

"If there had been any changes, Lennon, I would've called you."

"That's assuming you recognized them. Thanks again for filling in for me. I'll take it from here."

As he walked toward the door, Rogers said, "I hope you have plenty of pens to go around."

"Excuse me?" she said.

He stopped and turned around. "There's no telling how many death certificates you'll be signing before the sun comes up."

If Jack had learned anything about multiple physicians collaborating on a complex case, it was this: After a period of discussion, brainstorming, and cordial disagreement, the doctors have to agree upon a treatment course. Once that determination is reached, no matter what their personal bias, every doctor gets on board until the next treatment choice presents itself, at which point the process starts all over again.

Stopping her review of the monitors, she said in an even tone of voice, "We understand there are varying opinions, both pro and con, Dr. Rogers. But the decision to attempt prion neutralization has been made, so the last thing we need is the opinion of some self-important doom merchant."

Rogers didn't reply, but he chuckled under his breath as he walked out of the room.

"Asshole," Lennon muttered under her breath.

⊏――⊐

TWO HOURS LATER, the group reconvened in the classroom. Robert was the only one who chose to remain standing. In spite of the late hour, the news had spread through Oster's medical staff that there had been a major problem with the infusion, and serious consideration was being given to abandoning prion neutralization.

Robert said, "I've been beseeched by a few of our colleagues to immediately discontinue the infusions. They're convinced that, based on Kip's complication, we should abandon any plans to proceed. I've managed to keep them at bay for now but I need your opinions as to where we stand."

"Kip's completely stable," Lennon was quick to offer. "His blood pressure's normal, and we've managed to wean him off the dopamine drip. His breathing has slowed, and the level of oxygen in his blood is normal. Obviously, whatever this complication of the infusion was, it was short-lived and easily treatable." She pushed her palms together and added with confidence, "He looks good. My opinion is we should recommend completing the infusion."

"Jack, Althea, Madison...your thoughts?" Robert inquired.

"I agree with Lennon," Madison stated flatly. Jack agreed with a nod.

"I agree as well, Althea stated."

Kendric concurred, rubbing the stubble on his chin and nodding.

Robert took a step back and sat down on the front corner of a steel desk.

"Have you checked with Frank, just to make sure he hasn't had a change of heart?"

"We'll speak to him now, but I doubt he's changed his mind," Madison said.

"What about the other members of the focus group?" Kendric asked.

"I've spoken with each of them," Robert answered. "Except for two, they've agreed to go along with our decision."

"If we do complete the infusion without any further problems, what next?" Kendric asked Robert.

"I assume we'll proceed as planned and administer the infusion to the other patients."

Lennon returned to Kip's bedside to make sure everything was in order to administer the remainder of the infusion. Madison and Jack went into the parent suite and found Frank sitting on the end of the bed holding Kip's baseball glove with his fist in the pocket.

"He looks good, Frank. It's your call."

"I'm ready."

It took Lennon, Robyn, and Lisbet five minutes to complete the checklist and set the IV pump. With Jack and Madison looking on from the back of the room, Robyn opened the plastic roller clamp, allowing Leo's prion solution to course through the IV tubing, into Kip's port, and then into his bloodstream. Ten minutes later, the medication bag containing the prion neutralization infusion was empty.

THE NEXT FOUR hours passed uneventfully. Kip's cardiac and respiratory functions remained normal, and he required no medications to support his blood pressure. Adding to the delight of the nurses and doctors caring for him, his temperature remained normal, and the rash almost entirely disappeared.

Robert asked Jack and Madison to join him at the far end of the hall at the entrance to the atrium. Althea and Kendric were already there when they approached.

"I think we have the medical justification and more than adequate support of the focus group to treat the other patients," Robert said.

"In an abundance of caution, we may want to consider another couple of hours of observation before making a final decision," Althea said.

"If we wait, we may run into a problem with the potency of the infusion," Kendric countered. "Remember, Leo wouldn't commit to how long it would remain effective."

Althea nodded. "I think Jack said he mentioned twelve hours, but it was an educated guess at best."

"Recheck with every parent," Robert said, checking the time on his cell phone. "For all of those parents who still want to proceed, let's plan on beginning the infusions one hour from now."

"And the dissenting doctors?" Althea asked. "How do we handle them?"

"The last time I checked, there was only one chair of the board of trustees around here. The decision is ultimately mine, and I just made it." Dropping his arms to his sides, he added, "It's strange that everybody's so hyper-focused on whether these kids will tolerate the infusion. What terrifies me is, even if the kids live through the infusion, will the damn concoction do them any good or not?"

Part IV

Chapter 63

POST-INFUSION DAY NUMBER 3

TO THE DELIGHT of the caregivers and families alike, almost all the children were showing encouraging signs that they were recovering from leukemic malnutrition. Twelve of them had experienced the same immediate reaction Kip had, but they all recovered quickly and showed no signs of any further problems. Most notable was the disappearance of the insomnia and the marked decrease in agitation. Unfortunately, Charlee was among the few children who were not recuperating as quickly as the others. She continued to have a fever and remained difficult to arouse.

After a sunrise bike ride, Jack and Madison spent a lazy morning in the guesthouse. They ate a light brunch, then began a relaxed walk to the hospital to visit some of the patients. They still hadn't decided on the exact day they would leave Oster and return to Columbus.

"I'm surprised you aren't more excited about how great the kids are doing," Jack said.

"How can you say that? I'm overjoyed by their recovery."

"C'mon, Madison. I know when there's something bugging you."

"I hope the same thing's bugging you —there are too many unanswered questions. And, the one that most affects the medical side of things is how these kids got the prion infection in the first place?"

"I agree, but we've talked about this and decided that some things are better left to the authorities."

"What scares me the most is that, in a matter of a few weeks, everything that has happened here will be last week's news, and not too long after that, a faint memory."

"It's natural enough, Madison. Once the crisis is over, people move on," he said, tapping the crystal of his watch. "C'mon we have a bunch of kids and their parents to see. We can talk about this later." Madison reluctantly agreed with a hasty wave of her hand.

It was nearing noon when they reached the hospital.

One of their first stops was Priscilla Chang's room. Priscilla had been admitted eight days ago with classic symptoms of leukemic malnutrition. After an eight-month stormy hospitalization at Oster, she was finally discharged and had been at home for eight weeks before showing signs of LM. She had just recently celebrated her seventh birthday in Orlando with her parents and twin brother.

Her mother, Lilly, was asleep in the bedside lounger. The nurse, Eileen, an experienced, no-nonsense angel of mercy, raised her finger to her lips and took a few steps closer. "This is my nursing student, Jenette. She'll be spending this week with me. We're just getting ready to flush Priscilla's port. We're trying not to wake mom.

"How'd she do overnight?" Madison inquired softly.

"She slept a lot better. In fact, I'd call it pretty close to normal," Eileen answered, holding her hands up in a mock prayer. "Her vital signs were fine, and overall I'd say she had a great night."

"That's good to hear," Jack said, joining Madison at the computer.

While they spent a few minutes reviewing the latest lab results and other entries in Priscilla's chart, Eileen continued familiarizing Jenette with the port.

"She gets all of her meds and blood draws through the port. We flush it with a heparin solution every time after we used it to give a medication or draw blood. We also flush them if they're not used for a month. Do you remember why?"

"Heparin's a blood thinner. It prevents blood clots from forming in the port, which would block it up and make it unusable," Jenette answered, a proud look coming to rest on her face.

"That's exactly right."

"It doesn't look like she's required any sedation," Madison said.

"None at all," Eileen confirmed. "She's doing great. All the nurses feel the same way about the kids they're caring for. Telling you these kids' symptoms have simply improved would be the understatement of the year."

Lilly began to stir. Pulling off the blanket, she stretched her hands high over her head. The instant she saw Jack and Madison, she sprang to her feet as if a snake had just slithered across her ankles.

"She'd doing great," Lilly stated, in a voice swollen with joy. She walked to the bedside and interlaced her fingers with Priscilla's.

Looking at Jack and Madison, she asked, "What do you think?"

Madison strolled over to her. "We couldn't be happier, but while we're encouraging the families to keep a positive attitude, we're also reminding them that we're not across the finish line yet."

"I understand, Dr. Shaw, but compared to a few days ago, she's so much better that…well, for now that's enough. I know we'll be walking out of this hospital before we know it."

"Hooyah," cheered Eileen, a proud ex-Navy nurse. She strolled over and gave her a long hug. "I love your spirit."

"I owe all you guys so much."

"By the way, I'm glad you're up," Eileen said. "I keep forgetting to ask you; do you have your log from the heparin flush study? The research pharmacy is bugging me for it. They need to know the exact days you flushed Priscilla's port over the last two months."

"I have it. I keep it in my cell phone. My husband and I are very cooperative when it comes to enrolling our Miss Priss in all these research studies," she joked, removing her cell phone from her purse.

"You flush Priscilla's port with heparin at home?" Jack asked. "I thought that was strictly a hospital procedure."

"I've been doing it myself since the first time we were discharged. I had a great instructor," she said, winking at Eileen as she and her student finished flushing the port. "My husband and I are fully certified to flush Priscilla's port when she's not in the hospital, and we're keeping close track of the dates to comply with the study."

Eileen continued to smile as she helped her student finish flushing the port.

"What are they specifically looking at in the heparin study?" Madison asked Eileen.

"They're comparing different concentrations of heparin to see how effective each one is in preventing blood clots from forming in the ports."

"And they watch us like hawks," Lilly weighed in with a dramatic huff. I don't mind, but sometimes our discharge gets delayed a day or two because we're waiting for the research pharmacy to send us our supply of heparin flushes. I'm praying that doesn't happen this time."

"Is there really a separate pharmacy for patients on a research study?" Jack asked.

Eileen nodded. "We have two pharmacies. The main one is much bigger than the research pharmacy. In the past, when all the study drugs came from the main pharmacy, it got too confusing. So about five years ago they decided to build a second pharmacy, which only prepares the meds for the kids on drug studies."

"I've been to this picnic. I know what's going to happen," Lilly said in a sing-song voice.

"Take it easy." Eileen urged. "Let's not get ahead of ourselves. It's a little too soon to be worried about discharge planning. For now, let's concentrate on getting this sweetie of yours totally back to normal."

"Lilly, do you have any other questions for me or Dr. Wyatt?" Madison inquired.

"No. As usual, you guys have been great. When will I see you again?"

"We're not exactly sure. We'll probably be heading back to Columbus in a couple of days, so hopefully we'll be in tomorrow."

"I hope so, and I promise I'll be awake the next time."

Madison took Lilly's hands in hers. "Priscilla's doing fine, and I know how excited you are about it, but let's stay patient before we raise the victory flag," she said, knocking twice on a wooden chair.

"I didn't take you for a superstitious person, Dr. Shaw."

"Actually, it's one of my major faults," she said with a smile as she and Jack headed toward the door.

They spent the next couple of hours visiting as many of the patients as they could before heading across the campus to the daily debriefing of the physician focus group. After the meeting, they left the hospital and strolled along the rustic stone path that divided the Oster campus into its two main sections. It was a sundrenched afternoon. A swarm of loudly chirping sparrows swooped down, clearing their heads by a thin margin.

"You have that preoccupied look on your face," Madison said. "I assume it's about the talk we started this morning."

"When we first talked about how the kids might have acquired a prion infection, we considered their ports as a possibility."

"Which we dismissed, because all of them were outpatients when they got sick," Madison said.

"That's before we knew the parents were injecting their ports at home with a heparin flush. We assumed because the kids are spread out over a vast geographic area, an intravenous contamination from their ports was an impossibility."

"Obviously, you now have your doubts."

"From what we just heard in Priscilla's room, maybe all that's changed now," Jack said. "The heparin study they mentioned doesn't make any sense. Oster Children's is the biggest children's cancer hospital in the United States. They have a huge research program with dozens and dozens of clinical studies going on at any one time, and we both know research dollars are tighter than ever. The topic of clot prevention in ports using heparin has been researched to death. There are lots of studies already published addressing the issue. I can't imagine why Oster would have any interest in re-proving the proven. I just don't get it."

"So you're saying the heparin flushes the parents were sent home with contained a prion that could have possibly caused leukemic malnutrition."

"I think it's more than possible. I think it's likely," he said.

"We have to assume the parents flushed the ports per the instructions they were given, which meant they unknowingly injected their child's port with a prion infected heparin solution that went directly into their bloodstream," she said. When he didn't respond, she went on, "The only trouble with that theory is that Oster treats thousands of children with all types of cancers who also have ports. If the problem's a contaminated heparin flush, how come we haven't seen ten times the number of cases of LM?"

"Because I believe only a limited number of the flushes were contaminated with a prion."

Madison opened the front gate, and they started up the walkway. "Do you have any idea what you're suggesting?"

He took her by the forearm and they both stopped.

"I'm terrified to tell you that I know exactly what I'm suggesting."

Chapter 64

After hanging up their coats, they went into the den and settled into a pair of upholstered chairs that faced each other.

Jack picked up where he'd left off. "Supposing the only kids who got LM were the ones enrolled in the heparin flush study that Eileen and Lilly were talking about. I guess it's even possible it was a medical error of some type."

"Why don't we take the guesswork out of all this? We still have access to Oster's computer network, which includes all the research studies. All we have to do is take a look at the protocol and check the names of the patients enrolled in the heparin flush study."

Jack wasn't expecting her suggestion and was caught a bit off guard. For a moment, he considered the best way for him to tiptoe through what he feared could be a touchy political minefield.

Before he began tripping over his own words, Madison continued, "Nothing would make Oster's leadership happier than to put the entire problem of leukemic malnutrition as far behind them as possible. So, you're worried if we start snooping around, we run the risk of certain influential folks feeling a little chafed."

"Maybe, but I'm more than a little surprised to hear that possibility concerns you."

"Excuse me?"

"C'mon, Jack. You're the master of managing touchy political situations. I'm confident if we run into a problem, you'll use that silver tongue of yours to explain it away."

"While I appreciate the compliment, I think I may have a better idea," he said, reaching for the landline phone. "Before we go stumbling around in the dark, let me make a discrete call to Nellie. I've spoken with her several times. She's very familiar with the outpatient research studies."

"You know, Jack, if any of this turns out to be true, it's going to start a firestorm the size of which Oster Children's Hospital's never seen."

Chapter 65

Standing with his back to the granite stone fireplace with its white mantel, Jack waited for the operator to connect his call.

Dr. Nellie Grosvenor was a senior oncologist who served as the director of the outpatient clinic. At one time or another, almost every patient at Oster would be scheduled for visits at the clinic on a regular basis to have their progress monitored and receive their outpatient chemotherapy. In addition to monitoring each of the research projects, it was Dr. Grosvenor's job to ensure the unit operated in an efficient and seamless manner.

"Hi, Nellie. It's Jack Wyatt. You're on speaker. Madison's here too. Do you have a couple of minutes to talk?"

"Sure. How can I help you?"

"Madison and I are still trying to tie up some loose ends, and we have a couple of questions for you."

"No problem, go ahead."

"We're interested in learning more about the outpatient heparin study going on. It's our understanding that the flushes that the parents are discharged with come from the research pharmacy."

"That's correct. They're given a specific number of flushes with exact instructions regarding the date they're supposed to flush their child's port."

"Do you know how the patients were selected to be in the study?" he asked.

"I assume it was random, but there may be specific criteria for inclusion that I'm unaware of. I'd have to check the study's protocol to answer that question."

"And for the patients who aren't on the study, how do their parents get their flushes?" Madison asked.

"All our units keep an ample supply. At the time of discharge, the nurse just grabs a bunch off the shelf and gives them to the parents. It's obviously a lot simpler process compared to those kids who are on the study."

"Would you happen to have that study number?" Madison asked. "We may want to have a look at the protocol."

"I know it by heart: it's 71718."

"Thanks very much, Nellie. You've been very helpful," Jack said.

"My pleasure. If there's anything else you need, feel free to reach out to me again."

"Excuse me," Madison jumped in just before Jack hung up. "Do you happen to know who's in charge of the study?"

"The principal investigator is Dr. Abel Haas."

"Thanks again, Nellie," he said, as he swung a wary gaze Madison's way. With an exasperated groan, he replaced the handset on the dial pad.

"I guess we should've suspected." Madison moved nearer to the fireplace. "It's looking more and more like Dr. Haas had a hand in a lot of the strange events that went on around here."

"As my mother always used to say, it looks like the shadows are getting deeper and deeper. I'm starting to like your idea about checking out the heparin study on the hospital's research webpage," he said.

"Why don't I get started on it? You can grab a shower or work on your crossword puzzle. I'll fill you in when I have more information."

He grinned. "What are you trying to say?"

"Jack, you're hopeless when it comes to technology. You're just going to slow me down."

"Since, I already showered," he said, starting toward the living room, "I'll go look for a pencil with an eraser."

Chapter 66

"Any time you're ready," Madison yelled.

Jack tossed the magazine on the coffee table, stretched his hands fully over his head, and joined her in the dining room.

The moment he sat down next to her on one of the spindle-back chairs, she said, "In the past eleven months, Oster has enrolled a hundred and twenty-seven patients in the heparin study. One hundred and twenty-four have leukemia; the other three have lymphoma."

"That's a little strange," he said. "If the goal of the study is to determine the most effective heparin dose to prevent blood clots, why would the investigators enroll only leukemia patients?"

"Doesn't make much sense, does it? But, here's where it gets interesting. All ninety-five children with leukemic malnutrition are on the study, and they've all had their ports flushed at home. I went back six months and checked the dates to see if at any time they were clustered together." Madison lifted her hands from the keyboard, pushed her chair back. "Four months ago, every one of those patients had their port flushed over the same eight-day period."

"That's unbelievable, Jack said. "Assuming an infected flush is to blame for the infection, the question is was it some unavoidable medical mistake or an intentional act?"

"I don't know, but I wonder if any of the flushes in question are still around."

"I doubt it. And I suspect, even if there was one, the chances of us getting our hands on it would be zero."

Madison reached forward, picked up her can of black cherry soda, and took a couple of sips. "I keep thinking about Abel Haas and what we've learned about him. "Here's a researcher who, for unknown reasons, was in Max Kubicek's room taking notes the morning he died. And now we find out he's the principal investigator in a strange heparin study that could be shielding the cause of leukemic malnutrition. Add to all that, he was the scientist assigned to mentor and supervise Dr. Austin's research study, which turns out to be as phony as some charlatan selling bottles of snake oil out of the back of a covered wagon."

Jack grabbed her can of soda, took a long swallow and said, "I agree with you that all of this looks suspicious, but at this point, it's still a lot of guess work."

"I'm not sure I agree with you on that. It's not guess work that Haas is mysteriously out of town on vacation and has been unreachable for god knows how long now. I don't know about you, but I can't turn a blind eye to the fact that he may have intentionally figured out a way to infect a large group of innocent children with a deadly prion. None of this is passing the smell test, and it's very hard for me to believe that Haas isn't up to his eyeballs in some pretty unethical stuff. I'd call his little vacation a well-planned-out escape, and I seriously doubt he has any intention of ever setting foot in Defiance again."

"I'm not a psychiatrist," Jack said. "Maybe he's insane. On the other hand, it's possible there's a method to his madness. There's one thing I do know—prion strains don't exactly grow on trees. If this was an intentional act, whoever did it went to extreme lengths to get their hands on one. Which brings us back to the same question: how much of this is falls within the doctors' purview, and how much of it is a problem for the authorities to sort out?"

296

"I'm not sure I know the answer to that, but I think at a minimum we should share all this information with Althea and let her decide what to do with it."

"That's fine. We can give her a call first thing tomorrow morning," Jack said. He immediately noted the disapproving way she pressed her lips together.

"I don't think we should wait. I think we should call her now."

"Okay," he said, seeing no reason to object to something she obviously felt strongly about. "Would you like me to handle this?"

"I'd appreciate it."

Jack picked up his phone and made the call to Althea to explain their concerns. She asked him to hold while she phoned Robert. Five minutes later she came back on the line, relayed Robert's extreme concerns, and requested that Jack and Madison join them immediately.

"Sure, Althea. That sounds fine. We're on our way." He turned to Madison. "Get your coat."

Chapter 67

"Why are we meeting at the helipad?" Madison asked, as they left the guesthouse and started across the campus.

"We requested an urgent meeting, and we got it. Althea told me Robert's on his way to Akron on some kind of urgent family business, and this was the only time he could meet with us."

When Jack and Madison arrived at the helipad, they entered the well-appointed wood-frame building that served as a conference room and waiting area. Robert and Althea were already seated at a racetrack-shaped glass table.

"As you know, Althea called me to fill me in on your suspicions," Robert said. "I invited Kendric to join us. He should be here shortly. I wanted a few minutes with you alone first for obvious reasons. Abel Haas is a good friend of Kendric's, and I'm expecting this meeting to be difficult for him. The timing of this unpleasant matter couldn't be worse, but since that's not something within our control, we're just going to have to have to deal with it." Robert swung his gaze in the direction of the door. "It's my understanding that you haven't actually isolated a prion in any of the heparin flushes used by the LM patients when they were at home."

"We don't believe any of them still exist," Madison answered.

"So, as of right now, your theory is just that—a theory."

They both nodded.

"And it's your belief this...this contamination occurred in the research pharmacy."

"We don't see how it could have occurred at any other time," Jack said.

"Which begs the most troubling question of all: Was this an unfortunate medical error or...or some insanely deliberate act?"

"We can only speculate," Jack answered. "But we're very suspicious that both prion infections didn't happen by chance."

"Outside of pure insanity, do you have any idea why one of Oster's most respected scientists would have a motive to commit such a depraved act?"

"I'm sorry, we don't," Madison said.

Althea said, "I understand this is all speculation, but if word of this gets out, it will spread through the hospital like an old fashion chickenpox epidemic. I can't even begin to imagine the damage such a leak would cause to this hospital's good name."

Just then, the door opened and Kendric walked in.

"This is going to hit Kendric like a wall of falling bricks," Robert said softly as he approached.

"Am I late?"

"No, we just got here," Robert said. "Thanks for joining us. The reason Althea and I want to speak with you is because Madison and Jack have come across some rather disturbing facts that I fear will be distressing for you to hear." With a straight face and lips pressed together, Kendric said nothing as he took a seat. "I'm afraid the problem involves Abel Haas."

Robert then took a few minutes to brief Kendric on the entire situation. He held back nothing regarding Abel Haas' possible involvement.

"We'll try to keep an open mind, Kendric, but things don't look very good for Abel," Althea said. "Of course, as soon as he returns, he'll have the opportunity to address all of this. I pray we're wrong and that he'll be able to provide us with a logical explanation for what's occurred."

"I'm afraid that's not going to happen," Kendric said, blowing out a breath from the base of his lungs.

"Excuse me?" Robert said.

Kendric slowly raised his hand at the same time as he cast a downward glance. "I'm afraid Abel's possible involvement in this horrible event is a moot point. Earlier today, I received a call from his attorney. Abel is dead. I was going to call you later today, Althea, but when I was notified of this meeting, I thought I'd share the news with all of you in person. I'm so overwhelmed and shocked by this other matter you've just told me about, I hardly know what to say."

"How did he die?" Robert asked.

"He was killed in a car accident last week while traveling through Thailand. He always traveled with a document that laid out his wishes in the event of his death. Abel has no family that I'm aware of." With a pained grimace, he added, "His attorney had full authority and made the final arrangements for him in Thailand. I'm afraid that's all I know."

"I'm very sorry," Althea said. "Irrespective of what he may have done, I know you and Abel were good friends."

"It's hard for me to believe any of this could be true. Why in heaven's name would he have involved himself in such horribly immoral behavior?" There was a breathy timbre to his voice. "And how could all of this have been going on right under my nose? If what you're telling me is accurate, I fell asleep at the wheel and the whole thing's my fault."

"Spare yourself," Althea urged. "Abel was a trusted friend and colleague. You had no reason to be suspicious. The same thing could have happened to any of us."

Kendric let his arms drop to his sides and again looked past the group.

"I knew Abel as well as anybody. I can't believe he was a twisted homicidal maniac. I know this may sound insane, but I believe that in some misguided way he convinced himself that whatever he was doing would somehow serve a higher purpose— but there's one thing I don't understand. It was Lennon who proposed leukemic malnutrition was being caused by a virus. We all know her. She couldn't possibly have been involved in something as horrible as this."

"I spoke to Lennon," Madison said. "She told me she'd received an email from Dr. Haas the day he left on vacation informing her about Dr. Austin's research and its possible link to leukemic malnutrition. She was absolutely adamant that she never would've known anything about her work unless Dr. Haas had told her. We think it was all just a huge cover story that he created to shift the cause of LM away from a prion, and the blame away from himself."

Althea said, "I don't know if we'll ever really know what motivated him to do what he did. But one thing's for sure, Abel Haas is not the first scientist to lose their way and cross an inviolate ethical line."

"The problem we now find ourselves faced with is the best way to handle this sensitive situation," Robert said. "Obviously, we'll have to inform the authorities of our suspicions, but we still have almost a hundred children in our hospital recovering from a near-fatal illness. We can't be distracted by any of this. Our focus can't shift from getting our patients safely discharged from the hospital. As far as irregularities in our research procedures...well, I suspect we'll have plenty of opportunity in the near future to explain our lack of accountability."

It was at that moment that the air filled with the first chuff of the approaching helicopter's rotor. Robert came to his feet, and they all walked outside.

Forced to raise her voice to be heard, Althea said, "I agree with Robert and suggest we put the unpleasant matter of Dr. Abel Haas on the back burner for now."

The helicopter touched down on the pad. Jack and Madison wished Robert a safe trip and started back toward the hospital. Kendric stayed on to speak with Althea.

"You have to feel sorry for Kendric," Jack told Madison as they crossed the visitors' parking lot. "He's the one who's ultimately responsible for everything that's research related, and from what I just observed, it doesn't look like he's taking any of this too well."

"I don't know about you, but I thought his reaction to the news was a little strange," she said.

"Funny you should say that—so did I. I'm not sure I can put my finger on it exactly, but for some reason I almost got the feeling Robert didn't tell him anything that he wasn't already aware of."

"And I got a sense he was trying a little too hard to say the right thing." They swapped a curious look. Madison added with a grin, "Maybe the eye-opening revelations of the last few days have made us a little more suspicious than we'd normally be."

Chapter 68

POST-INFUSION DAY NUMBER 5

LEAH DUNNE HADN'T LEFT Charlee's side for more than a few minutes since she had received the prion neutralization infusion.

Rolling over in bed, she looked at the clock through heavy-lidded eyes left crimson by another sleepless night. It was ten minutes past five. She was encouraged that Charlee's condition was improving but at the same time concerned that her recuperation was lagging behind the vast majority of the other patients. Her sleeping pattern was improved, and her periods of agitation continued to diminish, but she was still unarousable, leaving Leah filled with trepidation.

She tried to go back to sleep, but after ten minutes of struggling to clear her grief-cluttered mind, she threw back the blanket, slipped out of bed, and strolled into Charlee's room. The room was warm and filled with the lasting scent of illness. She approached the head of the bed, hoping that when she set her eyes on Charlee, she'd see a difference. But to her dismay, Charlee's face was as pallid and featureless as it had been the night of the infusion.

After a few minutes, she decided to walk down the hall to the parents' lounge. Pouring herself a cup of black coffee, she sat down in one of the soft upholstered club chairs, where she nursed the caramel-flavored brew for a time before making her way back to Charlee's room.

Seeing that she was still sleeping, Leah strolled over to the window. A light glaze of condensation had formed on the outside of the glass, but she could still see the meticulously maintained park that abutted the west side of the hospital. Having spent many hours sitting under the shade of its massive oaks trying to keep her spirits up, the park had become her safe harbor.

After a few minutes, she returned to the bedside. Reaching down, she took Charlee's hand in hers. She tried to take solace in the only encouraging thing, which was the doctors' decision to take her off the ventilator and allow her to breathe on her own.

"It's only been a few days, Munchie. You're going to be fine," she whispered, crossing her fingers and touching them to Charlee's lips.

Leah sat at the bedside until six thirty. She wasn't sure why, but she suddenly felt a visit to the gym and a hard workout would help unburden her mind of the relentless stress she was suffering. Yesterday or the day before, the notion wouldn't have occurred to her, but today it seemed like a good idea.

Ten minutes later, she walked over to Charlee's bed, leaned over, and kissed her forehead. Usually it was speckled with perspiration, but this morning, it was dry. Another small but encouraging sign, she thought to herself. When she reached the door, she stopped, looked back, and said the same silent prayer she did every time she left the room.

———

AN HOUR LATER, Leah returned. She was making her way over to the bedside when Lisbet, came through the door holding a container of coffee.

With an encouraging smile, she said, "I saw you coming down

the hall and thought you might like some coffee." She handed her the container and added, "Cream, no sugar—just the way you like it."

"Thanks. Your timing's perfect."

At the same moment Leah lifted the container to her lips, she looked over at Charlee. At first, she was perplexed, but in the next instant, she felt a strange twinge in her gut. She was unable to trust her own eyes. Breathless from a mixture of hope and disbelief, Leah's grip on the container loosened until it suddenly slipped from her hand and tumbled to the floor. The lid instantly popped off, sending coffee splashing in every direction.

"Don't worry about it," Lisbet said, heading to the door. "I'll get some help. We'll have it cleaned up in no time."

"No, no," Leah pleaded, reaching out and placing her hand on Lisbet's arm. "Please, stay with me." Still consumed with doubt, she inched her way closer to the bed, praying with each step that her mind wasn't playing tricks on her. "Look at her lips."

Charlee's lips were barely moving, but they were doing so with an unmistakable purpose. "She's…she's reciting a poem she loves. A day doesn't go by that she doesn't recite it out loud."

Leah noticed the distressed look on Charlee's face had vanished. With a trembling finger, she reached down and touched her lips and mouth. Her jaw muscles were relaxed, and she wasn't clenching her teeth. When she ran her finger over the corners of her mouth, there wasn't a trace of saliva.

"Everything's different," she said between choked breaths. "Her breathing, her expression, her color…everything." She paused for a few seconds before a nervous laugh escaped her lips. She raised her gaze to the ceiling and said, "Thank you."

"I saw Dr. Armbrister on the floor. I'll get her," Lisbet said.

Leah quickly reached behind her. Pulling a plastic chair forward, she sat down, leaned forward, and moved her lips to within a few inches of Charlee's right ear.

"Hi, Munchie. It's Mommy. I'm right here. It sure looks like you're feeling better." There was no response. Fumbling to find her words, Leah gave no thought to giving up. "I've been so worried about you. Barry's been taking such good care of First Lady. Wait until you see her. She's getting a little fat because she doesn't have her best buddy to ride her," she said in just above a hush, her words starting to come more easily. "I saw Grandma yesterday. She's making you a new—"

"Mommy, I'm sleepy."

Leah's back straightened abruptly. At the same moment, her hand shot up and covered her wide-open mouth. She pushed back in her chair as a cascade of tears rained down her cheeks.

"Can you open your eyes? I know you want to go back to sleep, but can you look at me first?"

Charlee lifted her chin and opened her eyes. "What, Mommy?"

"Can you see me?"

"Of course."

She squeezed Charlee's hand just a bit little tighter. "Get some rest. I promise, I'll be right here when you wake up."

The door flew open, and Lennon and Lisbet rushed into the room. Leah watched as the two of them hurried to the bedside where they hovered over Charlee. From their reaction and the looks on their faces, Leah knew they believed she was finally showing indisputable signs of recovering.

Closing her eyes, she found herself overcome with a rush of sheer relief and bliss she never would have dreamed possible. After a short time, Lennon turned her head with a larger-than-life smile and winked her way. Choking back a renewed flood of tears, Leah looked at them through eyes that danced with joy. A moment later, she dashed across the room and gave them both an enormous hug.

Chapter 69

POST-INFUSION DAY NUMBER 6

FOR THE PAST TWO DAYS, the hallways of the leukemic malnutrition unit had been filled with a steady gathering of over-joyed parents impatiently waiting for the news as to when their child would be discharged. Jack and Madison's focus had shifted from medical matters to figuring out a way to possibly salvage any part of their vacation to the Caribbean. They had heard nothing further on the matter of Abel Haas from either Althea or Robert.

They were a day or so away from leaving Oster and returning to Columbus when they learned from Althea that Dr. Gabriela Addesso and Governor Sorenson had asked Althea to schedule a formal wrap-up session. At her request, they agreed to delay their departure to attend the meeting.

As it turned out, the meeting went as they expected. It lasted the better part of three hours and addressed every aspect of the illness from diagnosis through treatment. The governor and Gabriela made sure to express their heartfelt gratitude to the focus group for their vital role in curing leukemic malnutrition. As Jack and

Madison had predicted, the name of Abel Haas was never mentioned. Whatever measures the authorities and the Oster leadership had undertaken to investigate his illegal research and its possible connection to leukemic malnutrition were kept as hush-hush as possible.

When the wrap-up session was over, Jack and Madison took some time to say their goodbyes to some of the doctors they had worked with. It was five o'clock when they finished speaking to the last physician and were ready to leave the hospital. They were approaching the elevators when Kendric called out to them.

With his Dutch uncle smile, he said, "I spoke with some of your senior colleagues in Columbus this morning. We talked about the best way to collaborate in publishing the initial articles on leukemic malnutrition. I was going to invite you both back here next week for a meeting, but if you have some time now, it might help us jump-start the project."

"If you don't mind, Kendric," Madison began, "I have a few patients I'd like to see, so if you don't mind, I think I'll pass."

Kendric walked over to Madison and took her hands. "I understand, but in that case, would you mind terribly if I borrowed Jack for a little while?"

She feigned a grin. "I'll leave that up to Jack."

"Of course," he said, seeing no way out of the trap. "I think I have a little time before Madison and I grab dinner. Where would you like to talk?"

"It's a beautiful sunset. Let's walk over to my office."

"Lead the way."

For reasons Jack wasn't quite sure of, he suspected Kendric's request for a meeting had nothing to do with future research. He had no idea what his real agenda might be, but something told him to keep his wits about him and do a lot of listening at first, hoping Kendric would reveal what was really on his mind.

Chapter 70

Kendric's office was much warmer than Jack preferred. To make matters worse, an overstated aroma of a honey-scented freshener thickened the air. Slipping on the argyle gray sweater vest he always kept on the back of his chair, Kendric invited Jack to have a seat in one of the wingback chairs that faced his desk.

"If you don't mind, there is another matter I'd like to talk to you about before we discuss collaborating on a paper," Kendrick said. Jack was hardly surprised by his request.

"Of course."

Reaching forward, he removed one of his pipes from its rack and laid the tip in the corner of his mouth. "I may be way off base on this, but since our meeting with Althea and Robert I've gotten the feeling that you believe I haven't been totally forthcoming about Abel Haas's role in Oster's research lab."

"I won't deny that. I simply assumed you had your reasons."

"If you'll allow me I'd like to share some information with you."

Jack felt there was still too much at stake to decline his offer out of hand. He'd let Kendric begin to disclose whatever it was that was on his mind. If the conversation seemed to be going south, he could call a halt to things at any time.

"I'm happy to listen, Kendric, but I don't feel you owe me an explanation for anything."

"I appreciate your sentiment, but there are some things I'd like to share with you, and I'm sure, after I do, the first thing you're going to ask me is why. I'll save you the trouble by telling you I don't have a good answer to that question. The other thing worth mentioning is that I suspect whatever I tell you will be a matter of common knowledge in the not too distant future."

"As I said, I'm happy to listen."

Kendric set his elbows on the desk, cleared his throat, and began his explanation. "I knew Abel Haas for almost twenty years. He was a good friend and, until recently, I thought he was a valued colleague. Beginning a few months ago, his behavior changed dramatically. He became increasingly more anxious and argumentative. I was just about to set up a meeting with him to see if there was anything I could do to help when he requested a sit down with me." He leaned in, leveled his eyes on Jack, and went on. "In a near state of panic, he confessed that he'd been conducting unauthorized prion research right here in the Oster lab for the past thirteen years. Obviously, it was something I was completely unaware of."

"Unaware of? With all due respect, how would such a thing be possible?"

"That's the same question I've been asking myself every day since Abel first confessed." With a forced grin, he added, "It's not something I'm proud of, but nevertheless it's true."

"Did he give you a reason why he'd do something so unethical?"

"He told me he was working on finding a cure for leukemia and that he was very close."

"And, his theory for this was based on..."

"He was convinced he'd isolated a strain of prion that was capable of stimulating the patient's immune system to produce anti-bodies that were incredibly effective in killing leukemia cells."

"That makes no sense. Even if he was right, the prion infection would kill the patient in the process."

"Except for the fact that he was also positive the prion he'd discovered would be totally harmless to the patient." In a voice steeped in despair, he added, "That's when he informed me that a few weeks earlier he had administered the prion to a few of our leukemia patients to test his theory."

"When you say a few, do you mean three?" He cast his eyes down and nodded.

Jack could almost feel his heart flutter from Kendric's disclosure.

"Are you telling me for certain that Abel Haas was responsible for the prion infections that killed Max Kubicek and the other two teenagers?"

"Yes, but as I said Abel didn't tell me about it until weeks afterward. He said their deaths had left him so consumed with guilt that he was unable to function. He kept repeating he thought Max and the others would be cured." Shoving his chair back, Kendric pushed himself to his feet and walked over to his eight-foot high solid wood bookcase. With his back to Jack, he continued, "When I told him I had to report what he'd done, he begged me not to. He swore he'd ceased all his research activities and that his plan was to resign his position within the year and leave the country permanently."

"But, if we assume he was also responsible for creating the leukemic malnutrition epidemic, he lied to you."

"I realize that now. But at the time, he played on our friendship, begging me to look the other way. For a few months, I turned a blind eye to what he'd done. Eventually, I told him I couldn't continue protecting him. That's when his entire behavior changed. He threatened that if I breathed a word of his research to anybody he'd swear that right from the beginning I was completely complicit in every aspect of it including the illegal experimentation on the three children."

"But it was untrue. The authorities never would have believed him."

"I was terrified they would, and that I'd wind up spending the rest of my life in jail...or worse," he said with complete conviction as he set his pipe into a large crystal ashtray. "The problem was that the appearance was that I could've easily been complicit. When it came to the oversight of Abel's research, I was totally derelict in my responsibilities. I knew he was a bit of a rogue in the way he worked, but I trusted him. He was a prolific researcher who was held in the highest esteem by everybody. It never entered my mind he was capable of such contemptible behavior. I had no idea there was a connection between leukemic malnutrition and Haas's research until you and Madison informed us that you believed a prion was the cause. By that time, Haas was long gone."

"Did you ever ask him why he chose not to follow established ethical procedures in carrying out his research?"

"That was the first question I asked him. He insisted the circumstances surrounding his work were highly complicated and prohibited him from following normal procedures or discussing the matter with me. The only thing he made clear was that, in his mind, finding a cure for leukemia trumped every other consideration—the end justified the means."

"I'm sorry, Kendric, but no ethical scientist would embrace such an absurd rationalization. I would have assumed you felt the same way."

"With all due respect, Jack, that's easy for you to say. You weren't the one threatened by a cunning madman. Are you sure your high-minded principles would trump being arrested, publicly disgraced, and having your entire life's work obliterated, not to mention the real possibility of your life coming to an end by lethal injection in some shadowy prison?" Before Jack could offer a response, Kendric's voice strengthened. "Now that Abel is dead and all the children he infected are cured— what's the point of sacrificing myself?"

"So, you're just going to pretend none of this ever happened, put your head in the sand, and hope it all goes away?"

"It doesn't matter what I do because everything that happened here is going to be front-page news whether I admit to it or not. As I mentioned earlier, that's the only reason I'm baring my soul to you now." He paused long enough to walk back to his desk and retake his seat. "There's another important point to be made: because of your discovery of prion neutralization, you've opened the door to possibly curing other deadly prion diseases."

"And you see that as some kind of twisted get-out-of-jail-jail card for what you've done?" Jack posed.

"I know what I did was cowardly and immoral. I'm not seeking exoneration, Jack. But the fact remains I didn't know about Abel's role in leukemic malnutrition, the phony Dr. Austin, or Hayden Kubicek's death until it was too late."

"Which begs the question: are you going to offer the same shabby excuse for the matter of Dr. Austin? I hope to god you weren't involved in creating that cover-up."

"I had nothing to do with that. Abel never breathed a word of it to me. But I think it's obvious he was trying to cover his tracks by diverting everybody's focus away from the real cause of Max's death." He leaned back in his chair and raised his hands to his face. "The irony is that whatever happens to me is irrelevant. My legacy will be one of shame and immorality."

"Your legacy is an irrelevancy and I still can't believe how blind you are to what you've done. If the real reason you decided to disclose all of this information to me was in the hopes I'd under-stand or forgive you, you're sadly mistaken."

"I thought you'd at least be openminded enough to consider it. It's easy to be judgmental, Jack. I shouldn't be surprised you'd take the moral high ground."

Jack finally realized he was not about to change Abel's distorted take on things. To argue the point with him any further would serve no useful purpose. Having endured all he could, he came to his feet. As he did, he watched Kendric sluggishly swivel his chair and stare through hollow eyes at the diplomas, certificates, and awards that hung on the wall in military order.

That there was nothing more to be said was obvious to Jack. He emptied his lungs of a heavy breath, and without so much as another word or a backward glance, he marched out of Kendric Nash's office.

Chapter 71

During his walk back to the guesthouse, Jack couldn't help but relive every word of his conversation with Kendric. He was forced to conclude that the man was a pitiful figure cursed by a flawed character and undeserving of forgiveness. Stepping into the foyer, he hung up his coat and went into the living room where he found Madison reading her monthly tennis magazine. As soon as her eyes caught his, she tossed it aside.

"I wasn't sure you'd feel like going out to eat after talking to Kendric, so I ordered in," she told him, as she slid down to the end of the love seat. Her eyes were bloodshot, and her voice was despondent.

"Is everything okay?"

"I got a call from Becky Walt. I don't know if I ever mentioned her to you."

"The name sounds familiar," he responded, kicking his shoes off and sitting down next to her.

"I met her at the oncology center in Columbus. She was diagnosed at about the same time I was. We started treatment together and attended the same leukemia support group." With a slow shake of her head, she added, "She hasn't done as well as I have, and she's still on therapy. Unfortunately, her last round of chemo wiped out her bone marrow. Her oncologist spoke to her today and told her she definitely needs a bone marrow transplant before she can receive any further treatment."

"I'm sorry to hear that," Jack said, taking Madison's hand in his. "How low are her blood counts?"

"They've pretty much bottomed out, especially her platelets. Her condition's very serious. Unless they find a donor and she gets some healthy bone marrow pretty soon, she'll be prone to infection, bleeding, and a host of other problems. To make matters worse, she developed a cough and fever yesterday, and her oncologist admitted her to the hospital."

"I'm a little rusty on bone marrow transplants. Are they still as risky as I remember?"

"They've definitely become safer over the years, but there are still lots of possible complications, including death. Even so, most experts feel the benefits far outweigh the risks. They've saved thousands of lives and are an essential part of cancer treatment."

"When's Becky's transplant scheduled?"

"In a few weeks. She'll require quite a bit of preparation for the procedure."

"Hopefully, everything will go smoothly."

Madison crossed her fingers and held them up. "I hope so. The first thing I'm going to do when we get back to Columbus is visit her."

Jack hesitated briefly but then asked, "How is all this affecting you?"

"A day doesn't go by that I don't get scared of relapsing. Obviously, hearing stories like this doesn't help. It's just something you try to live with."

"Anything I can do?" he asked, full well with the knowledge that, since he'd never walked in a cancer patient's shoes, there was only so much he could understand about her endless fears and anxiety.

"I wish there was," she said, as she came to her feet. "C'mon, let's eat some dinner. I'd like to hear what Kendric really wanted to talk to you about. His story about writing papers on LM together was about as thin as a tissue turned sideways."

Chapter 72

Jack followed Madison down the hallway toward the kitchen.

"I'll tell you this," he said. "That was hands down the most bizarre conversation I've ever had with another doctor."

Madison sat down across from him at the farmhouse-style table and set the two wrapped subs, a bag of potato chips, and a large bottle of lemon iced tea down between them.

"Another night of gourmet dining, I see."

"C'mon, it's your favorite—turkey and provolone." She removed the paper wrapping from his sub and handed it to him.

Jack spent the next twenty minutes recounting the details of his conversation with Kendric. Madison stopped him from time to time to either pose a question or offer an opinion. From the disbelieving look on her face, Jack gathered she considered Kendric's explanations and rationalizations pitifully lame.

"Do you believe his story?" she asked, handing him a napkin to replace the shredded paper towel he'd been using.

"I think so, but that doesn't change the way I feel about his corrupt behavior. My charitable side keeps reminding me that he's not the first human being to panic and make a bad decision."

"I don't know, Jack, I'd say he made a whole bunch of bad decisions. I don't think I'm as sympathetic to his situation as you obviously are. One's principles only mean something when times are tough and it's a challenge to stand by them." She paused to take a couple of swigs of her drink. "It sounds to me like Kendric knew exactly what he was doing. It's not as if a group of terrorists threatened his family or put a gun to his head. His actions may not have reached the level of depravity of Abel Haas's, but they sure as hell are light-years away from being forgivable."

As he listened, Jack gathered up the paper plates and tossed them into the trash.

"Does Kendric really think you're going to keep his dirty little secret? I mean, why in the world did he confess all of this to you?"

"He said it was because all the information was on the brink of becoming public anyway, although he made sure to tell me that I'm the only one he's confided in." He drummed the table for a few seconds. "I guess it's possible he thinks I'm in a position to help him."

"Why would he think that?" she inquired.

"I wouldn't know, but it's a moot point. He's right about one thing—everything that happened will soon be public information. Nothing's going to save him. In the end, Dr. Kendric will be taking a trip to the woodshed."

"Hearing all this makes me wonder about something," Madison said.

"What?"

"Did it cross your mind that maybe Haas isn't dead? I mean, all we know is that Kendric got a call from somebody claiming to be his lawyer. If Haas believed his death would dissuade the authorities from looking for him...well, it's possible he arranged for somebody posing as his lawyer to make the phony call."

Jack thumbed his chin. "Anything's possible, but I still think he was probably killed in Thailand."

"I wish as I was as convinced as you are. You'd think that from all we've learned about this guy, especially considering the whole Dr. Austin scam, we'd be a little more circumspect about what we so willingly swallow hook, line, and sinker." She stood up, wrapped up the half of her sub she hadn't eaten, and put it in the refrigerator. "I don't know about you, but I'm ready to call it a day. We can talk more about this tomorrow."

Suspecting he wouldn't be able to sleep, he said, "I'm really not very tired. I think I'll stay up for a while. There's an old Spencer Tracy movie on that I'd kind of like to watch."

"Come to bed. You're exhausted. As usual, you just won't admit it."

He turned away from the sink with a small frown. "I hope this isn't your way of bringing up physician burnout again and my total inability to establish a healthy work-life balance."

"Now that you mention it, you do work all the time. You only have two real hobbies—doing the New York Times crossword puzzle and tennis."

"So what's wrong with that?"

"Nothing, other than they're about as exciting as watching a synchronized swimming competition. I'm just saying that you'd benefit from a few more leisure activities."

To steady himself, he sucked in a huge breath. "Perhaps, we can add my boring lifestyle to the other topics we plan on discussing tomorrow."

She laughed. "Good idea."

He started to get up but stopped. "By the way, how come you're so tired? Didn't you take a nap earlier?"

"So?"

"I just want to make sure you're feeling okay," he assured her, trying his best not to sound alarmed.

"I'm fine, Jack. We've talked about this, and I've given you my word that I'll tell you if I'm not feeling well."

"You know me—trust but verify."

As she was finishing a low groan, Jack stole a second look her way. Her color was good, and she didn't seem to be short of breath. When she looked his way, he quickly averted his eyes, but he knew he hadn't done it fast enough.

She walked over and gave him a hug. "I'm fine. I promise. Enjoy your movie."

He sat at the table for a couple of minutes after Madison had gone to the bedroom. He checked the time. The movie started in five minutes. He made his way out of the kitchen and down the main hallway. Just before he reached the den, he grabbed his phone and placed a call.

Chapter 73

Even though Jack had seen the movie version of *Inherit the Wind* more times than he could count, he thoroughly enjoyed watching it again. He was usually pretty careful about sticking to a healthy diet, but during the film, he finished off an entire bag of sea-salt-and-vinegar potato chips.

He turned off the television and put his feet up on the ottoman. Maybe Madison was right. Maybe Haas was lurking around Defiance and still posing a threat to the patients of Oster Children's. He allowed his head to fall back and was just about to close his eyes when his phone rang.

"Hi, Doc," Frank said. "Sorry about the hour, but I just picked up your message and wasn't sure if it could wait until morning. What can I do for you?"

"I have a quick question for you. I found out a few days ago that a colleague of mine was recently killed in a car accident in Thailand. He has no family, and the message I got said he wasn't traveling with a cell phone. When I tried to find out what happened, I learned the accuracy of these reports can be pretty unreliable. I was hoping you could steer me in the right direction to confirm if he died or not."

"You're right to be concerned. All kinds of mistakes, including the victim's true identity, are reported every day in these types of situations. If you're really interested in finding out if your friend was killed or not, give me what information you have, and I'll give it a shot. It'll be a lot easier for me to find out than you. It's not a big project. It'll take me less than a day, but I can't guarantee I'll be able to find out what happened to this guy, if anything."

"Thanks. I'll text you the info I have," Jack said. "By the way, when's Kip being discharged?"

"Lisbet's looking after him tonight. She told me they're planning on sending him home before the end of the week." With a chuckle, he added, "If I know my kid, he'll be pitching batting practice at the high school this weekend."

"That's something we'd all love to see. We'll stop in to see you guys tomorrow."

"Thanks, Doc. We'd both like that. Have a good night."

Jack was reaching for the remote control when Madison called out to him. "Is your movie over?"

"Yeah."

"Come join me in the kitchen. There's something I want to bounce off you."

"Be right there," he told her. Since he thought she'd been asleep for the past two hours, he was a little surprised by the request.

He rubbed Moose's belly. "C'mon, pal. We've been summoned to the throne room."

Chapter 74

When Jack walked into the kitchen, Madison was making herself a mug of hot tea.

"I thought you were asleep," he said.

"I've been thinking about your conversation with Kendric, and there's something that doesn't make any sense to me."

"I thought you didn't want to talk about any of this until tomorrow," he reminded her.

She joined him at the table and handed him a strawberry frosted donut. "I got my second wind."

Pleased to see she'd recouped some of her get-up-and-go, he smiled inwardly.

"You told me that Kendric claimed Abel Haas was trying to discover a cure for leukemia. Do you think that was an assumption on his part, or was he sure?"

"He said Haas insisted he was on the brink of finding a new prion strain that would cure childhood leukemia."

"That's what has me scratching my head," Madison said. "The thought that a unique strain of prion could cure leukemia goes beyond preposterous and crosses over to insane. We've both read Dr.

Hartmann's journals pretty carefully, and I don't remember anything in there that even hinted at a cancer treatment."

"So you're saying what?"

"I'm saying I think there's a pretty strong chance Haas was lying about working on a cure for leukemia. I don't think he wanted Kendric to know what he was really up to," she answered, adding another squirt of lime juice to her tea. "I'm betting he was researching something entirely different, and whatever it was, it not only had nothing to do with curing cancer, it also completely escaped our attention."

"I see. Anything else?"

"Yeah. I also think we can comfortably assume Haas was the one who gave the journals to Hayden."

"Which begs the question: Why would he do that?" Jack asked.

"Maybe the reason's simple. Haas knew Hayden was digging for information about Max's death. Once he decided to flee the country, perhaps he was so overwhelmed with plain old-fashioned remorse that he simply gave the journals to Hayden to purge his guilty conscience and vindicate himself."

"Since they're both dead, I suspect we'll never know."

"Look, Jack. I realize the LM crisis is over, and in a matter of days these kids will be going home, but from a scientific standpoint, I still think it's critically important we do everything in our power to figure out what the hell Haas was so desperately searching for." Madison lifted a cautionary finger, wagged it a couple of times, and added, "There are too many unanswered questions. As I said before, we don't know for sure if Haas is really dead. We also have no idea if he was working alone." She pushed her chair back and stood up from the table. "Until we have those answers, I'm not sure we've seen the end of Abel Haas or what disasters might still be out there as a result of his depraved research."

Chapter 75

POST-INFUSION DAY NUMBER 7

8 p.m.

Jack and Madison had spent the day visiting several of the LM patients and tying up a number of administrative loose ends. They'd split a pizza for dinner and planned on a relaxing evening.

After answering a dozen or so emails, Jack strolled into the den, where he found Madison sitting on the couch playing tug of war with Moose with his cloth rope.

"I was thinking of taking him for a walk. Any interest in joining us?" he asked.

"A long one or a short one?"

"I think he and I could both use a large dose of fresh air. I was thinking of going over to the dog park."

"In that case, don't be surprised to find me sound asleep when you get back."

"Understood," he said, looking at Moose. "Where's your leash, pal?" Having only a two-word vocabulary, which consisted of cookie and leash, Moose jumped off the couch, started barking, and trailed Jack to the entranceway.

With Moose leading the way, they made their way across the

Oster campus. It was a raw, gusty night, and it took a full twenty minutes to make the walk. They had just entered the park when a man walking a small white dog approached. Jack thought he recognized the man's silhouette but wasn't positive it was Frank until a few seconds later when he passed under a lamppost.

"How are you, Doc?"

Frank's perfectly groomed dog began yapping at Moose, who instantly backed up and took shelter behind Jack's legs.

"I'm fine. Is that a Maltese?"

"Actually, she's a miniature Maltese," Frank answered, picking up the dog and tucking her under his arm. "Her name's Camille. I hope she's not scaring your dog."

"He'll be fine. Both his bite and his bark are nonexistent," Jack said, feeling a twinge of embarrassment. "I didn't know you had a dog. I thought I was the only one the administration broke the no-dogs-allowed rule for."

"Since she's very well behaved, and I was beyond insistent, Security agreed to look the other way. She stays pretty quiet and is happy to sleep in the parent suite as long as I sneak her in to play with Kip a couple of times a day."

"Do you walk her here every night?" Jack asked.

"Not usually, but Robyn's working tonight. She told me the word's out that you're here most evenings around this time and that I could probably find you here. We're scheduled to be discharged tomorrow, and I wanted to make sure I got back to you about your colleague who reportedly died in Thailand."

"Did you have any luck getting the information?"

"I hate to sound like a politician, but I can neither confirm nor deny Abel Haas was the victim of a fatal accident. Unfortunately, when dealing with certain foreign countries, we frequently hit a dead end with these types of inquiries. You almost have to be physically present on their soil to confirm a death."

"I appreciate you trying, Frank."

"If you feel your source was reliable...well, that's probably your best bet that the information's accurate."

"Since I got the news thirdhand, I'm not sure."

"If I come across anything more, I'll let you know, but it's not likely," Frank told him. "I was hoping Dr. Shaw would be here. I wanted to thank you both in person one last time before you leave— any idea when that will be?"

"We're not exactly sure yet, but I imagine sometime in the next couple of days. I'm pretty sure we'll be able to visit Kip at least one more time before we leave." They strolled over to the far side of the green space to a grassy, fenced-in area that had been designated as a dog park. "Do you have an idea what time you'll be discharged tomorrow?"

"It's kind of up in the air," Frank answered. "Robyn told me that Kip's scheduled to get a dose of IVIG tomorrow. I imagine our discharge will depend on what time that happens."

Jack was familiar with IVIG. It was a mixture of antibodies obtained from human plasma that is given to patients to boost their immune system. He wasn't a pediatric oncologist, but even so, he was in a muddle to explain why Kip and the other patients who were fully recovered from their prion infection would require IVIG, especially when the antibodies had no effectiveness against any prion infection known to modern medicine. What bothered him more was that the medication wasn't without possible side effects. Many physicians had learned the hard way not to prescribe it without good reason.

"Did any of the doctors explain why Kip needed IVIG?"

"No, but I can't say I asked. After everything that's happened the last few weeks, it didn't seem like a big deal. Kip's gotten IVIG a few times in the past. He's never had a problem with it."

"Did Robyn give you any idea what time he's supposed to receive it?"

"She mentioned the research pharmacy thought they'd be able to send it over at around ten." He grinned. "Since they're not the most reliable organization when it comes to punctuality, I have my doubts."

"Research pharmacy?"

"That's what Robyn said."

The research pharmacy only prepared drugs for children who

were on studies. He had no idea how a last-minute decision to give a medication could possibly be part of a research protocol. All studies were subject to extreme scrutiny by a number of hospital committees before they were approved. The process generally took at least six months from the time it was proposed until it began.

By this time, Moose and Camille had become fast friends and were chasing each other around the park.

"It's getting a little late. I think I'll head back," Jack said.

"Me too. I'm sure by now Kip's wide awake watching the Cavs game." Frank hesitated for a moment, but just before Jack turned to leave, he said, "There's something I want to share with you, Doc. I had pretty much decided not to burden you with this, but after giving it some further thought, I realized it's possible the information might be important."

Frank took a few minutes to recount the attack he'd suffered in the veterinary school's parking lot. He was only as detailed as he had to be in his description of the assault.

"I...I don't know what to say," Jack responded, his chin dropping toward his chest. "It was at our suggestion that you made the trip. I'm beyond relieved to hear you're okay."

"I can't be sure that what happened was anything more than a botched mugging...but in all honesty, it wouldn't be my first guess."

"Unfortunately, I suspect there are events related to leukemic malnutrition that will eventually wind up in the hands of the authorities."

"I understand, Doc. I'm glad I filled you in on what happened." He checked the time on his cell phone. "Well, I should get going."

Jack hooked Moose's leash onto his collar, exited the dog part, and started back to the guesthouse. Making his way past the main parking garage and a state-of-the-art playground, his mind filled with more questions about leukemic malnutrition. As he continued along the footpath, he fell deeper into thought, barely noticing the squally wind that briefly swirled around him.

He couldn't shake his uneasiness as to why Kip had been scheduled to receive IVIG. Even if there was a reasonable indication for its use, that still didn't explain why it was being prepared in the

research pharmacy. Adding to Jack's trepidation was his conversation with Madison about the growing mysteries surrounding Abel Haas and the true extent of the conspiracy. He found himself more plagued by the possibility that he was alive, may have returned to Defiance, and still be up to no good.

He was about halfway home when he reached for his phone and called Madison.

"I just ran into Frank. He told me one of the doctors ordered an IVIG infusion for Kip. My understanding is that all the LM kids who are ready for discharge are infection free. Can you think of a reason why Kip might need IVIG?"

"Not off the top of my head, but maybe there's been a clinical change that we're not aware of that prompted one of the doctors to order it for him."

"I guess that's possible."

"Are you on your way back?"

"Yeah. I'll be there in about ten minutes."

"We can talk more about this when you get here."

"Sounds good— see you in a few," he said.

Coaxing Moose along with a gentle tug on the leash, Jack found himself again racking his brain, trying to make sense of things. He was familiar with the feeling—the pieces were there, but they were scattered randomly along the edges of his mind. One thing he was certain of—he was unconvinced Kip was in dire need of IVIG.

He was a few steps from the front gate when all of a sudden he came to an abrupt stop and dipped his chin. There was no blinding flash of lightning or crash of thunder, but the eye-opening thought hit him that hard.

Pinching his lips together, he muttered, "Of course."

He reached for the thumb latch and opened the gate. Eager to speak with Madison and savoring his revelation with a gratified smile, he hurried up the path.

Chapter 76

Jack entered the guesthouse and walked down the main hall, past the antique-style grandfather clock, and straight into the living room where Madison was sitting fireside.

"I thought about it some more," she said. "I still can't think of a good reason why Kip would need IVIG."

"Maybe that's because there isn't one."

He felt her probing eyes moving across his face.

"Okay, Jack what's going on.?"

"I'll be right back. I just want to get something." He left the room and quickly returned with Dr. Hartmann's journals in hand. He set them on the coffee table. "I've been thinking about a few things. Since you posed the possibility, I've been wondering if you're right about Abel Haas never having had an interest in curing leukemia."

"I thought you already agreed with me on that."

"Let's say I'm more convinced now," he said, kicking off his shoes and joining her in front of the fireplace. "While I was walking back to the guesthouse just now, I remembered looking at Haas's CV and being impressed by the hundreds of scientific articles he'd written. They covered a wide range of topics, but do you know what he wrote about the most by far?"

"I can't say that I recall."

"Bone marrow transplantation."

"A lot of researchers have an interest in one particular area. What's the big deal?" she asked

"I remembered what you told me about your friend Becky being scheduled for a bone marrow transplant." He picked up the third journal and carefully opened it to the last several pages. With certainty in his eyes, he pointed to the top of the page. "This experiment was one of her last. Do you remember it?"

Craning her neck, Madison began reading the description of the experiment but stopped after only a minute or so.

"I remember it, but to tell you the truth, it struck me as relatively unimportant compared to the rest of her work, especially when you consider the other strains of prions she discovered."

"Forgive me for disagreeing, but I believe this particular one was very special."

"I'm all ears." she said, pulling her legs into a seiza position.

Exhaling a resonant breath, he said, "I never gave it much thought myself until a little while ago. You said it yourself yesterday, when we were talking about Haas and what he'd really been up to. You said the answer was in Dr. Hartmann's journals and that we must have missed it." Pointing at the journal page again, he said, "I think I know what we missed. According to this experiment, Dr. Hartmann was able to isolate a strain of prion that was not only fifty percent less deadly than her other strains, but it also had the ability to stimulate the bone marrow to produce healthy new blood cells at an extremely high rate. She also found that the infected animal's bone marrow became highly resistant to the damaging effects of certain chemicals like benzene that are very similar to our modern-day chemotherapy drugs. In her own words, Dr. Hartmann called the bone marrow *energized and indestructible*." Closing the journal carefully, he added, "At the time she isolated this particular prion strain, I don't think she realized the magnitude of what she'd discovered."

"I'm not sure I do either, Jack," she said, throwing her hands up. "Where are you going with all this?"

"That's a fair question," he assured her. "Let me back up a little bit and ask you something." She nodded. "What's the purpose of a bone marrow transplant?"

"Basically, it replaces the damaged marrow making it possible for a cancer patient to receive more chemotherapy. It also replenishes it with healthy *stem cells*, which are not only the necessary raw material to make new healthy blood cells, but also are believed to kill cancer cells." She stretched her legs out and leaned back against the couch. "What does any of that have to do with Haas?"

"I think he had a very specific interest in Dr. Hartmann's prion, but with one modification—he had to find a way to make it harmless to the patient, which is exactly what Kendric told me he was trying to do. Do you see what I'm getting at?"

"I do, and if I'm reading you correctly, that would make Haas even more insane than we ever imagined."

"Maybe so, but there was a method to his madness, and I suspect that after thirteen years of prion research he was ready and willing to test his theory."

A look passed between them.

"So, you're suggesting he somehow isolated a prion that had the ability to make the patient's bone marrow resistant to chemotherapy, and at the same time stimulate it to make new, healthy stem cells that were capable of killing the leukemia cells? Do you know what you're saying, Jack?"

"I'm saying I believe Abel Haas's intent was to alter Dr. Hartmann's prion and use it to develop a cancer treatment that would make *bone marrow transplantation obsolete*."

"I'm not an oncologist, Jack, but that sounds beyond impossible to me."

"Whether it would be possible or not is irrelevant. The only thing that matters is Haas's disturbed state of mind and what he believed." He blew out a weighty breath and continued, "The more I think about it, the more I'm sure he was hell bent on using his prion strain to ensure no cancer patient would ever require a bone marrow transplant again."

"If you're right, and he was using innocent children as his laboratory rats...well, that would make him a certifiable madman...a modern day Dr. Moreau," Madison said.

"But, you'd agree—if there was some way of eliminating the need for bone marrow transplantation, it would revolutionize cancer treatment on a global level."

"It would be considered one of the greatest medical breakthroughs of the century."

"And the scientist responsible for the discovery would be hailed as a medical genius."

"There's a terrifying irony to all of this," Madison said in just above a whisper. "Haas's reason for fleeing the country was almost certainly because he'd failed to create a strain of prion that was harmless to the patient. It no longer mattered whether that strain had the ability to render bone marrow indestructible." Opening her hands, she continued, "Assuming he's still alive, by curing LM, we put the son of a bitch right back in business. We were his unwitting accomplices. Now, with all the kids surviving the prion infection he gave them, everything changes. All Haas has to do is test their marrows to see if the prion that caused leukemic malnutrition had rendered the patients' marrows resistant to the effects of chemotherapy.

"How hard would that be?" Jack asked.

"Not too hard at all. All he'd have to do is figure out some way to give them a chemotherapy drug like Busulfan, which is usually used in the treatment of adult leukemia. In a high enough dose, it'll predictably destroy anybody's bone marrow," she said. "Two weeks later, he brings the kids back to the hospital on some pretext to have their blood drawn for a few routine tests. The results would give him a very accurate picture as to whether their marrows were normal of if they'd been destroyed by the Busulfan."

Jack stood up, grabbed a brass poker, and nudged the top log farther back on the grate. "So, we can assume the blood tests would be a highly accurate predictor if their marrows would stand up to the damaging effects of chemotherapy."

"I hate to tell you this, buddy—and I'm not trying to be the naysayer in the room, but everything we just tossed around may make for interesting conversation, but in the end, it's all conjecture. I know what I said about Abel Haas, but in reality, we have no real proof he's still alive."

"To which I'd say we have no real proof that he's dead, either." Jack continued to fuss with the logs. "There's something else that's a little bothersome. Robyn told Frank the IVIG infusions are being prepared by the research pharmacy."

"Did she say why?"

"No."

"On the surface, that makes no sense, but maybe there's a good reason for it that we're unaware of."

"I'd like to know what that good reason is," he said, his mouth turning downward.

"Look, Jack, Oster's upper echelon is taking the attitude that the leukemic malnutrition outbreak is last week's news. All they want to do is to leave it as far behind them as possible, get back to business as normal, and forget the entire event ever happened. So, where do we go from here?" she asked.

"From a medical standpoint, I think we've done about all we can. Unless we come across some new, critically important informa-tion…well, I think things are out of our hands."

Madison didn't respond in words, but her exasperated frown spoke volumes. They got up together and headed down the hall to the bedroom. Jack suspected she felt the same way he did about the enormous sense of accomplishment that comes with solving a chal-lenging diagnostic dilemma.

Regrettably, in the case of leukemic malnutrition, that feeling was noticeably absent.

Chapter 77

With his mind filled with thoughts of Abel Haas, Jack suffered another restless night's sleep and was up before the sun. Instead of lounging around, he decided to grab a shower, get dressed, and eat breakfast. As he was finishing a lightly toasted English muffin, he remembered his promise to Frank about visiting Kip before he was discharged. Hoping Robyn would have an idea what time the research pharmacy was sending over the IVIG, he picked up his phone and called the LM unit. It was five a.m.

"This is Gwen. How may I help you?"

"It's Dr. Wyatt, Gwen. Would you please connect me to Robyn?"

"I'd love to, but she's been having trouble with her hospital phone all night. Is there a message I can give her for you?"

"Would you please ask her to call me? I'd like to find out what time she's planning on giving Kip the IVIG."

"I'll give her the message, but since we have so many of our kids scheduled to get it, I'm not sure she'll be able to give you an exact time. We have nineteen patients to treat before they're discharged today. We're all running around here like chickens with our heads cut off so we'll be ready when the infusions arrive from the pharmacy."

Jack felt his back stiffen "I...I was unaware that any patient other than Kip was scheduled to receive IVIG."

"We just found out about it ourselves last night," she said.

"Are any of the patients ill with a new infection?"

"No. They're all doing great, thanks to you and Dr. Shaw. We were told it's just a precaution."

"Do you happen to know who ordered it?"

"It was Dr. Camspoker. She phoned in the order late yesterday, but I don't know if it was her decision alone." Jack was again taken aback. He and Madison had attended all the care plan meetings for the LM patients, and he hadn't heard a word about it. What bothered him more was that he had never met Dr. Camspoker, or for that matter ever heard her name before.

"I thought I'd met all the oncologists on the team," he casually mentioned to Gwen. "I don't know why, but her name doesn't ring a bell."

"Dr. Camspoker's great. You probably never met her because she spends most of her time in the lab doing research. She's a pediatric oncologist, but her main responsibility is research. She only covers a couple of clinical shifts a month."

"I hope Dr. Shaw and I will have the chance to meet her before we leave. Thanks, Gwen."

"My shift's over in a couple of hours. I'd like to say goodbye to you and Dr. Shaw. What time do you think you'll be in the hospital?"

"Sometime this morning, but I'm not exactly sure when."

"Are you planning on being here when the kids come back for their first outpatient visit? It should be in about two weeks. We're planning a surprise celebration for the families."

"We'll certainly try to make it, but are you sure about the date? At the last clinical care meeting, we decided the first outpatient visit would be in six to eight weeks."

"The nursing administration let us know yesterday the date had been changed."

"Any reason why?"

"None was given. I guess everybody's just trying to be as cautious as possible."

"Thanks for the information, Gwen. We'll do our best to see you in a couple of weeks. Please ask Robyn to give me a call when she can."

"I will."

Jack set his phone down on the central island. He was starting to think that maybe their wild theories about Abel Haas weren't so wild after all. From the moment Gwen mentioned Dr. Camspoker's name, he'd been combing his memory as to why it sounded so familiar.

Making his way into the den, he sat down in front of his laptop and did a search on her. From what he could find, her academic career had been praiseworthy. When she completed her combined MD-PhD program and residency training in Canada, she had accepted her first, and what turned out to be her only, job at Oster Children's. That was eleven years ago.

Jack brought up her bibliography of medical publications. As he made his way down the list, his apprehension soared. Similar to Dr. Haas, she had written dozens of articles on bone marrow transplantation in children. But what raised the red flag even higher was that Haas had co-authored every one of her scientific publications on the topic. It seemed highly likely that they worked closely together in Oster's lab.

Consumed with angst, Jack chose not to waste any time wondering if his imagination was running away with itself. Why would a physician who worked a couple of shifts a month take it upon herself to order an IVIG infusion for nineteen healthy patients? He suddenly remembered he hadn't heard back from Robyn. He reached for his phone to call the LM unit.

"Hi, Gwen. Sorry to bother you again, but I haven't heard back from Robyn about the IVIG infusions."

"I told her to call you, Dr. Wyatt, but I guess she hasn't had a chance to get back to you yet. By the way, a couple of minutes after you and I got off the phone, the courier from the research pharmacy walked on the unit with the infusions." Before Gwen could say another word, Jack was on his feet. "We should be ready to hang them in the next few minutes."

"Thanks, Gwen."

Jack was just about to make his way to the bedroom to wake Madison when he heard her voice from behind him.

"What's going on?"

"I was just about to wake you. I'm going to head over to the hospital."

"At this hour?"

"I don't have a lot of time to explain, but I think there's a chance the IVIG's been tampered with. Maybe our theory about giving the LM patients Busulfan to see if it damaged their marrows wasn't so out-there after all. Get dressed and meet me on the unit as soon as you can."

"Have you called anybody about this?"

"Not yet, but you're reading my mind," he said rushing toward the entranceway. "Can you give Lennon a call and see if she knows anything about all these kids getting IVIG?"

"All these kids?" she asked, chasing him down the hall.

"It's not just Kip. Eighteen others are scheduled for the same treatment this morning."

Jack grabbed his coat and bolted out the front door.

He reasoned that, even at his best pace and taking the shortcut across the main campus, it was still faster to drive. Pulling the door to the van open, he jumped inside, slipped the key into the ignition, and fired up the engine. Backing out of the driveway, he estimated he'd be at the hospital in seven minutes— he prayed he'd make it under the wire.

the only way Kip's care will be jeopardized is if we allow him to receive the IVIG."

"You have no—"

"Robyn, while we're standing here arguing, the other nurses might be starting their IVIG infusions. If that happens, we'll have a catastrophe on our hands. Stop and think about it for a second. IVIG is not an emergency drug. If I'm wrong, we can always give it in a few hours."

Turning a deaf ear, she picked up her phone. "I need Security in room 4407, stat."

"You're making a terrible mistake."

"My decision's final, Dr. Wyatt. I won't tell my nurses to hold the infusion without a bona fide order from an Oster physician."

"You just got one," came a voice from the doorway. Lennon Armbrister walked to the center of the room with Madison a few steps behind her. "I'm placing an immediate hold on all the IVIG infusions," she announced, pointing at the IV bag. "No questions, no discussion, Robyn. Just stop the infusions right now. And check with the other nurses immediately. I want to know the name of any patient who received the IVIG—even if it was only a thimble-full. Make a list." Lennon paused and swung her gaze flush on Robyn's face. "Is all that clear?"

"I'll get started right now, Dr. Armbrister," she said, stopping only briefly to disengage the pump and attend to Kip's port.

"Oh, and don't forget to cancel that call to Security," Lennon said.

Robyn's face flushed with a mixture of anxiety and confusion. She sank into silence and quick-stepped out of the room.

"Thank you," Jack said to Lennon.

"I came running as soon as Madison called me." She tapped her fingers together and added, "I hope for all our sakes you two know what the hell you're doing." She removed the infusion bag from the pump and started toward the door. "I'm going to call the toxicology department over at Defiance Memorial and tell them to expect a sample."

Just then, Frank walked into the room. Both he and Kip had

somehow managed to sleep through the chaotic events of the last five minutes.

"What's going on? What's all the commotion about?"

"Just a clarification of a medication order," Madison said. "It's all straightened out now."

Frank walked over and eased Kip's blanket a little higher on his chest. He cast a sideways glance their way. "You're sure everything's okay?"

"We're sure. There's nothing to worry about, I promise," Lennon said, as she headed for the door.

After speaking with Frank for a few minutes, Jack and Madison exited the room and went straight to the core desk. As they approached, Lennon was just finishing her talk with Robyn, who turned and started down the hall without making eye contact with either Jack or Madison.

"She feels terrible," Lennon said. "I assured her she was absolutely correct to stick to our protocol. She was beyond relieved to tell me that none of the patients received any of the IVIG."

"She's a great nurse. I'll track her down later and do some damage control," Jack promised. Frank suddenly appeared and gestured to Jack. He stepped away to speak with him.

Lennon turned to Madison. "I realize you and Jack haven't had much of a chance to fill me in on just what in god's name went on here tonight, but I really need to know the details as soon as possible so I can brief Althea."

"I doubt anybody's in the conference room," Madison said. "We can grab some coffee and talk there."

Jack walked up and rejoined them.

"Lennon and I were just about to grab a cup of coffee and have a long talk about Dr. Abel Haas and his unusual interest in the future of bone marrow transplantation. Would you care to join us?"

"I'd be honored," he said, as they started down the hall. "By the way, wait until you hear who ordered the IVIG— you're not going to believe it."

Chapter 79

It was twenty minutes to eight when Kendric Nash opened the door to his office. The first thing he did was walk over to the only window and tap the switch that lowered the sunscreen. After hanging up his hat and umbrella on the standing coat rack he'd had since the day he began working at Oster, he strolled over to his desk and sat down in his tan leather manager's chair and spent some time checking his latest emails.

When he was finished, he stood up and walked over to the black credenza that sat against the far wall. First diagnosed with diabetes when he was a student at Stanford, Kendric had been taking insulin for well over three decades and was well versed in the procedure. Sliding the top drawer open, he removed the cloth case that contained his insulin supplies, removed a syringe from its paper package, and uncapped the needle. He then drew up his customary twenty-two units, pulled up his shirt, and injected himself next to his navel.

Just as he was zipping up the case, Lisbet appeared in his doorway.

"Good morning," she said. "Thanks for agreeing to see me."

"Of course. Come on in and have a seat. Have you heard from Fay?"

"Every day," she answered, sitting down across from him. "She's really enjoying the cruise, but I'm sorry to report she doesn't miss work. She's in Barbados today."

He chuckled. "She's an incredible personal assistant. I'd put her up against any other one in the entire hospital system. I'm lucky to have her. It's nice you two have such a close friendship."

"You won't get an argument from me on that. She's always been a great friend."

He closed the drawer and strolled back to his desk. "So tell me, how can I help you?"

"I was just thinking about the first time we met thirteen years ago, and I wanted to talk to you about it."

With a slight head tilt, he asked, "Thirteen? My senility's getting worse by the day. How long have you been working here?"

"Let's see... It'll be five years in March."

"I'm afraid I'm confused," he said, regarding her askance. "If we met prior to you coming to Oster, I'm embarrassed to say I have no recollection of it."

"I'm not surprised," she told him with a knowing grin as she watched him thumb the corner of his mouth. "Our meeting didn't last too long, and my appearance was a lot different in those days. I was sixty pounds heavier, and my hair was short and very prematurely gray."

"I hope you'll take this in the right spirit, but that's probably why I don't remember meeting you. But you look terrific."

"My appearance wasn't the only thing I changed. If I told you my real name is Elise Hartmann, it might jog your memory a little." She watched as the color practically drained from his face. "Thirteen years is a long time, but you weren't the only one who made a solemn pledge to my dying mother that afternoon in Ithaca. The only difference between us is that I kept mine."

He looked at her silently. She wasn't surprised to see him nervously drumming his fingers on his desk pad. His panicky eyes betrayed his loss for words.

"It is you," he finally said. "I'm not sure why, but you've obviously gone to enormous lengths to pull this little charade off. What I can't figure out is why, but I think we'll have to agree to disagree on the matter of my promise to your mother. I haven't betrayed her. I've honored her."

"Honored her? Listen to me, you miserable son of a bitch. I know every unconscionable thing you've done. I don't think I've ever met anybody as disconnected from the truth as you are."

Interlocking his fingers behind his neck and leaning back, he asked, "Wasn't it her dying wish that her research pave the way to great medical discoveries that would save the lives of thousands of suffering children? I'm the one she entrusted to carry out her dream, and I can honestly say I've dedicated my career to it. And, if you don't mind me saying so, I find it perplexing you'd have the nerve to come to my office and sling accusations at me."

"You swore to her that you'd build on her work ethically and with uncompromising integrity. That was a bald-faced lie."

With a cynical crease to his lips, he removed his black bifocals and reached for a cleaning cloth. Calmly polishing the lenses, he said, "I'd be the first to admit your mother was a brilliant and gifted researcher who provided us a road map to a crucial medical advance, but if you're trying to convince me she embraced morality and integrity, you're wasting your breath." He replaced his glasses and fiddled with them for a few moments before going on, "I suspect we could debate all day about the oddities of the way you see things, but I don't think we'd accomplish much." With arched eyebrows he added, "Look, Elise, everybody in the hospital knows about your relationship with Abel Haas. Even though you two are involved, I'd beware of putting a lot of faith in his wild stories. He's a very disturbed man."

"I assume you haven't spoken to anybody about what happened on the LM unit last night."

"Why would I—"

"I'll save you the trouble of coming up with some lame denial. None of the patients received the IVIG, which also means they didn't get whatever you put in there to wipe out their bone marrow."

She paused, studying his face. "You look surprised. I spoke to Robyn. I'm guessing it was Busulfan, but we'll soon find out, because even as we speak, the IVIG is in a toxicology laboratory being analyzed."

"I have no idea what you're talking about."

"I guess Doctors Shaw and Wyatt really screwed up your plans when they figured out your lab was conducting illegal prion research."

"My lab, or do you mean Abel's lab?"

"You're the director, aren't you? I mean the buck stops with you."

"This is a fascinating bedtime story. Keep going," he said with a staged yawn. "I can hardly wait to hear how it turns out."

She could feel her blood starting to boil, but she'd had a long time to prepare for this moment, and she wasn't about to lose her cool. "What were you going to do if you found out your plan worked and the bone marrow you tried to wipe out remained normal?" She waited for a response, but when it became clear he preferred to hold on to his silence, she continued. "I'm guessing your plan was to shut down all further research at Oster for a couple of years and then fire things up again in a new research lab in Europe or Asia where you'd find some other patsy like Abel to help you pick up where you left off. Another year or so goes by, and you proudly announce to the world you've developed a way to eliminate the need for bone marrow transplantation in cancer patients. You get all the glory, tons of money, and nobody would ever make the connection to Oster Children's or leukemic malnutrition."

"That...that fairy tale you came up with makes for good theater," he said, as he chuckled between clipped breaths. "But you left out the part where you appointed yourself the avenging archangel to right all injustice and hold the guilty parties accountable for their vile behavior."

"Something like that."

"Did it occur to you that your boyfriend was up to his eyeballs in all of this, and I really knew nothing about it?" he asked her.

"That's crap, and we both know it. Abel was no match for you.

There was only one mastermind behind this conspiracy, and that was you. He was a hapless pawn in your scheme, but you needed him, because you didn't have the brains or the research skills to pull any of this off on your own."

"So what are you doing here in my office when you could be sitting in some police station spilling your guts?" He laughed harder this time. "C'mon, Elise...or do you prefer Lisbet? I think we both are well aware why you can't disclose any of this to anybody, so why don't you stop wasting both of our time with this ridiculous end run."

"Not until you tell me who speaks for Dr. Hayden Kubicek. Who should his parents see about both of their sons being murdered?"

"Not my problem, but I will say this: Sometimes inconsequential people become expendable when the stakes are extraordinarily high." With a shrug, he added, "It's an unfortunate reality."

It was at that moment that Elise noticed the first physical signs of what she had done. There was a jitteriness to his hands, and the skin on his face had faded to the color of cotton. She watched him wring his hands and wipe at the flood of sweat pouring down his neck. "You don't look well, Kendric," she told him with a dramatic sigh.

Realization dawned on his face. "What have you done?" he demanded, tearing at his collar.

"Fay really admires you. She talks about you all the time. She even told me how you do absolutely everything on a strict schedule and with military precision. That includes taking your insulin without fail at exactly nine o'clock every morning."

"You...you sadistic bitch. Tell me what you've done."

"You look just like a man having a heart attack. If I were you I'd save my breath, Kendric. You're going to need it." She came to her feet and took a few paces closer to his desk. "You know, you should really lock your office door when you go home at night. If you must know, I replaced your usual bottle of insulin with one that has five times the concentration," The corners of her mouth curled in an easy smile. "Instead of your usual twenty-two units of insulin, you just gave yourself well over a hundred."

She couldn't contain a smile. "You're right about one thing. It never crossed my mind to go to the authorities. That would have been too good for you. I prefer the solution I chose."

"You'll...you'll never get away with this," he said with an intense gulp for air that stepped on his words. Grabbing his throat as if somebody was garroting it with a piano wire, he jerked his head back, trying to force air into his lungs.

"Everybody loves you, Kendric. For goodness' sake, you don't have an enemy in the world. Why would anybody want to murder you? And it's well known your health isn't the greatest. You're a brittle diabetic and have had two heart attacks. How many cardiac stents have you had put in for goodness sakes—four? Plus, with everything going on around here, somebody's going to raise the possibility you decided to commit suicide. With a casual shrug, she added, "I'm sure the medical examiner will assume you died of natural causes and deem it unnecessary to perform an autopsy."

Suddenly, he thrust his upper body across his desk. Wildly thrashing his hand from one side of his desk pad to the other, he desperately struggled to get his fingertips around his phone.

"You won't be needing that. Nobody's going to save you," she said, calmly sliding the phone well beyond the reach of his flailing hands. With one final misdirected lunge, he slammed his hand against the marble base of his pen set and a framed photograph of him shaking hands with the governor. The impact launched the two items off his desk and sailing to the floor.

A steady froth of saliva bubbled between his lips before it spilled over his quivering chin. The first seizure took him with a powerful fury, throwing him against the back of his chair and leaving his stiffened torso shaking violently. His jaw muscles clenched, sending his upper and lower teeth slicing into his tongue, producing a torrent of hot blood and saliva that found its way into his windpipe.

Choking and spewing plum-colored secretions through his nose and mouth, he slumped forward into a flaccid state. With his brain starved for oxygen, his neck muscles could no longer support the weight of his head. It was the side of his face that impacted his desk with a dull thud. He drew his final breath. A few seconds later his pupils became dilated and fixed.

Stone-faced, Lisbet tilted her head to one side and stared at him. She took a minute to slip on a pair of surgical gloves and tidy up the area around his desk. Before leaving, she strolled to the credenza, opened the drawer, and removed his cloth insulin case. With a steady hand, she removed his usual bottle of insulin from her pocket and exchanged it for the one she'd placed there last night. Without so much as an inquisitive backward glance, she strolled out of his office and quietly closed the door behind her.

She exited the building and started down the street to where she had parked her flat-bed truck. Things had gone exactly as she'd planned, leaving her unconcerned she'd ever have to answer for the death of Kendric Nash. She felt no remorse. To the contrary, she liked the term he'd used to describe her—an avenging archangel. She deemed her act of revenge a righteous one. She turned her face to the sun, inhaled a large breath of the moist morning air, and climbed into her truck.

Chapter 80

At eleven a.m., Jack, Madison, and Althea quietly entered the Oster Children's Hospital chapel, a sanctuary of unique beauty and spiritual inspiration. The exterior walls were finished in lightwood that framed out a glorious collection of magnificently crafted stained glass. The white chancel sat beneath a steeply pitched teak ceiling.

As soon as they started down the center aisle, Jack spotted Dr. Gabriela Addesso standing next to a young man with a crew cut who was dressed in a dark suit. Without making eye contact, the man walked past them, locked the door, and then accompanied them to the front of the chapel.

"I hope we didn't keep you waiting," Althea said to Gabriela.

"You're exactly on time. Thanks again for calling to let me know what happened and agreeing to meet on such short notice." She paused, looking around the chapel. "A few years ago, my husband was hospitalized in Cincinnati for two months from complications after a bout of meningitis. He was as healthy as a Greek god, so his illness came completely out of the blue. I spent a lot of time in Hamilton General's chapel. It was the only place I could sort out my thoughts and hold things together." She shook her head, seeming to bring herself back to the present. "When do you think we'll have an answer on the toxicology profile?"

"I was told by noon today at the latest."

Gabriela rolled her wrist over and stole a peek at her watch. "I'm sorry, I seem to be running late. I wonder if you'd mind walking me to my car? We can talk on the way."

"Of course," Althea said. Gabriela reached for her purse, stood up, and hoisted the strap over her shoulder. Her aide approached and accompanied them out of the chapel and across the campus to her waiting limousine. "I have some hot coffee in the car. Let's continue our talk inside."

The aide opened the door. Jack was the last one to get in. He was just starting to rotate his body to sit down when he caught sight of Governor Vernon Sorenson sitting on the seat that faced the rear of the car. A stone-faced man sat next to him.

"Thanks for joining me and Gabriela," he said. "I apologize for all the secrecy, but for the record, you should know I generally don't request emergency meetings unless my level of concern is tickling the red line." He placed his hand on the shoulder of the man sitting next to him. "I'd like to introduce you to Special Agent Jeffrey Taylor. He's in Charge of the Cleveland FBI office. I asked him to sit in our meeting. Now, I'm sure you can all imagine my surprise when Gabby told me that, in spite of what I understood, we still have a major problem at Oster." He removed his reading glasses and dropped them into the inside pocket of his sports coat. "I understand there's a conflict between professional discretion and disclosing everything that could in any way be helpful in the rather large investigation that we're about to launch, but now's the time to get past that. So I'd very much appreciate it if somebody would take as much time as they need to explain to Special Agent Taylor and myself just what in the name of all that's holy happened here this morning." He took a breath and watched as all eyes fell on Jack.

"Doctor Wyatt, would you care to get this ball rolling?" Taylor asked.

· · ·

"WHERE WOULD you like me to begin?"

The governor answered, "We understand from Althea that you had an interesting conversation with Dr. Kendric Nash recently. I, for one, would like very much to hear more about it."

"It was productive, except for one minor detail," Jack answered. "He lied right to my face."

Chapter 81

A few hours later, Jack and Madison were sitting at the kitchen table enjoying a late lunch when the doorbell rang.

With a sardonic wince, he reached for his iced coffee. "Are we expecting company?"

She grimaced and snapped her fingers. "I forgot to tell you. Gabriela Addesso called about half an hour ago and asked if she could stop by."

So they could greet her together, Jack swallowed the final bite of his salad and trailed Madison to the front door.

"Let's sit in the den," Madison suggested. Can I get you something to drink?"

"No thanks," Gabriela said, settling into the sofa. "I just wanted to let you know we received the official report from the toxicology lab. Kip Dale's IV contained a very high dose of Busulfan."

"We heard," Madison said. "With the level they found, there's no question it would have destroyed the bone marrow of every patient who received it and put their lives at risk."

"The governor's instructions to Special Agent Taylor left no doubts. He wants answers. Don't be surprised if you get a call in the next day or two to set up interviews. He's leaning toward your theory that Haas wasn't working alone. I suspect the big question's going to be if he's still alive. If that turns out to be the case, and they can find him, I suspect he's the only one who'll be able to provide the information that will put all the pieces of this horrible puzzle together. This is going to be one of the biggest investigations and legal proceedings in Ohio's history. Based on the information you provided us, Kendric Nash had better start lawyering up. Misguided, insane, or whatever, he's going to have a lot of tough questions to answer."

"Can we assume the authorities will be taking a much closer look at Hayden Kubicek's death?" Madison asked.

"There's no question about it. I spoke with Special Agent Taylor after you guys left. He made it clear they would also be talking to the young lady in Ithaca who attacked Frank Dale. Taylor already called the hospital. She's still a patient. He's obviously suspicious she was working for Kendric and was the one directly responsible for Hayden Kubicek's death."

"And the matter of Abel Haas's alleged death?" Jack asked.

"I assure you that won't remain a mystery for long. If he's alive, the FBI will find him."

Madison said, "All of this is going to raise some pretty controversial questions of medical ethics, especially as to how to handle unscrupulously produced medical research."

"The governor has already raised that possibility and is adamant that his administration is not going to become involved in any thorny debates of medical ethics. His interest lies solely with accountability and enforcement of the law."

"I can't say I blame him," Jack said.

"By the way, we reached out to Dr. Camspoker. She categorically denies ordering IVIG for any patient," Gabriela stated with a sigh rich with a mixture of fatigue and frustration. "I'm sure she's telling the truth, so it looks like we're dealing with more deceitful behavior on somebody's part."

"So, it seems as if the conspiracy is growing," Madison said.

"Actually, Taylor's gut feeling is this wasn't some huge conspiracy. He suspects there were a very limited number of people involved. Obviously, that's pure guesswork at this point, and only a detailed investigation will reveal the truth."

They spoke for another few minutes before Gabriela rose to her feet.

"Well, I'd better get going. The main reason I stopped by was to personally thank you two again for all that you've done to help these children and their families. You have the gratitude and admiration of more people in this state than I could ever express in words." As they walked her to the door, she said, "I almost forgot. When we met with the governor, you were just about to tell us about Kendric lying to you when I had to step out of the car and take that call. Can you fill me in now?"

"When I spoke to him a couple of days ago in his office, he told me that, until our meeting with Robert and Althea, he was totally unaware of Abel Haas's illegal activities. And almost in the next breath he claimed he didn't know anything about Hayden Kubicek's death. It stuck in my mind because he mentioned him specifically by name."

"What's so strange about that?" Gabriela asked.

"I never mentioned Hayden's name to Kendric or anybody else at Oster except Althea. Other than one of our nurses who was very friendly with Hayden, I'm not aware of any person at Oster who would have reason to know about his unexpected death."

"I came back to the meeting on the tail end of the conversation and got the impression you thought Kendric wasn't exactly being forthcoming about what he knew of Abel Haas' depraved activities," Gabriela said. "Was there anything else?"

"I was embarrassingly gullible about the actual research," Jack said. "The study of prions is a highly complicated, expensive undertaking that requires sophisticated scientific equipment, a trained staff, and lots of laboratory space. I don't care how oblivious Kendric insists he was—it's inconceivable that he had no clue as to what was going on in his own research facility, right under his nose." With an unfinished shrug, he added, "I was slow on the uptake. It was obvious he was lying when he claimed he was completely unaware of Haas's research. I should have realized it immediately."

"Interesting," Gabriela said. "Dr. Kendrick will get the chance to explain himself in the next few days. Special Agent Taylor has him on his short list of the folks he's most anxious to interview."

Just as they were approaching the entranceway, Gabriela's phone rang.

"I should take this. Excuse me for a moment." After listening for a brief period of time, she said, "Thank you for letting me know." She returned the phone to her purse. An exasperated look came to her face. "I'm afraid things just went from bad to worse. Fifteen minutes ago, Kendric Nash was found dead in his office. They think he had a massive heart attack, but I suspect suicide's going to be up there as a possibility. I'd better give the governor a call. I'll speak with you later."

Jack and Madison walked Gabriela to her car and waited until the SUV pulled away.

"Well, that was an unexpected piece of news."

"To put it mildly," Jack said, as they started up the pathway.

Chapter 82

NEXT DAY

JACK AND MADISON had finished dinner and were attending to some last-minute packing when the doorbell rang. Zipping up her leather carry-on bag, Madison looked at Jack and wagged a finger in his direction.

"Don't look at me, buddy" she said. "I didn't invite anybody over, and nobody called." Having said all their goodbyes, Jack was equally in the dark as to who had decided to pay them an unannounced visit. His best guess was Althea.

"I'll get it," he told her.

"I'll be there in a sec. My curiosity has the best of me."

When Jack opened the door, he was greeted by a draft of wet, chilly air and Lisbet holding a large black umbrella over her head.

Having no idea what would bring her to their door, he pushed a mannerly smile to his face.

"Good evening, Dr. Wyatt."

"To you as well, Lisbet. Please, come in out of that horrible weather."

"Thank you." She shook her umbrella free of water and stepped forward into the foyer.

"I know I should have called before barging in on you and Dr. Shaw," she began as Madison joined them. "I wouldn't want you to think I'm totally without manners, but my time is limited, and I was afraid you might not agree to see me. What I'd like to discuss with you is extremely important." Madison helped her off with her coat, set her umbrella in a stand, and escorted her into the living room.

"May we offer you something to drink?" she asked.

"I'm fine, thank you." She sat down on the couch and placed her purse at her feet. "I'll be leaving the country tomorrow. I have no plans to return. I've come here tonight to ask you to return an important family possession to me."

There was an awkward silence for a few moments. Jack and Madison traded an intrigued look.

"This is all very difficult."

"Take your time," Madison suggested.

"I should probably begin by telling you that my real name is Elise Hartmann."

"Hartmann?"

"That's correct, Dr. Shaw. Anna Hartmann was my mother. I've come here tonight to reclaim her journals."

Jack was equally as stunned to learn her true identity as to hear her unexpected request. Absent a further explanation, he was hesitant to even admit they had the journals.

"I'm sorry," he stated, "But I'm not sure I understand what—"

"Please, Dr. Wyatt. I don't mean to appear impertinent, but I wouldn't be here unless I was certain you and Dr. Shaw have my mother's journals. You see, Abel Haas and I were quite close." She reached down and took hold of her purse's handle. "If you'd prefer to insist you have no idea what I'm talking about, I'll be on my way, and we can pretend I was never here."

From her disclosure regarding Abel Haas and the conviction in her voice, Jack was convinced she was telling the truth and hadn't come to see them on a fishing expedition. Over the past few weeks, he'd seen enough misdirection and blatant dishonesty to last him a lifetime. He decided to be as forthcoming with Elise as possible without disclosing any facts that might be sensitive to the formal investigation the authorities had launched.

He turned to Madison. By the expression on her face and seeing the slight nod of her head, he was sure she agreed.

"Please understand, handing over the journals to you may not be a simple matter."

"I don't see why, Dr. Wyatt. I'm not making an unreasonable request. I'm merely asking you to return my mother's journals to their rightful owner."

"As I just said, it—"

"If you'll allow me, I'd like to share some information with you. Hopefully, after you've heard what I have to say, you'll have a better understanding of why I'm here."

"We'll be happy to listen to whatever you have to say," Madison assured her.

She folded her hands together and placed them on her lap. "My mother kept her early life a tightly guarded secret. She was, in fact, a gifted young doctor and a highly talented medical researcher. She was working in Hamburg in the mid–1930s when she discovered the existence of an abnormally shaped, toxic protein that accumulated in the brains of mice. As you know, it wasn't until five decades later that other investigators would discover similar proteins and name them prions. She eventually isolated a strain that had a very short incubation period and the strange effect of causing very rapid and fatal starvation in mice. It was a couple of years later when she discovered another prion that had a powerfully protective effect on bone marrow and was less lethal than her other strains." Halting briefly, she reached down and removed a tissue from her purse and enclosed it in a fisted hand.

"But, to our knowledge, she never published any scientific articles about her discoveries," Madison said.

"For good reason, Dr. Shaw. Unfortunately, her prion's starvation effect drew the attention of certain Nazi physicians who were intensely researching techniques of medical genocide. One of them, a Dr. Pfannmüller, was working at the Eglfing-Haar Hospital. When he learned of my mother's work, he immediately moved her and her research activities to his laboratory. His hope was she'd be able to perfect a technique of using accelerated starvation to suit the depraved purposes of the Nazi fanatics. It was there where she was forced to continue her research under his watchful eye. And it was there that her research eventually led to innocent people being subjected to inhumane medical experimentation."

"Are you saying the subjects your mother referred to in her journals were not mice—they were human beings?" Jack asked.

"I'm afraid so."

"My god," Madison uttered as she raised a hand to cover her mouth. "Did your mother ever say why she agreed to participate in such despicable acts?"

Jack immediately wondered if the question had offended her. If it had, she disguised it well.

"She hardly had a choice in the matter, Dr. Shaw. My mother was well advised by Dr. Pfannmüller what the SS would do to her and her family if she refused to cooperate. She was young and not a particularly strong-willed individual. There's no question she was ill-equipped to deal with such threats or the turbulence of her time." She edged forward on the couch and raised her eyes. "I'm not trying to make excuses for her participation in unforgivably cruel treatment of her fellow human beings, but none of us sitting here could possibly fathom what it was like to live under the tyrannical rule of the Nazis." With a flushed face, she tipped her head forward. She appeared as if she was struggling not to become unglued.

"Are you sure we can't offer you something to drink?" Jack asked.

"No, thank you," she told him. After a short pause to steady herself, she continued. "As the war came to an end, my mother was able to escape Germany and come to the United States. Fortunately, her prion strain was never used at any of the Nazi death camps. It wasn't until many years later, when she was a veterinary professor at Cornell, that chemotherapy and bone marrow transplantation became an essential part of cancer treatment. It was then that she realized her prior discovery of her prion strain's revitalizing effect on bone marrow could be the key to an enormous scientific break-through."

"I assume you're referring to the possibility of eliminating the need for bone marrow transplantation," Jack said.

"Yes, Dr. Wyatt. My mother was a visionary. But she was conflicted to the point of self-torture because, even if the research had been conducted in a highly ethical and professional manner, her fear of revealing her past stopped her from beginning any new prion research. She knew she couldn't be the one to lead the research. It would raise too many ethical questions, not to mention the long list of personal consequences she would have to face. But she was desperate to find an alternative. Finally, she decided the only way to proceed would be to offer another researcher the opportunity to carry on her work in the hope that they could find the answer to eliminating the need for bone marrow transplantation."

"But it must have been decades from…"

"I know, Dr. Shaw. It was only after a period of intense emotional turmoil that she decided to wait until much later in life before searching for somebody to carry on her work. It wasn't until her death was approaching that she gathered the strength and the wherewithal to make the necessary arrangements. She devoted herself to finding a researcher who was not only trustworthy and ethical to a fault, but who also possessed the scientific skill to build on her work."

"If you don't mind me asking, when did you become aware of all this?" Jack inquired.

"I didn't know about any of it until a month or so before my mother died. I was working on my nursing degree at the time," Elise said, as her shoulders drooped. "I know what you and Dr. Wyatt must be thinking."

"We're not making any judgments," Madison was quick to say.

She raised both hands, as if she were holding back a crowd. "It's understandable that you're wondering why I didn't put a stop to all of this before it started…and maybe even inform the FBI about my mother's unethical research." She looked directly at Madison and asked, "Could you have done it, Dr. Shaw? Could you, Dr. Wyatt?

Could you have gone public, vilified your mother, and been the one to guarantee she'd be remembered forever as a despicable monster? My god, she'd have shared a legacy with the likes of Dr. Mengele and Adolph Eichmann. Did the world really need another Angel of Death?" She grew silent, pushed her palm against her lips, and then swept a few tears from her cheeks. "I know it doesn't amount to much, but in the end, my mother believed she was doing the right thing by giving the journals to Kendric Nash."

"You mean Abel Haas," Jack said with no hesitation. "You meant to say your mother gave her journals to Abel Haas."

Drawing back, she said, "My god, you really have no idea, do you? How much do you know about Kendric Nash and his relationship with Abel Haas?"

"Only that he became aware of Haas's research around the time the first cases of leukemic malnutrition started coming into the hospital. Other than that, he claims he had no knowledge of Dr. Haas's illegal activities," Jack answered.

"Kendric Nash is a masterful manipulator, amoral to his core, who knows how to be very economical with the truth," she told them in an even tone of voice. "No, Dr. Wyatt, my mother gave her journals to Kendric Nash, not Abel Haas. She contacted Kendric when she knew she didn't have much time left. He had already become a nationally recognized scientist and an expert in childhood cancer research, especially leukemia. I was there the day he came to see her in Ithaca. I stood in the bedroom and listened to his unconditional assurances that he'd follow her every wish to the letter. Unfortunately, what he vowed to an old woman fighting to redeem her life on that rainy day in Ithaca turned out to be nothing more than an endless trail of outright lies and broken promises."

"If what you say is so, how did Abel Haas become involved in the prion research?" Madison asked.

"The truth is that Kendric's reputation as an outstanding researcher was more imagined than real. Once he got back to Oster and tried to pick up where my mother left off, he realized he wasn't up to the task. That's when he approached Abel, who was a gifted investigator. Kendric was a very persuasive man. He convinced Abel that, when the research was completed, they would never divulge anything about Anna Hartmann or her journals. Abel is a weak-willed man who is easily intimidated and manipulated by others. I'm not claiming he's innocent in all of this, but at the same time, he was more of a victim than anything else. Kendric was absolutely convinced they'd never be caught. To the contrary, he told Abel they'd be viewed as iconic researchers who had provided the world with one of the greatest discoveries in medical history—a discovery that would save thousands and thousands of lives.

"Why did you decide to come to Oster?" Madison asked.

"The day my mother gave her journals to Dr. Nash, I made a solemn pledge to her that I would do everything in my power to make sure her research would be used to save lives and never again lead to human suffering. She never completely trusted Kendric, and by various means, I was able to keep an eye on things. After eight years, I finally accepted something was wrong. That's when I made the decision to make the necessary preparations and move to Defiance."

Jack switched gears and asked, "It's always been my under-standing that the Nazi physicians who participated in unethical medical experimentation came under enormous scrutiny by World War II historians. How is it possible your mother escaped detection for her entire life?"

"Almost all of the Nazi medical experiments were done in concentration camps. My mother was at one hospital and worked with only one other physician who committed suicide in 1945. She was positive the only record of her experiments was her journals. As far as eyewitnesses… Well, by time the war ended, there were none remaining."

"I spoke with Kendric at length. He was adamant that he got duped, just like everybody else. He portrayed Abel Haas as the villain."

"Kendric told you what he wanted you to believe. It was a blatant deception with little bits of truth sprinkled here and there. He wanted you to believe he was a weak man, guilty only of trying to avoid going to jail." A tired look appeared on her face. "My only goal is to leave here tonight with my mother's journals. They've already been the source of enough misery. It would serve no useful purpose if the truth about my mother and her work became public information. Trampling on her grave at this late date would benefit nobody."

"It's just not as simple as you think," Jack stated.

"That's just the point, Dr. Wyatt—it is that simple. Those responsible for what occurred at Oster are either dead or will pay a heavy price for their vile actions. There's nothing in my mother's journals that you and Dr. Shaw aren't fully aware of. After all these years, their physical existence is an irrelevancy. I want to believe the one and only copy of the journals is right here in this house." She reached forward, picked up her purse, and stood up. "I don't mean to sound abrupt, but I'd appreciate an answer to my request."

"I'm sure you can understand there's a strong likelihood the authorities will want them," Madison said.

"For what purpose? Both Abel and Kendric are dead. Anybody else involved was a minor player who knew nothing about what was really happening. They can be brought to justice and pay the price for what they did. My mother's journals won't be necessary to make a case against any of them." The room went silent as she walked over to the fireplace and stared through the screen at the twirling flames.

Madison laid her hand on Jack's forearm. "Would you excuse us for a minute?" she asked.

"Of course."

While Jack and Madison were talking in the kitchen, Elise continued to gaze at the fire. Ten minutes later, they returned.

"Jack and I have an idea we'd like to propose to you. It may not be exactly what you had in mind, but we think it's an alternative worth discussing."

"I'd be happy to listen to anything you might have to say," she said, returning to the couch and calmly retaking her seat.

Chapter 83

After a few weeks of being out of the country and constantly on the move, Dr. Abel Haas returned to the United States. It was not a decision he'd made lightly. Even though his journey overseas had been extensive, at no time had he set foot in Thailand. Only through extreme vigilance did he managed to elude the two men he'd first encountered in Paris. But he knew his good fortune was almost certainly temporary, and irrespective of where he chose to hide, his future was hardly a rosy one.

Once he was back in the U.S., he chose Southern California as his safe harbor. He had spent time there in the past, reveled in the desert environment, and believed it would offer him tranquil surroundings to consider his options. After his third long day of hiking in Joshua Tree National Park, he came across a flat granite boulder beside an isolated patch of thorny bushes. Slipping off his backpack, he sat down on the boulder and pulled his knees to his chest. The hazy twilight of dusk provided him just enough light to gaze out at the rocky slopes that stretched above the arid desert flats.

The abundance of media attention addressing the strange goings-on at Oster Children's Hospital had allowed him to keep up with the latest events. Even though the children he had infected with the prion had recovered from leukemic malnutrition, he remained haunted by unrelenting guilt and depression. He was a shell of his former self, struggling in vain to recover from his emotional freefall.

With the fading warmth of the sun on his shoulders, he closed his eyes. After a few minutes, he reached into the top pocket of his plaid flannel shirt and removed the same cyanide capsule that he had kept within easy reach since the moment he'd fled Defiance. As he had become accustomed to doing, he rolled it gently between his fingers. But this time, instead of returning it to his pocket, he placed it between his lips. A few moments passed before he repositioned it between his teeth.

Right until the moment he crushed the capsule, he felt no fear. Having read extensively about acute cyanide poisoning, Haas wasn't surprised when he was instantly overcome by an intense wave of nausea. Gagging violently, he felt his throat stiffen and narrow. A few more seconds passed, and every cell in his brain was drained of its oxygen supply. His mind flooded with lurid visions of rabid dogs madly tearing at his torso and face.

Robbed of any awareness of his surroundings, he toppled forward and rolled off the boulder to the desert floor below. Face down on the bedrock and cracked clay, his heart fluttered for a few seconds before it became agonal and pumped its final beat. Abel Haas had fulfilled his final wish of dying in the country of his birth.

Epilogue

Twenty minutes after Jack and Madison had excused themselves to speak privately, they escorted Elise to the front door.

While she was putting her coat on, he asked, "Do you know if Abel Haas is still alive?"

"I don't. I haven't heard from him since he left the country. I don't have the first clue what's become of him. Even if he is still alive, I can't imagine I'll ever see or hear from him again."

"We wish you the best," Madison said. "We'll keep our fingers crossed that your new life in Europe turns out to be everything you could hope for."

"If you don't mind telling us, where will you be living?"

"There's a small town in the Czech Republic I visited many years ago that I instantly fell in love with. I decided right then and there that, when the time came, I'd spend the rest of my days there."

Handing her the umbrella, Jack said, "Safe travels, Elise."

They stood in the doorway and watched her walk cautiously down the slippery driveway and get into her truck. After she pulled away, they returned to the living room where Madison fell into the corner of the couch. Jack strolled over to the fireplace and reached for one of the brass prong-ended pokers.

He said, "The ethical question of whether medical science should use research that was conducted in an unethical or illegal manner as a platform to discover new and beneficial medical treatments is certainly a fascinating one. I'm not sure what the answer is."

"If it makes you feel any better, that question has crossed the eyes of the brightest medical ethicists for a very long time."

"What's your opinion on the controversy?" Jack asked.

"I'm opposed to allowing the use of any medical research born out of immoral scientific practices where innocent people suffered and died."

"Even if that research meant the possibility of saving thousands of lives in the future?"

"To my way of thinking that's a weak justification because it creates a horribly dangerous precedent for future research. The justification that the end justifies the means has no place when it comes to medical research."

"So those victimized by unethical research methods...the price they paid should have been for naught?" Jack asked. "There are lots of researchers and ethicists who would vehemently disagree with you. They'd argue that any medical breakthroughs based on Nazi research that could be used to save future lives would be the only legacy of the victims who died in the concentration camps. In Anna Hartmann's case, they'd claim it would be a tragic mistake not to use her work because it would deprive future cancer and prion disease sufferers of the possibility of being cured." Jack pulled back the chain fireplace curtain. "Do you feel sorry for Anna Hartmann?"

"She had five decades to come clean and do the right thing, but she chose not to. I have no sympathy for her."

"What would you have done differently?"

"All I can do is pray that, if I'd been in her position, I would've found another way," she answered.

"She was a tragic figure, Madison. I can't begin to imagine the horror her life must have been during the war."

"Worse than the millions of concentration camp victims? You asked me a tough question. I have one for you. Do you and I have a responsibility to disclose what we know about Anna Hartmann? Is the world entitled to know about an individual who has committed unspeakably heinous and unforgivable acts against her fellow human beings?"

"As an inviolate rule, I don't think so. I'd base my opinion on the individual in question," he answered. "The Anna Hartmann story is a complicated one. Right now, I tend to agree with Elise. I don't know what a full disclosure of every detail would accomplish, but I also don't know if I'd answer your question the same way tomorrow, next month, or in the years to come."

"Do you think it would change the way you feel about things if you had a relative who perished in one of the death camps?" she asked.

While he pondered Madison's question, Jack stared into the fireplace. Becoming lost in thought, he stirred the smoldering pile of feathery gray ashes that were the last physical remains of Dr. Anna Hartmann's journals.

About Gary Birken, MD

When I first set pen to paper as a novelist, I was a busy full time pediatric surgeon. I completed eight years of surgical training at Ohio State University and Nationwide Children's Hospital and remain to this day an ardent Buckeyes fan. Upon completing my training, I relocated to South Florida and joined the medical staff of Joe DiMaggio Children's Hospital, where I served as the Surgeon-in-Chief.

Now that my schedule is more relaxed, I'm able to devote greater time to writing and getting more involved with my readers. My approach to story-writing has always been to utilize fiction not only as a means to entertain, but also to offer some insight into an interesting or controversial topic in medicine. I'm often asked by aspiring authors for suggestions as to the best way to get started. The best advice I can offer any individual who seriously want to write is to take the time to learn the craft of fiction writing, and then - read a lot and write a lot.

I am a member of the Mystery Writers of America and have had the opportunity of teaching writing at various conferences and other forums. I have also had the pleasure of serving as a panel member at the SleuthFest Conference. In addition to spending time with my family, including my ten grandchildren, I am a private pilot, and an avid tennis player. I also enjoy auditing university level courses and just hanging out with my English Setter, Eliza Doolittle. I hold a black belt in martial arts and frequently teach courses in women's self-defense.

Made in United States
Orlando, FL
06 May 2025

61092626R00225